"Kimberly Brock ... what splendid writing ought to a...... .....at linger in the reader's consciousness. Such is the power of Roslyn Byrne, who retreats to Manny's Island, Georgia, in search of herself, only to discover her great need of others. Tender and intriguing, often dazzling in its prose, this is a mature work of fiction worthy of the celebration of praise."
—Terry Kay, author, *To Dance With The White Dog*

"There is magic and wonder in The River Witch, but the real enchantment here is the strength of the characters Roslyn and Damascus. Their voices are the current that carries the reader along in this compelling tale of healing and discovery."
—Sharyn McCrumb, New York *Times* Bestselling Author, *The Ballad of Tom Dooley*

Kimberly Brock has an amazing voice and a huge heart; The River Witch welcomes the reader to a haunted landscape, authentically Southern, where the tragedies of the past and the most fragile, gorgeous kind of love-soaked hope are equally alive. This is one debut that you absolutely should not miss.
—Joshilyn Jackson, New York *Times* Bestselling Author, *Gods in Alabama*

"With lyrical prose, Kimberly Brock explores the hidden places of the heart. The River Witch is a magical and bewitching story that, like a river, winds its way through the soul. In the voices of her wounded characters, Brock takes us through both the breaking and the healing of a life."
—Patti Callahan Henry, New York *Times* Bestselling Author of *The Perfect Love Song*

Can the river heal her?

Roslyn Byrne is thirty years old, broken in body, heart and soul. Her career as a professional ballet dancer ended with a car wreck and a miscarriage, leaving her lost and grieving. She needs a new path, but she doesn't have the least idea how or where to start. With some shoving from her very Southern mama, she immures herself for the summer on Manny's Island, Georgia, one of the Sea Isles, to recover.

There Roslyn finds a ten-year-old girl, Damascus, who brings alligators, pumpkins and hoodoo into her sorry life.

Roslyn rents a house from Damascus' family, the Trezevants, a strange bunch. One of the cousins, Nonnie, who works in the family's market, sees things Roslyn is pretty sure she shouldn't, and knows things regular people don't. Between the Trezevant secrets and Damascus' blatant snooping and meddling, Roslyn finds herself caught in a mysterious stew of the past and present, the music of the river, the dead and the dying who haunt the riverbank, and a passion for living her new life.

The River Witch

by

Kimberly Brock

Bell Bridge Books

This is a work of fiction. Names, characters, places and incidents are either the products of the author's imagination or are used fictitiously. Any resemblance to actual persons (living or dead,) events or locations is entirely coincidental.

Bell Bridge Books
PO BOX 300921
Memphis, TN 38130
Print ISBN: 978-1-61194-123-4

Bell Bridge Books is an Imprint of BelleBooks, Inc.

We at BelleBooks enjoy hearing from readers. Visit our websites – www.BelleBooks.com and www.BellBridgeBooks.com.

10 9 8 7 6 5 4 3 2 1
Cover design: Debra Dixon
Interior design: Hank Smith
Photo credits:
Cover photo (manipulated) © Oxilixo | Dreamstime.com

:Lwr:01:

Dedication

For Daniel

"Though I do not believe a plant will spring up where no seed has been, I have great faith in a seed. Convince me that you have a seed there, and I am prepared to expect wonders."

—*Henry David Thoreau*

Prologue

These were the first things I heard, the sounds of women and water on a cool November morning just south of the Cumberland River. My grandmother and two ladies from the Glenmary Baptist Church sat in the living room and sang Wayfaring Stranger, Number 459 from the Sacred Harp as my mama labored. Later, the midwife, who was also a Keller cousin, told the story of how there'd been a storm that flooded the hollow, and the rising water threatened to come in the door all night. Stranded in that little house for three days, they swaddled me in a flour sack quilt, decided what to name me, and predicted all the days of my life. Granny Byrne always said they'd never ate as well, fellowshipped as sweetly, or sang with hearts that full of the Spirit.

I was a grown woman, lost and stranded by my choices, before I realized I'd forgotten that story. And then I heard my Granny Byrne. Day and night, she began to sing to me again, an old song, a lesson of water and time.

Listen.

Kimberly Brock

Chapter One

Roslyn

The realtor Mama recommended was a friend from her days on the Appalachian craft fair circuit. Verna had a hairless Chihuahua named Mistake and a distended tattoo of the Tasmanian Devil running across her belly. I knew this second hand, thank God. The point is, in my hour of need, this is who Mama turned to for sound advice.

I showed up to sign the lease with my hospital grade cane and my dark hair dirty and falling out of a ponytail. No make-up could hide the dark circles under my gypsy eyes, the pallor of my olive complexion. Two Percodan an hour before kept me from rolling-on-the-floor- cart-the-woman-off out-of-my-mind. I surprised myself, really, how I managed the whole thing sitting upright in a wingback chair like I was booking a Caribbean cruise. Someone might have suggested I needed a day at the salon or a fresh T-shirt. Nobody in the world would have looked at me and said *my stars, that woman just lost her child and look at her, what a tower of strength.*

I imagined that was why Verna kept her nose to the listing when she said, "Honey, considering what you've been through, I don't know if I'd be doing as well."

People had ideas about me, and they didn't know the half of it.

"Every day's a little better," I said. I'd practiced the words until they sounded about as genuine as a toothpaste commercial.

"Never did see you dance myself, but it's about all my

granddaughter can talk about, and her little ballet class. Shelly's just turned six, and it's so sweet at that age. Wish we could all just stay that innocent."

Apparently, I was due for a dose of reality. Sugar Plum fairies were reserved for the young.

"When your Mama called, I told her I'd do whatever I could for you."

"I appreciate that, Verna."

"Of course, Shelly'd love to have you sign her ballet bag. Got it right here under my desk. But we'll do that after."

"That'd be fine." No telling what Shelly's Mama would do with that bag. Burn it, bleach it, pawn it for twenty bucks and book a day at the beauty shop. Shelly sure wouldn't be carrying my name around. I was no example for any little girl.

Verna finally looked up at me with a little more interest. "Now this is Manny's Island we've got here."

"Right off the coast, I know."

"Well, this property's been owned for the last decade by a family name of Trezevant. Seems they inherited. A brother and sister. Now, I know the girl, and she's a sweet thing. Says they just can't part with the old home place. My guess is these folks can't afford to live on it for the outrageous property taxes. That's a pretty common problem down there. They'll get ungodly offers every other day from developers, but they hold out. They won't break up the twelve acres or sell it off."

"I don't want to buy anything," I reminded her. I pushed my hands between my thighs to keep them from shaking. "I just want it for the summer. This is remote, right?"

"Hell, my guess is this here's the place they've got Elvis Presley hid out. As islands go, it's about as undeveloped and remote a spot as you're going to find. There's a resort, but it's pretty exclusive. Not like you'd be mixing with the snowbirds unless you wanted to play a few holes."

"I don't want commercial. I don't want to run into anybody for miles. For days."

I wanted to be separated from the world by oceans. By decades. Planets. I wanted an alternate reality.

"Nobody's going to get within a hundred yards of that place." Verna watched me carefully. "People claim some old conjure woman used to live there."

I couldn't have cared less. Verna had no idea who she was dealing with.

"Do you believe in that sort of thing? People can be superstitious, that's all. But there's not a thing wrong with the house. Sits on an estuary of the Little Damascus River. As far as I'm concerned, it's a steal."

"I grew up on a river," I said.

All Verna saw was a crying shame. She didn't make a peep if she noticed the dirt under my fingernails as I signed. She didn't mention what she'd heard happened to me and my child. Verna Oldham was as close to an angel of mercy as girls like me were likely to come by.

Not even a year ago, at thirty, I was leading a charmed life. Charmed. That's what people called it, the gift or blessing or obligation that brought a little Appalachian urchin to the sophisticated stages of Atlanta, Georgia. Then I'd screwed up my life with a ridiculous affair with an older man, gotten knocked up, been in a car accident that ruined a promising dance career, and landed myself on my Mama's couch to recuperate, twenty-two weeks pregnant and barely showing. These days, I was running short on charm.

"I don't know why people want to bring children into this world in the first place," I said the afternoon in late June before everything changed. I was trying hard to come up with a way to undo the inevitable. "What kind of person in their right mind thinks it's a good idea to have babies?"

"Mamas." Mama sang, her alto voice still strong and steady while she set me up with soft yellow yarn and a crochet needle. I'd dumped all the music from my iPod, the favorite scores from years in the ballet, and replaced them with my Granny Byrne's music, a sound I hadn't heard in years. I guess it had Mama remembering, too.

Granny Byrne's people—not just family, but the community within the cove—sang from the Sacred Harp songbook by shape notes, sitting in a square, facing one another for the call and respond of a fugue. I hadn't heard the sound since we'd left, years before when I was just a little girl. Back then I'd been terrified of it, and loved it just the same, the power of a sonorous layering of voices, the steady climb and crescendo of a miraculous human instrument. Now, somehow everything that had happened made me remember and obsess. I downloaded hours of the haunting Sacred Harp hymns, and got carried away on the glory train.

"Motherhood is not a choice," Mama said, when the song ended. "It's a condition. Here, let me show you." She pulled the needle in and out, looping the yarn so that it formed an even stitch, over and again, crocheting the corner of what would be a square.

Her fingers were methodical, hypnotic as they pulled together a line of neat knots. Surely, we were both thinking of Granny Byrne. She'd died last spring, when I was dancing Swan Queen, and my stepdad, Jackie, had gone in the hospital with a collapsed lung, a complication of the emphysema. By the time Mama got the call, a Keller had already set up the services, and there was no time for either of us to make it back for the funeral. We knew they'd rushed the whole thing just to keep us away, and we'd had such excuses for staying away that we thought we could live with ourselves. But we knew better than to talk about it now. When we did say her name, we always talked about her as though Granny was fixed permanently in time, just as we'd left her, years ago.

"I won't be any good at this," I said, feeling Granny's ghost over my shoulder. "I shouldn't even be allowed."

I meant motherhood, and Mama knew it, but she simply demonstrated the stitch once more and pushed the needle into my hands.

"This baby's going to blame me for every damn thing one day."

"That's just natural," she said, waving away my dramatic

declarations. "Don't buy into all that look-at-what-this-world's-coming-to business. The world is what it's always been."

"They preach that fence-riding at the Unitarian Church?"

I wanted to pick at her new interest in formal religion, which she'd formerly clawed her way out of in Glenmary, TN, and basically taught me was next to brainwashing. But she didn't even look at me.

"A baby's going to change everything," I said. My cycles had never been regular because of the stress of dancing, and so I was already two months gone by the time I realized what had happened. I still wasn't used to the idea. Even now, if I faced front-on in the mirror, I could almost pretend it wasn't even a part of me.

Mama only laughed. "Oh, don't fool yourself, kid. It already has."

Thooe words echoed in my ears, later.

When my water broke, I was alone. Mama and Jackie were gone to town. I didn't want to believe it. But I know part of me knew what was happening and made a choice.

I did not call for help. The flood forced me off the sofa and into the tile floor of the bathroom, but I just dragged the sewing bag with me. I finished the square I'd been working on, sat it aside and started a new one. I worked madly. I did not stop until the pressure in my womb made it impossible to continue. The crochet needle dug into my palm, and I could feel the yarn tangled in the fingers of my other hand, stretched across my belly like a web, but it was so easy to lie back. You wouldn't believe what little effort it took.

It was amazing really, how quickly life could change into something worse than you ever imagined. I cried over her, I'll tell you that. She was perfect, a little wax figure, a baby doll. I don't know how long before I realized I wasn't going to be able to just lie there forever, but everything had grown cold. Knowing I couldn't go back, seeing clearly there was no way to move forward, I guess it was right about this point when I went a little sideways.

In my mind, I found my way back to Glenmary in another time. I was walking a steep path up a sweet old rise to sacred ground.

Three blocks from the house, I made my way slowly toward the far west corner of Lenoir Baptist Church's cemetery, past the concrete statue of Jesus. He'd been holding his arms out to the world all my life and longer, long enough to have lost every finger he had. Watching over the Baptists had obviously cost him a lot already. I wasn't afraid. I'd had firsthand experience with the grave as a child, and I was remembering Granny Byrne and a dark hillside long ago when we'd buried her regrets.

It was getting late in the afternoon, and the light wasn't so sharp. I wondered hazily where the day had gone. Underneath a sheltering stand of pine where I hoped the ground was softer, I brought out Mama's potting shovel from my bag. I wished I could remember one of Granny Byrne's hymns, but I only had bits and pieces come to me. While I was trying to call up a tune, I realized I'd forgotten the yellow blanket at the house. I'd meant to tuck those crochet squares around my child, and I regretted bitterly that I'd forgotten them.

The ground was harder than I'd expected, and my arms were shaking before I'd barely managed to turn up a few little chunks of dirt. It didn't seem like I'd ever get a hole big enough. I could not even do this one thing for my daughter.

When Mama's hand touched my head, I looked up to meet her eyes, and for minute, I thought she was Granny Byrne, come down from Paradise. But Mama wasn't a saint, and she wasn't singing any sacred song. She was only crying my tears for me. That's when I saw what she saw. Once before, she'd taken me up, and we'd run. But here we were, back on our knees.

"I just wanted to put her to bed," I said.

Mama knocked the dirt off the shovel and stuck it in the back pocket of her jeans, then tucked the little shoebox holding her grandbaby in the crook of her arm.

We didn't say one word about what had happened to me. There was no going back to change it, so what was the point in telling the story? Mama handled all the questions from the coroner and set up a time for the interment at the end of the week. She said we needed to pick out a stone. The baby deserved a name, at least.

"I can't. Not yet. I don't know who she was."

I didn't know who I was.

We went over to the gravesite to stand over the small hole in the earth that had been so impossible for me to dig up on my own. When I tried to sing, Mama shushed me. I'd never known her so silent. And she did what she'd always done when my life was a mess. She started making decisions to clear a path.

She was scared, I think, that I'd run straight back to Glenmary and the poverty, the crazy Kellers, the desperate relatives she'd always resented. She heard me humming the old songs deep in my throat. But Mama knew if I went back there, it wouldn't be what I remembered, and I couldn't stand one more disappointment. She couldn't have me going north, and so she sent me south. She knew something I hadn't learned yet. If I wanted to sing the Sacred Harp, I had to learn to listen first.

So, maybe I was crazy the day I parked in a lot at a dock and waited for a ferry boat, swatting at mosquitoes and sighing over the expanse of the Little Damascus River. Nearly two months had passed since Granny Byrne had died, leaving so much unresolved, like the fractured bones that burned like fire inside me and the frightening red scars that had only begun to knit back together on the outside. It was three weeks since I'd lost the baby. The first week of August was bearing down on the Georgia coast, and my life and body seemed completely unrecognizable.

"Home sweet home," I murmured, staring across the wide water. It looked nothing like the Cumberland River of my childhood.

Manny's Island can't be found on most maps. If it's there at all, if a person isn't careful to inspect, it's likely to be mistaken for a coffee stain or the remains of an unfortunate insect. Truly a peninsula, but separated from the mainland by an estuary and thick marshlands, the island lies just off the eastern coast of St. Simon's, and most people never happen upon the curved spit of land, unless they've taken a seriously wrong turn.

But one river was as good as any other when you were a drowning woman.

Chapter Two

Damascus

Three months earlier, when the summer nights were so heavy with humidity everybody was making deals with God for one stiff breeze, Damascus' eyeballs were all dried out from trying not to blink, getting ready to make her mad dash. She watched her babysitter's head nod, a woman who usually worked the reception desk at the resort, her jaw growing slack and her fingers wrapped loosely around an empty V-8 can that threatened to hit the floor any minute. Damascus' blood rushed in her ears, filled with the game show music as they cut to a commercial.

Go to sleep, old woman.

Damascus couldn't risk being found out. Her daddy would put a quick stop to her plans. If he noticed. Of course, that wasn't very likely. Most of the time, Daddy hardly even noticed her, except maybe to have her hand him the paper, or bring him a glass of ice water when he worked in the yard. He was a disappointment to Damascus so far as fatherhood was concerned. But she'd only known him ten years, so she guessed it wasn't fair to pass judgment on a man's whole life when you hadn't been around for most of it. She'd heard people say Urey Trezevant was a charmer, a man's man, a hard worker, a sly dog. But not once had she ever heard one person say how much he'd loved her Mama. But love could eat you whole. Just ask the alligators. That was only one of the secret things Damascus knew.

People told their secrets, one way or another, and not just with their words. Damascus knew how to lay low and still.

Daddy called it testing the waters. He was a man with currents and tides and that made people nervous, but Damascus was named after a river. And that's how she knew her mama'd understood about Daddy, too. She'd bestowed the name Damascus on purpose.

Images of a dark-haired woman with soft arms and perfectly rounded fingernails were the fragments Damascus kept tucked in a precious corner of her heart. She had learned a hard truth. People die in pieces, slipping away, wearing off at the edges until they are thin as the reeds in the marsh, clicking and empty. Each time she allowed herself to think of something besides her mother, she came back to the memory to find it faded further, the smell of her mother lost, the exact color of her eyes indistinguishable now from those of the lady at the check-out line at the grocery.

But to remember Mama fully, she had to remember the day she'd lain in that sweaty bed, crying and sick from the poison that was supposed to kill the cancer, shouting at her father until it seemed her mother had sucked all the noise out of the world and blown it from her lungs. Until there was no air at all. Mama had been taking it out on Daddy, fighting to live, but she knew she would not. And then, weeks later when it came to an end so quietly, it felt like she'd bequeathed Damascus and Urey nothing to breathe but grief. The cancer had left only the poison.

Damascus could not remember a father who swung her up on his shoulders and strolled through the autumn sunlight, or one who laughed from a place that vibrated like a drum, or clapped his hands to see her dance. Hers was a shadow father, a dark thing that slid past her, just out of her vision. Damascus lay in bed with her eyes shut, drifting, and tried to imagine what that other Daddy might have been like, but she didn't remember a time when he wasn't tired out from work, grisly around the edges, and saving his best smiles for the women he took out some Saturday nights. He did not want to be with her. He saved his free moments for a barn owl he'd trained to hunt the small things that came out at night.

She alone knew what her mother's death had done to Urey

Trezevant, how he had stopped bathing and had grown a beard, Damascus believed, just so he could pull it out in tufts with his own two hands. Their love must have been fine. She imagined he held her Mama for five hours after she'd gone to God, cold, the color of a stormy sky, and so small. Damascus held those images close. So close, they had blocked out most all other memories that came before.

The babysitter squinted in her direction, made a there's-no-sense-to-it face and shook her head a little before turning her concentration back to the TV. Damascus chewed a nail.

Within thirty minutes, the old woman's thin chest rose and fell with a deep breath. Two minutes after the sitter started snoring, Damascus scrambled to retrieve the tray of peat pots she'd kept hidden for weeks on top of the refrigerator. Clutching the trays, Damascus was quiet as the creatures that hid from her father's owl. She went out the back of the cottage, a two bedroom house provided by the resort where her father worked as grounds manager, padding softly across the short grass of the twelfth green. She dashed through the wood that separated the old Trezevant farm from the *damn* High Dunes Resort. Damn High Dunes, that's what her daddy called it, and so Damascus did as well. She liked saying it just that way, knowing she was cursing the place just a little.

"Damn High Dunes," Damascus whispered aloud.

The cool evening breeze made her neck cold where the jagged little wisps of her self-fashioned hair-do did little to keep her head warm. But she liked it. No fuss. And it was shocking. Her daddy rolled his eyes when he first saw it—a boy cut that made her look like some dirty blonde clipper-job gone wrong.

She pulled the bill of her ball cap down low over her eyes the way she'd seen her father adjust his hat all her life. He'd fought to save Mama, but he couldn't. He'd fought to keep this farm and the island the way he remembered, but he couldn't. And now, just this morning, Damascus had overheard him arguing with Aunt Ivy. It was about Damascus, how Daddy was neglecting her. That's the word Aunt Ivy used. Everything her daddy loved got taken away. Now, they wanted to take her, too.

That's why she'd opened the seeds. He'd had to fight by himself 'til now, but her mother had left a secret for them, and Damascus believed she was finally old enough to understand it was her fight, too.

About a hundred years ago or something like it, the Trezevants had farmed the wild riverbanks all along the Little Damascus River. They'd been tenement farmers making a living off the place. But by the time Daddy came along, the farms were disappearing, and people were building big beach houses and then a golf course, instead of planting tomato fields, and Daddy became a grounds manager instead of a farmer. Urey Trezevant had never raised a single crop, except his daughter, and he wasn't doing a bang up job of that.

Damascus knew the whole story from cousin Shayna, who liked to tell anybody who'd listen. When the old woman who had raised her father and aunt died, she left the house and twelve acres to Aunt Ivy, and Damascus' daddy was furious. Anybody would have been burned up by that after all the work her daddy'd done for Aunt Delia. That's when he left the island, just took up and went on the ferry one day, nobody knowing where he'd gone. They still didn't know, really, since he wouldn't talk much about it. He was gone without one word for seven years, until Aunt Ivy and Uncle Will nearly lost the farm.

Daddy showed back up just like he'd left, without a word to anybody. He brought the owl with him, and it scared Aunt Ivy, who said it was a bad omen. And he brought Damascus' mother, a girl named Fawn, without any family of her own. He had money enough to buy the farm from Aunt Ivy and Uncle Will and pay off some bills they couldn't pay. Uncle Will'd yelled at her daddy in the yard, even though he was helping them, and a truck had come and moved all their things out so daddy could move in.

He'd married Fawn after that, and had Damascus a few months later, but they'd only spent three years there before she got sick, and pretty soon there wasn't an extra penny from his paycheck for savings or taxes or bills. They used up everything they had, everything he made at Damn High Dunes, and the money he got for the extra fishing charters he took on the weekends only kept them fed. And Damascus hadn't felt full since.

When Fawn died, they left the farm and moved into the cottage at High Dunes. Ever since, old Otis Greene had lived as tenant on the farm, and Urey had become the landlord, just like the men he'd hated his whole life. When old Mr. Greene went in the nursing home last fall, the house sat empty until her daddy decided to rent the place again, at least for the summer. "Then we'll see," he'd said to Damascus.

But Damascus knew things weren't going to change. They never would. Not unless she changed them.

Scuttling down the bank to the water, she held a tray of pots close, careful not to trip and fall, following the path by memory in the dark.

Inside a seed, there is a miracle.

Those were her mother's words. She'd scribbled instructions on the back of a brown legal envelope. Inside, she'd left seven pumpkin seeds.

You must search for the perfect spot to plant your seed and then you can't forget about it. Care for it every day, without fail.

On the envelope, Fawn Trezevant's handwriting looked like flowers and ribbons. For years Damascus had traced the loops and slants, loving them for their sweet shapes alone. Before she could read, their meaning was a mystery that kept her tied to Fawn, an inky umbilical cord reaching from this world to the next. But two years ago, third grade changed everything. She didn't go to public school. Daddy was afraid of how the kids there would treat her, what they'd say about the Trezevants and how people talked about what happened to Mama. So Aunt Ivy homeschooled Damascus, and it was so easy. Damascus about did her work in her sleep, and, since Aunt Ivy worked so much, she didn't have time to come up with extra stuff. But third grade meant penmanship, and Damascus was excited about that. She actually spent extra time practicing on notebook paper when she ran out of room in the workbooks. Out with block letters and in with cursive writing. Time to grow up.

She hadn't expected it when the words came clear with purpose and meaning. Damascus had simply pulled the envelope from her underwear drawer as she had hundreds of times before. But this time the words came at her in a rush. Without warning, she'd read her mother's message.

It felt like a kick in the stomach, like falling without catching yourself and having all the wind knocked out of you. She hadn't realized until that instant that she didn't want to know what the letter said. It was better to be able to imagine anything she liked, just what she needed, any time she needed to talk to her mama. Sure better than stupid instructions for growing seeds, like she couldn't figure out how to do that by herself. But once you know something, you can't un-know it. Even now, she felt terrible about how carelessly she had wasted her mother's words, their last conversation gone in a blink. And she didn't know what to do with it, so she'd done nothing. That was the worst part. Except she'd decided for sure that she didn't want to learn anything more than she had to. She did the work Aunt Ivy gave her, but that was all. And even when the required tests for the state showed good scores, she refused to even talk about public school when Aunt Ivy brought it up.

You can't be hasty. You can't be careless. Once you plant your seed, it will have to make the best of your choices.

Still, she'd made it a ritual, reading the words of Mama's letter. She'd memorized them, but she read them anyway, forcing her eyes to slow down and follow the letters even as her mind tried to race ahead.

Seeds need warmth, light and water to survive. They grow best in soil that has something to give, but not so rich that the seed doesn't have to work at making something of itself.

And then, weeks ago, she'd overheard Aunt Ivy in the yard at High Dunes. She was rattling a paper at Daddy, telling him he might could let his own life go straight to hell, but she'd be damned if he would take Damascus with him. Damascus waited to hear her daddy chase Aunt Ivy off. She listened hard, but he didn't say one word. That silence about scared her worse than anything before, and worse, she felt sick because part of her wanted to go with Aunt Ivy. That's when she knew she couldn't wait anymore. If seeds were miracles, her daddy needed one.

She'd put the seeds on a paper plate and dampened them, giving them a head start to sprout. They had started to smell funny. They were peeling in translucent layers, and she'd been worried it had already been too long since the day her mother put them in the envelope and sealed up their secrets. But Damascus hid them on top of the refrigerator to keep warm, sending them all good thoughts. The first green shoots were enough to make her feel like she'd done the impossible.

When the first little sprout appears, it will demand your protection. It will scare you to death, how easy it can be squashed. But when everything seems to work against you, when the world tries to kill your vine and the hungry things come, remember a good fight makes the strongest fruit.

She remembered the day her mother dug them out of the biggest pumpkin Damascus had ever seen. They had glistened, moist and buttery pale, smelling sweet and new. Her mother had sat these seven aside on an open newspaper. She had chosen these seven seeds from all the others for reasons Damascus could only imagine.

Watch over what you've planted. Treasure it and it will grow. And most important of all, don't be afraid to cut deep and cut loose when things ripen. Don't be a girl who lets her gifts rot on a tough old vine.

Damascus had already let so many growing seasons pass while the seeds waited for her to be old enough to understand what she had to do. But this spring she'd looked to the moon, a pale sly wink starting to climb into the evening sky. The almanac said it was a new moon, the time to start the seeds. She had searched out a book at the library that said to let them sprout inside peat pots and grow strong before she'd put them in the ground to work things out for themselves on the banks of the Little Damascus. There were so many doubts, things she did not know that might ruin everything.

One she did know, the worst she could never have imagined. Her daddy had rented the farmhouse to a woman, a dancer who'd gone and wrecked her car and herself, and people were talking about what kind of trouble sends a woman like that running down here. So Damascus was listening, and what she heard just about did her in. Nonnie talking witchy ways, looking nervous so her eyes rolled up white in her head while she whispered to Aunt Ivy how she'd seen that woman coming in her dreams. "She gone set up a nest in your house, gone call up those gators from deep, deep with her broken heart. They gone rise up and put the dead to rest."

Damascus had to see for herself if this Roslyn Byrne could be a new conjure woman, if she could call the alligators. The Seminoles believed alligators could speak for the dead. The thought gave Damascus a chill. Because if it was true she knew how to speak to an alligator, then Roslyn Byrne had a power in her, one that could change everything. But besides that, Damascus needed to know where that woman stood on pumpkins. That was all.

Anxiously, she scuttled across the resort grounds and followed the river until she was standing at the edge of the yard where the security light pooled. She stopped just there, in that spotlight. In the dark, the living mystery of the ancient tributary that was her namesake swirled before her. No telling where that water had been. No way a girl like her would ever know the secret depths in the belly of the sea where this river sprang to life. But when she closed her eyes, Damascus could hear the water running, a promise, a sense of her own beginning.

It made her blood run to her head just thinking about all the things crawling around out here that made the grownups in her life stomp their feet and point their fingers in crazed worry over her. But as far as Damascus was concerned, if she got eaten up sometime by one of the alligators that had become a menace on these islands, the river could have her then. She wouldn't care. She'd grown up listening to Nonnie talk about the old folk crossing the water when they passed, and Damascus wanted more than anything to know what was on the other side, where her mama'd gone. Was it beautiful? Was it lonely? Was her mama happy there, or worried, watching them on the island? She needed to know. When you got there, did you forgive the people that went right on living without you?

She imagined the other side of the water like a mirror reflecting the island and the life her mama'd lived, only on her side, everything was perfect. Maybe if she followed the river, Damascus thought, it would carry her soul past the curve that bordered the resort, the current rocking her, guiding her toward the open waters, toward that greatest mystery of all, a middle place where she could touch both sides.

On her knees in the cool, sandy soil, she counted the precious plants, although she knew the number of her hopes. Seven reasons to believe. She'd laid them out with purpose, as God Himself must have lined up the first days of this world. Here was the promise of life that would depend solely on her care; seven ways her mother had trusted her to be able.

She'd built her sacred mounds, same as the Indians, and dug into their soft centers. She'd told herself that she was that kind of girl, someone who deserved to hold the future in her hands. She'd imagined pumpkins sprouting overnight, enormous and juicy, undeniable, big enough to hold a little girl. Those seeds held more than the promise of pumpkins. They were keepers of memories and wisdom as old as the earth. They were the return of the Trezevants to this farm, a sign to her father that when summer was up, it would be safe to come home.

Chapter Three

Roslyn

It didn't seem possible I could be here, so far from home and the things I knew. The dance company had replaced me with ease. There was always a line of eager young things waiting for my fall from grace. I might have come back from the pregnancy, but not the accident. The stitches were out, the fractures were healed, the torn ligaments in my knee would recover so my limp would hardly be noticeable. But at my age, I'd never regain the endurance to dance professionally. And after the stories got around about what followed the accident, no studio would hire me to teach.

I had until October to recover quietly, lick my wounds on this far-flung island, and come up with a brand new life for myself. I looked at the wild coastline with a sense of panic. The mysterious marshland and the far horizon seemed boundless. I wondered what I could possibly discover of myself in such a place.

I shouldn't have let Mama arrange my life for me again. I should have somehow managed to talk to Stephan about what happened. He'd know, of course, about the baby and what followed. Probably he was relieved I'd disappeared. What could we say? But I felt ashamed, and it was mixed up with the way I felt that I should have gone back to Glenmary. But Granny was gone. What would be the point?

The only thing that seemed clear was that while Mama and I had walked away from just about any place or person that wanted to settle us down, like her love for Jackie that had trapped her in the role of caretaker to a convalescent, I'd never believed I could just walk away from my one true gift. And now that the choice was taken from me, I had no idea what to do. My only comfort was knowing my car was parked on the other side of the bay.

But, sweet Jesus, it was beautiful here.

I drove the golf cart slowly along the sandy path, trying to avoid the ruts, gritting my teeth when my knee absorbed the little shocks. Waist-high chord grass swayed underneath a grove of half a dozen live oaks. The house sat off the water, half-hidden behind the low-hanging moss, a squat, two-story structure made of shale with a screened porch tacked across the front.

I'd have gone straight inside, but the door was locked, so I wandered down to the water to survey and acclimate myself instead of pulling out luggage. At the river's edge, I stood and stared over the gray-green expanse, at least two hundred yards across. It flowed strong and certain; a live thing, it crawled toward the open sea, around the tip of the island. I stretched my arms overhead and imagined morning exercises under the arms of those trees. Out of habit, I attempted a few steps and a turn. The wind off the water kicked up in a warm breeze, and I lost my center. I swear it was a voice I knew, a strong, low alto as familiar as a lullaby. My head jerked round, and I called for someone I knew wasn't there.

"Granny Byrne?"

My legs tangled, and I landed in a heap. I wasn't a child. I knew what was real and what was plain craziness.

But I wasn't alone. As if I'd called up the Reaper himself, I looked to see a tall man casually carrying a rifle at his side, step from the forest, closing the distance between us with ease. Humiliated, I could only hope he hadn't seen me, and I scrambled to my feet, wincing at my uncooperative joints.

He was darkly tanned from hours in the sun, and he stood a good head and shoulders above me, straight and intense, with a brooding expression and a wide mouth turned down in an uninviting grimace.

"Ros-Lyn? That what you go by?" He dragged the syllables

out, ebb and flow.

"It is. I mean, yes, I am." I could've jumped and run like a rabbit, but I made myself look hard enough at him until he was only a man.

"Urey Trezevant." He gave a brief nod, and the wind played with the dark hair that had grown out long over the collar of his work shirt. He clutched a slouch hat, wore fishing boots pulled over stained khakis. Gray was settling in at his temples, and his face was strained and drawn with worry lines. He held the rifle, barrel to the ground, in one hand while he pulled a key ring from his pocket and handed it over. There was no small talk. He seemed distracted, an unhappy man barely invested in the moment.

"This is for the shed out back, and an extra duplicate to the one you got with the confirmation in the mail. You got that all right?"

I said I had, and he knocked some mud off one boot and generally looked ill at ease. He was coarse, with sun-darkened skin, hands and forearms run through with large veins, feet rooted firmly in the ground. But I found myself deeply affected by his discomposure. Honestly, I wasn't sure which of us wanted out of the other's company worse.

"Look," he said, ticking the details off on his fingers. "I've got a brother-in-law that'll handle the yard, and he's the one that's set you up with the golf cart. So if you need repairs, he's your man. Number's on the fridge inside. He and my sister run the market down by the ferry. You'd have seen that. My sister's supposed to've been out here to clean up. Should have already been done, and I apologize about that."

"It's fine. That's fine."

He seemed to take notice of me for the first time and let his gaze wander far enough in my direction to take in the shape of my stance and the cane I was still using.

"I'm recovering from a car accident."

He was rubbing the back of his neck like the universe was completely out of hand. "Yeah, I heard some about it. So, there's this other thing. I've got a kid, ten years old. You ain't going to want a little girl under your feet. If she bothers you, tell her to get home. She's called Damascus."

"For the river? That's really nice." It was like telling a nervous dog he's a good boy and just waiting to get a chunk bit out of you.

"Her Mama came up with that name. She sure as hell didn't give the girl much else."

What could I say to that? A silence fell that would have been awkward with anyone else, but it seemed natural for Urey. He took a moment to look out over the river, and I wondered if I ought to just turn around and go back to Mama's before I had the chance to learn what kind of man greeted his renters with a rifle in hand.

From where we stood, I could see a tree near the house, its leeward side stunted and bare while the side closest to the house flourished, thick branches hanging low to the ground, reaching wide, adorned heavily in green leaves and dripping moss. From the lower limbs a collection of colored glass dangled, twisting in the island breezes, throwing strange and brilliant color across the ground and into the shadows on the porch. And I heard the chime of hollow vessels just before a wild little golf cart came tearing up the drive.

A brightly painted business logo for Lucky Mo Jo House Blessing covered the side, and the woman behind the wheel stirred up a plume of dust when she skidded to a halt at the front steps.

"Hey," she said, briskly, red hair floating away from her face where it had come loose from a braid. "Roslyn, right?" I nodded and smiled as she climbed down and crossed the yard to shake my hand. "Ivy Cain, this one's sister."

Urey kept quiet, turning the gun over in his hands, inspecting it.

Ivy rolled her eyes. "I'm here, ain't I?" she said to him. "Urey'd have you think I make a habit of lazing about and letting people wait on me. I had a big job at the other end of the island that's got me way behind," she explained. "Else I'd have already been done and gone from here. Everything okay? Urey helping you get moved in?"

"Yes," I lied.

She wasted no time in sizing me up from head to toe. I was glad of the loose-fitting sundress to hide a multitude of sins. Still, I could not escape the blue eyes, the twin pair to her brother's.

From closer than I'd like, a deep bellow made me forget all else. I let out a low sound of dread.

"Alligators," Urey said evenly.

"Seriously?" He shrugged and handed me the gun. "You think I'm going to use this?"

"Just don't shoot my kid," he said. "Or yourself."

Ivy spoke up then. "Lord, Urey. You'll scare her to death."

"She don't scare easy, or she wouldn't be here," he said. It surprised us both to hear him speak up so plainly in my favor.

Ivy looked at me more closely and said, "I guess you've got a point. Well, Roslyn, next few weeks or so, they'll be carrying on like that. Just a lot of boys making noise."

I smiled, and she hurried inside, lugging a heavy basket of cleaning supplies.

I started to follow Ivy, feeling awkward for not having stopped her in the first place. "I could clean up, myself," I said. But Urey's grip on my elbow stopped me.

"Stay out of the water," he said. He was all seriousness and, when he didn't let go, I listened. "If you're going to walk down there, look for slides. That's marks their bellies leave. Got a pet, keep it inside. 'Cause it ain't true, what they say. They're not more afraid of you."

He let go and stepped back as though he were embarrassed.

I tried to say something that made me sound as tough and dark as him. "Same with most bullshit people say. Like how this house is haunted," I said, testing him. But there was no change in his expression.

I watched him wipe his brow with the back of his hand. They were large, dark hands lined with scars that almost gave the impression of an animal hide, working hands. His grip was harsh, yet somehow sensual. Nothing like Stephan. I imagined waking up tomorrow with bruises like Urey Trezevant's fingerprints.

Ivy's voice calling made us both look to the house, and when I turned back, he'd gone.

And so this is how I met Urey Trezevant, while the alligators roared, and the breath of evening pressed on the back of my neck. I did not take my eyes from him as he disappeared down a footpath, so much a part of the place that he appeared to be absorbed into the thick maritime forest rather than passing through it as I was. He was going someplace I could not follow.

I'd abandoned my stash of caffeine pills when I left Dalton and the party was over, but I felt compelled to look useful next to the woman bumping around inside the conjure woman's house, busy making it fit for the likes of me. I decided to stay out of her way and start at the top. Upstairs I found a small space, a narrow loft area with two twin beds and an old throw rug on the floor. A small window showed a view of the front lawn down to the water. In my childhood, it would have been the hiding place of my dreams.

Back downstairs, in the back corner there was a small bedroom with a double bed and an ancient pine dresser. The mirror's glass was wavy as sea water. My clothes filled one deep drawer. In the other, I put away the yellow crochet squares with a twinge in my chest. I pulled out sheets and made the bed.

Ivy was a blur, wiping down counters and mopping floors. I found my luggage thrown wide open, my things already sitting out so the house looked inhabited. It would take me hours to figure out what kind of reason prompted her to put my toothbrush on the kitchen windowsill, shoes at the top of the stairs and, worst of all, sitting on the hearth was the cast of my feet Mama'd done when I first came home from the hospital.

Ivy came through the living room and caught me looking at the sculpture. She stopped, clutching a bottle of disinfectant to her chest, and cocked her head. "I didn't know where you'd want that," she said.

"I don't. You want it?"

A slow smile broke out on her face, and she shook her head. "Nope. What is it, anyway?"

"My mama trying to tell me something. She's an artist, sort of. Those, I'm sorry, are my feet."

I wanted to take a hammer to that sculpture, or a gun. I looked to the corner behind the kitchen door where I'd propped Urey's rifle and the thought crossed my mind to use it.

I couldn't help the green streak of envy as I watched Ivy bound up the stairs. She ran the vacuum over the throw rugs. The light was changing when she lugged her equipment out to load up her cart.

"I'm gonna go now, if you're good," she said. "I've got one more place to get to before my own." How she'd gotten everything out of the house and back onto that cart so fast, I'd never know. I stepped onto the back step, and Ivy smiled, face flushed behind her freckles. "Really, Roslyn, I'm impressed you're here. This place has a reputation, you know."

"I keep hearing that. Verna told me. She had nice things to say about you, though."

"So are you desperate or crazy?" Ivy said, then laughed and shook her head. "No, don't answer that. I wouldn't. Head on down to the store. It's open another hour, so you can run through tonight. It was a real pleasure meeting you."

I thanked her and watched her pull down the drive before I went inside for my purse and got a good taste of the conjure woman's house.

The kitchen cabinet to my left slowly opened of its own volition. If I'd been the kind of girl to faint, I might have fallen out right then. Instead, I bent down to get a better look. Two orange kittens mewled from a five-quart soup pot.

"How'd you get in there?" I asked, peering inside the cabinet in search of an explanation, not to mention their mother. The first was obvious, once I saw the lack of insulation around the kitchen pipes running inside from underneath the house. They must have climbed inside the pot or been put there by their mother. But there was no sign of the mother cat, and I thought of the predators prowling the riverbank and shuddered. I could only hope she'd show up and prove me wrong.

The kittens were nothing but skin and bones, their eyes barely open. I squatted down to reach for them, but I lost my balance and sprawled on the floor, my knee throbbing. The kittens didn't have much sympathy. They just continued to complain. Apparently, they didn't know they were alligator bait.

I kept quiet as I reached my hands toward them. They paced and wobbled, unsure as I eased the pot out and into my lap. "Looks like we're in this together now," I whispered over their pitiful cries.

None of us appeared at all reassured by this.

Cain's, the island market, was hardly even that, with only a few aisles of odds and ends, dimly lit. But I wobbled around in a hurry, picked up staples for myself, formula, an eyedropper, and baby bottles—the expensive brand, old-fashioned glass. A thin mahogany-colored woman behind the counter rang up the items while she cut sullen, astonishingly black eyes up at me.

"You got a little one?" she asked.

I was twitchy and unprepared to make conversation, but finally admitted, "No. Kittens."

While she made change, she eyeballed my cane. She was bagging my purchases, but I was entirely aware of her eyes; they were that impressive. Her features were sharp. and the planes of her face were smooth and wide. "You're the one renting the farm," she said.

I nodded, helping bag. I couldn't be sure of her ethnicity, although her speech was a mix of deep south and an unfamiliar, island accent.

"We grew up in that house, you know. Ivy's Mama and mine was second cousins."

"Oh. Roslyn Byrne." I gave her a tight smile, nothing encouraging, but she wasn't through with me.

"I'm Nonnie. Well." She considered me a little longer. "Ain't nobody told you about that place?"

"I've heard some."

She laughed, unconvinced. "Likely not enough." She was peering into my bag like she expected to find a shrunken head.

"It was a great deal," I said. "And I'm not superstitious."

Amused, her eyes were bright. "You don't believe what you heard, so that makes it so?"

"No, I believe," I corrected her. "It's just I travel with enough ghosts of my own. A few more don't worry me."

She nodded like I seemed sensible. "You need that stick?" she asked.

I let out a sharp bark of laughter at her nerve, startling her. "Yeah, I do. But I came out on the good end. Totaled the car," I said.

"That's a bitch." It was truly a sympathetic comment, and I almost liked her for it.

"No, that would be me. Wasn't my car."

She enjoyed that and leaned toward me over the counter. She had a way about her that made me nervous. "Ah, and Jesus knows he deserved worse, eh?" she said and winked.

I smiled. I couldn't help it. It was nice to have somebody take my side. But I regretted saying too much. I needed to get out of there.

She called after me, "Plug that cart up tonight, or your battery'll go dead on you."

I sang the first verse of *Farther Along* about fourteen times while I used the eyedropper to feed the kittens, dripping warm formula down their throats until their bellies were round and warm. I sobbed my way through the whole thing. "Don't die," I told them. They looked content in their milk stupors. They had no idea I was taking advantage of their misfortune to make myself feel better. I was a real saint. "Cats don't imprint, do they?"

I shut them up in their cabinet, safe for the night, blind as little moles.

Even in the dead of night, life was fresh and potent, crawling around out there, and instead of falling asleep I lay in the little room off the kitchen staring at the ceiling, biting at the edge of my thumbnail, a nervous habit that left my fingers looking raw and ragged. My mind wandered to the memory of my new landlord, the image of him stepping from those woods, the set of his broad shoulders, his tall, straight back and the firmness of his grip. I hadn't known a man like Urey Trezevant, not since I'd left Granny Byrne's cove with its taciturn farmers and rough neck miners. Maybe that was why I'd felt familiar with him so immediately.

He was a far cry from the self-absorbed, flamboyant dancers in the company, with their perfect physiques and enormous egos. Urey Trezevant wouldn't look you in the eye when he warned you not to let his island eat you up. He apologized for his daughter, like he was sorry he'd had any hand in her.

I wondered about her. That was something that stuck with me after he'd gone. But while he was before me, he demanded all my attention. He was organic, visceral, and might have sprung right up from the earth, beautiful as Adam after the fall.

Whatever Urey Trezevant called up for me, I couldn't handle it. But it aggravated me, why he'd affected me so deeply. Probably because he was the one distraction finally strong enough to keep my mind from wandering back to mirrored walls, wooden floors, yawning stages where I would never stand again. I didn't know. Wrestling with the emotion, I bit too far into the quick of my nail. The sharp sting shocked me out of my thoughts. I'd drawn blood.

A thin soprano rose up far over the water, an eerie sound that found an echo in a mate farther off, probably a bird. I sucked on my fingertip and pulled out the crochet squares. I sat them side by side on the dresser top. I mean, rationally I understood that if I opened the door, there would be nothing waiting for me.

I drew myself a bath.

It was a fine idea, and I walked around naked, just because I could, while the tub filled. I ran my hands over my abdomen. Life had come and gone, but it had changed me. Marked me.

When the tub wouldn't hold another drop plus me, I sank deeper and deeper into the silent waters and traced the cracks in the porcelain with my toes. But the plaintive chorus would not be silenced. It seemed to seep in through the walls and rise up from beneath the floor. In the midsummer heat, I felt something raw and real, like I'd only ever known in Granny's church. Perhaps I had called her here as surely as I'd watched her call Grandpa each morning.

Grandpa Byrne died years before I came along, but in the early morning I would sometimes wake to hear Granny softly singing love to her husband over her Folgers, the tune a little off for lack of his harmony. His ashes sat on the windowsill instead of being scattered over the mountain like he'd asked. Granny said she'd expected to have more time with him when they'd married. She wasn't giving it up because of a little thing like death. The one time I remember Mama trying to convince Granny to do the respectable thing ended in Mama saying hoarding a dead man's ashes was exactly the kind of thing a Keller would do, Keller being Granny's maiden name. Being compared to a Keller was the worst kind of insult.

But Granny Byrne didn't turn a hair. She left Mama standing in a sweat and hauled me down the road to a neighboring field and let me play all afternoon long. She was never idle, and the fact that we piddled around all those hours flat amazed me. I loved the field because every year about a million daffodils broke loose like gold all over the place. I picked them until I couldn't carry any more.

"I'm going to live here when I grow up. We'll be neighbors and just walk to see each other any time we want," I promised.

I meant it, too. I thought I'd have been happy as Grandpa Byrne to sit on her windowsill forever. I'd heard her telling him all the things he was missing when I would walk into that kitchen and see her talking to those ashes. There was no doubt even for a child as young as I'd been, that she'd raised his ghost. I knew then, the only thing that really ever haunts a person is a regret.

I thought I'd be with her forever. She loved me better than anything. But it didn't turn out that way for either one of us.

That was my first ghost. The first promise I broke.

I wondered about the ghosts in this house and if any of them haunted Urey Trezevant.

"Make yourself at home, Granny," I called to whatever was listening. We were sitting up in that house, for better or worse, because I sure didn't know anything better to do with myself at the moment. I wondered if maybe that's what brought those sorry Kellers to Granny's doorstep. Maybe Mama ought to think of that. I wanted Granny there so bad, telling me what to do, I was willing to pretend. Even when I no longer heard the sad calling outside. "We're going to be here a while."

Chapter Four

Damascus

The farm stood pale in the moonlight before Damascus, who crouched a few yards away from the house, barefoot and sweating behind the saw palmetto. She pulled the baseball cap down lower, a nervous habit, and waited. She'd been here each night since she'd put her garden in, checking on her vines, never failing to care for them, just as her mother had told her, saying a secret prayer over them. She wasn't sure where she held with God, but figured it couldn't hurt, since she wasn't praying for herself, but for seeds that were mostly his business once they were in the dirt, anyway. And then mostly, she was watching to see what was going on at the house. She was waiting to see if the things Ms. Nonnie said about Roslyn Bryne were true.

Damascus had seen the pictures in a newspaper, images of a ballerina like a queen. But something had happened, and now the woman in this house had changed into something else entirely. Magic, like glitter, like dust, could slip right through your fingers. Before you knew it, a wonder could mix with the plain old earth beneath your feet until you could no longer tell the difference at all.

Damascus hunkered down, so still she could barely feel the rise of her chest with each breath. She would have to bide a while. She'd seen her pumpkins were safe. But the curiosity that drove her kept her watching to see if the rumors she'd heard could be true. Roslyn Byrne was a true conjure woman with the secret language of the dead, whose broken heart brought the alligators with her to the river this year. She might not like a little girl with a bunch of pumpkins getting in the way of her alligator business.

She didn't know which impressed her more, the idea of a real ballerina, or a hoodoo woman. But she was inclined to believe the latter, since she'd seen it with her own eyes, the woman standing on the river bank. Her voice carried back to Damascus, sorrowful and wordless calling, a watery, monstrous language of grief. Who else would live in this house, after all? She'd seen the woman call her words over the water, and just like that, her daddy had shown up. Her daddy, who didn't come when anybody called his name, stepped out of the woods and got busy doing every little thing to get that woman moved into his house like she wanted.

This night the woman did not open the door. She did not step out onto the porch. Patience wasn't supposed to be a Trezevant trait, and Damascus got tired of waiting for the perfect moment, and decided the one she was living in would do just fine.

Dashing on bare feet right up the crumbling tabby steps that led to the back door, she pressed her face to the glass window, but could make out nothing beyond an empty kitchen countertop and a sad, single chair. In the light spilling out from the kitchen, she saw a blue-tailed lizard scurry across her toes and into a crack beneath the door. No alligator, that was for sure, but Damascus let out a squeak just the same. She clamped her hand over her mouth, but there was no movement from the dark rooms inside. No sound came from the house at all.

She didn't give herself time to be chicken shit about it. The door wasn't locked. She slipped inside and stood on the cool wood floor in the dark, letting her eyes adjust.

Tonight, sweet green tendrils were already curling their way across the sand of Damascus' pumpkin patch, life sprouting out of the earth. Her dream had taken root before this woman had come here, and now Damascus had to protect it at all costs. She said the sacred words over them, words she couldn't even understand, the ancient prayer, a blessing from people who'd lived on this island about a gazillion years ago, and hoped it would be enough.

There were signs of the woman in the house. Curtains at the window, dirty dishes in the sink, Aunt Ivy's business card stuck to the refrigerator with a magnet. She poked through the cabinets, finding little more than paper plates and a couple of cans, a bag of chips, and a bottle of milk, half empty. All a little disappointing. The hum of the refrigerator kicking on startled her, and she bumped her knee on the table that sat in the middle of the room. When that noise brought no one running to discover her, Damascus tiptoed through the other rooms downstairs until a flicker of light caught her eye. At the back of the house, a door stood half open. If she'd tried, Damascus couldn't have imagined what she would find behind that door.

A candle burned on the sink, and the scent of hot wax and gardenia was so thick Damascus gasped. But it was the milky white ankle that dangled from the side of the footed tub that caused her to hold her breath. She crept closer. She was not afraid of death. Damascus had already seen the worst it could do. The woman lying beneath the water was the Queen herself, the Roslyn Byrne from the newspaper clipping Damascus had tucked inside her jeans pocket.

Roslyn's eyes stared up at the ceiling. Not moving, her arms floated out beside her, her long, dark hair fanned around her head. A thousand times, Damascus had imagined her mama just that way, her soul being carried across the river. But there were mean little questions that came at Damascus in the night when she closed her eyes, and they came for her now, under that old, yellow light. They had teeth like wasp stings.

What if you'd been there so your Mama could have seen your face? If she'd seen you, maybe she would have remembered she had to come back to you. What if you could have given her all the beats of your heart, pulled her from the river, and combed the little knots of death from her hair with your fingers? You wouldn't have let that river take her.

Damascus didn't stop to think before she grabbed the chain attached to the plug and opened the drain. In that instant, the woman's eyes swiveled toward her.

"Hey," Damascus yelped. "You trying to kill yourself?"

Roslyn Byrne sat up in one quick move, sloshing water onto

the floor. The sound that came from her made Damascus think of the screech in the steering wheel of her daddy's Chevy.

"Well, you ain't dead." She stepped forward to pull a towel from the hook on the wall and offered it, but the woman only coughed and stared at her with a dazed look until Damascus had no choice but to try to help her from the tub. "Come on. You need to get out of there before you shrivel up and go down the drain," she said, the same words her mother used to say. She slipped her small fingers around the woman's hand. Roslyn Byrne's grasp tightened like a clamp, and she stared hard at Damascus.

"I thought . . . shit," the woman said.

Damascus smiled. She'd made the ballerina cuss, and that was something. Roslyn Byrne was still hanging on to her.

She seemed amazed at the solidity of Damascus' hand. "I mean, you're not what . . . who I thought."

"Well, *shit*," Damascus said, enjoying the taste of the nasty word. "Neither are you. That don't change nothing."

"No. No, I guess not."

Roslyn leaned to grab a towel and stepped out. The woman was no ethereal fairy. There was weight to her. Where wings should have been, her shoulder blades poked up, fragile and ugly. Damascus had read the article over again and again. *Car accident ends Swan Queen's reign.*

Damascus tried not to look at the woman's nakedness, embarrassed by the sight of titties and hips and the dark curls that made Damascus think of her own little girl's body. There were things she wished she'd known to ask her mother. But it was the sight of angry red scars along the length of one leg and across her abdomen and shoulder that burned in the little girl's mind.

"You look bad. Not like I thought. Not like the picture. I thought I'd like looking at you, but I sure don't."

Roslyn laughed hoarsely, but Damascus didn't think it was funny. In fact, she thought Roslyn looked like one more messed up grownup, and she'd had about all of that any ten-year-old could take.

The woman was shaking like she was going to come apart. The way her teeth chattered made Damascus want to hold her jaws shut with her hands. At least Roslyn had wrapped her hair up in a towel and put on a robe. Damascus watched her do it all, then head out to the kitchen where she poured Damascus the last glass of milk and sat down at the kitchen table.

"That's about all I've got," Roslyn Byrne said. "If you're hungry, you came to the wrong place."

Damascus sipped her milk while Roslyn watched her. It was silly how neither one of them was saying what they were really thinking, like how come Roslyn was underwater at this hour, or what Damascus was doing busting in on a complete stranger like a little burglar. Damascus figured now she was sure Roslyn wasn't about to kill herself, she might as well find out what she'd come here to know.

She leaned back in her chair like she'd seen her daddy do all her life, like she was easy as anything, and said, "We ain't seen this many alligators since way back, like two hundred years or something." They were brave words. They sounded like a real big question. A great big dare.

Roslyn Byrne blinked at her. But instead of saying she knew what Damascus was getting at, she just said, "I bet I know who you are. Little Damascus. I'm supposed to watch out for you. That's what your daddy said."

"So. Watch."

Damascus about jumped out of her skin when a big crash came from the front room.

"Who's in there?" Roslyn demanded, coming around the table to go see. "Who did you bring in here?"

"Nobody." Damascus followed close behind, bumping into Roslyn when she stopped short and sucked in a quick breath.

And then nobody breathed again for what seemed like a long time.

Right there by the couch, hissing mad, with stout legs sticking out like it was ready to jump on them, was an alligator about three feet long. The noise had been the three-tier curio table in the corner getting knocked on its side. A couple of little sea shells were scattered on the floor, and a piece of pottery had broken.

"I left the door open," Damascus whispered, disbelieving.

All of a sudden, before either one of them could do anything, the alligator darted one direction, then another, making them squeal and grab at each other. Damascus tried to pull Roslyn toward the front door while the alligator banged itself smack into the wall a couple of times before it made for the hallway. But Roslyn wasn't moving, crazy lady! In fact, she pushed Damascus off and skirted around like she was going after the thing! That's when Damascus noticed the trail of blood the animal was leaving. It must have cut itself on the broken pottery. It didn't really seem to have good sense.

Roslyn snatched up a metal walking stick, the kind Damascus had seen old people use to get around, and poked at the alligator to try and turn it around. When it started back toward Damascus for a moment, she ran and jumped on the couch, cussing Roslyn.

"I've got to keep it out of the kitchen! There's kittens in there!" Roslyn hollered.

"You didn't call it here?"

The alligator came after Roslyn's stick, nearly knocking her over in the hallway before it scooted past into the kitchen anyway. It didn't seem like it wanted a bite out of them. Damascus even felt a little sorry for it now she'd noticed its eyes might be the trouble, all milky white and staring. That's when Roslyn saw it looked like the alligator had already had a bite of something. She wailed over the mess at the foot of the stairs, but while Roslyn chased the gator around the doorframe into the kitchen, Damascus stepped over and saw it was only a little pile of chicken bones. Not alligator leftovers, but three clean, white bones tied together with a raveled piece of red string.

Damascus didn't touch it. She just eased through the house and watched, not even believing when Roslyn Byrne hiked her leg over a kitchen chair and the top of that alligator so she got around in front of it. Then she put it in a corner with the edge of her walking stick just like she was taming a lion in the circus.

The two of them were breathless, sweat popping out all over, and the alligator looked plain worn out to Damascus by the time this was all over with. Its mouth was wide open, but it wasn't knocking its head around into everything anymore.

Roslyn's long hair hung down, a dark curtain that hid her face. It was like a spring released inside her when the woman said, "Damascus, I think you better go get somebody."

Damascus' feet hit the porch steps in fast slaps, and then the sand in silence where she stopped.

Where was she going? To whom? Nonnie? She wouldn't come out here at night to some strange white woman, not to help. Her daddy was gone to town. Besides that, he'd skin her alive if he found out she'd come over to the farm after he'd told her to leave Roslyn Byrne be. There was only one person, and Damascus flew down the path toward help.

When the porch light flipped on, Damascus' legs were burning from the five minute run to the little house near the ferry dock, just behind Cain's Market. She took a step back so the moths wouldn't get caught in her hair and called out, "Aunt Ivy? It's Damascus. You've got to come. An alligator's got in on that woman Daddy's rented to, and she says to hurry up and get somebody. And you're the only body I got."

Aunt Ivy's golf cart bumped down the drive throwing headlight beams all over the place. Damascus could tell her aunt wasn't happy. She was likely to lecture Damascus about scouting around in the dark without her daddy's permission. But none of that could be helped now. Aunt Ivy'd thrown her bag at Damascus, and she'd brought a ball of ground beef wrapped in cellophane, now in her lap.

"Is that poison?" Damascus dared to ask.

Ivy scowled at her. "Not if he's lucky. I don't know how much belladonna I used exactly, but it ought to just knock him on his butt long enough so we can get him outside. Damascus, what are you doing out here?"

"I couldn't just let her die in there," Damascus said, feeling the weight of the bag on her thighs.

"Die?" she nearly shouted. "It's that big?"

"No, I ain't talking about that, the alligator. I mean before, when I got here. She was in need."

"Damascus, you're going to have to make some sense. She called you over here?"

"No, ma'am. I come on my own. I let myself in, 'cause I always did before, only I didn't know she was in the tub. I believe she was thinking of hurting herself."

Aunt Ivy shook her head and mumbled under her breath. "Honey, it's the middle of the night. What were you doing in that house?"

If Daddy signed that paper, Aunt Ivy wouldn't let any girl of hers out running this island in the dark. Damascus had looked everywhere she knew, but she hadn't found that paper. She didn't know what Daddy had done with it.

It was probably something like four o'clock in the morning by now, and Damascus shrugged. It wasn't like she could lie her way out of anything now. "Snoopin'." Damascus wondered what on earth was in that bag. Aunt Ivy called it her bag of tricks. "Is there something in here to help?"

Ivy sucked air through her nose. "Well, I don't guess I know. Are we going over here because this woman's trying to do herself in, or because of an alligator?"

"Both. I mean, just the alligator. I'm not making it up or anything. It's not real big, but it's mad like crazy."

"That don't worry me like the other."

Ivy had been running one thing or another out of that house her whole life. Damascus figured a little alligator didn't stand a chance. But what about Roslyn Byrne?

"I heard about her. Nonnie's got a story from the paper." Damascus didn't say she'd heard plenty more, listening in on Nonnie's gossip. Aunt Ivy sighed and groaned some more, but Damascus carried on with her explanations. "I wanted to see her. And then I thought she was about to drown herself, only she wasn't," Damascus sighed. "Least she said she wasn't. She put me at the table with a glass of milk, not mad at all.

Everything would have been just fine if it weren't for her having a bowl set out for those kitties. I reckon that little gator smelled a meal and crawled on in."

"There's kittens now?" Ivy groaned, and Damascus tried harder to shed a better light on things. "I just left here! When did the whole earth crawl in the house?"

"Just two of them. They're not hardly a couple weeks old, either."

"Oh, hell." Ivy shifted in her seat and quickly added, "You shouldn't hear me talk like that."

Damascus rolled her eyes. "Whatever. Anyway, she was doing all right when I left, even with her leg being stiff like it is, 'cause she's got that cane. But the gator, it about had the house tore apart when she said for me to get on and find help. I leaped out the back door to come find you. I told her just come on with me, but she wouldn't leave them kitties."

"How big is the gator?"

"I just saw it a minute. I guess about three feet." Damascus waited to see what Aunt Ivy made of that, thinking she might slip up and give away more of her superstitious ideas about Roslyn.

But Aunt Ivy only said, "Your daddy can kiss the rent goodbye."

"Maybe he don't want it," Damascus grumbled. She knew Aunt Ivy was the one responsible for finding a renter. "Maybe he don't want that woman in our house. He's moving us back. Soon as this summer's done. He told me so."

Aunt Ivy didn't say anything. She glanced at Damascus like she might argue, but then she just pushed the cart's peddle all the way down so they were having to clench their teeth through the ruts to keep from biting their tongues off.

They pulled up in the yard, and the cart hadn't even come to a stop before they jumped out. The wind barely stirred, a silent flight swooping past in a rush just above their heads, Urey's henchman.

"There's Elder," Damascus said. That was her daddy's barn owl. The old folks said an owl was a bad omen, a sign of death to come. When it settled, it called in search of a mate, a lonely sound that split the darkness. It could raise the hair on your arms, hearing that sound.

"Oh, I hate that bird." Aunt Ivy started toward the house.

Taking her bag from Damascus, she flung open the screen door.

Strange to say, but everything was quiet except there was music playing, and it was coming from the kitchen. They might as well have walked right into some kind of revival for all the spooky voices carrying on like an angel choir.

"Good God," Aunt Ivy said.

"Ha!" Damascus laughed, totally entertained. "Maybe she got him saved."

Aunt Ivy glared at her and unwrapped the meatball on her way through the house. They found Roslyn in the kitchen, feet wide apart, brandishing the cane at the cornered alligator.

"Help's here!" Ivy called out over the music. Roslyn jerked around to see them but Aunt Ivy didn't waste time with how do you do. She tossed out her meatball, and then grabbed the gun leaning by the doorframe. The alligator hissed and jumped around on its short legs, unsure how to defend itself.

"Don't kill it!" Damascus screamed, leaping for the barrel with both hands.

Ivy pushed Damascus off.

"Stop it, Damascus," Ivy said, keeping her eye on the animal. "That's a gun, girl! You don't grab a gun like that."

But even as her aunt warned her, Damascus watched to see that the alligator wasn't even close to finding that meatball, so she reached down and grabbed up the poison. Wrapping her arms around herself, she hopped up and down and hollered, "I know, but look at it! It's just little. It don't know from what! It can't even see, and it's my fault it's come in here. I left the door open."

"It can't see?" Ivy stammered.

The alligator must have smelled the beef, and it was throwing its head around, irritated, but it was easy to tell by the milky white of its eyes that it was blind.

Finally, Roslyn, who hadn't taken her eyes off the animal, spoke up in a cool, calm voice that surprised everybody with its command. "Shut up arguing and move. Ivy, get around to the left, and we'll drive it out the door. It's going to take the two of us because it's blind as a bat. That's why it's nearly killed itself crashing through the house. It ran all through that glass on the floor after it knocked into the table, and it cut up its belly. I don't want it hurt any more than it is."

Ivy crept next to the animal while Damascus opened the door. All she could do was watch, amazed as Aunt Ivy poked the alligator with the butt of the rifle. Roslyn spoke softly, whispering sometimes to the creature as she stomped one foot along to direct the procession. The alligator scuttled this way and that, but followed Roslyn Byrne right outside, and the whole thing was over pretty quick. Only once on the porch did it dart in the wrong direction and nearly fall off the edge. Then down the steps and through the yard it ran, faster than you'd believe.

Both women threw their hands up with a whoop of victory and laughed, breathless, but Damascus followed the animal, even with Aunt Ivy hollering at her from the porch. She heard the sound of it moving through the tall grass at the side of the yard and a quiet slosh as it slid into the slough in a low spot she'd crossed many times. She stopped short, not wanting to disturb it if it had found itself a hole. She'd have to be careful there now.

For a moment, Damascus stood still, her skin and hair damp in the humid morning air. Dawn would break any minute. The birds were starting to wake, and she could hear the river beyond the shadowy yard. She felt everything, as though she'd grown new nerves under her clothes. She thought of the seeds she'd put in the ground to dissolve and open and send out something live to reach up to the light. She thought of the alligator, heart racing, finally sinking into the mud and finding its home after running for its life. She was aware of each breath and felt she had turned inside of herself somehow and found something sweet waiting there, something she'd never expected, that might have been her soul. Her alligator soul.

The light was creeping over the world when she came back

to the house. Aunt Ivy was sitting on the porch with Roslyn, and they were drinking coffee. Damascus knew she should hurry home before her daddy found her missing, but she couldn't decide to leave. She wanted to stay there with the women. It was as if what they'd done together in the night had bound them some way to one another. Even when Aunt Ivy told her she'd better take her sneaky self and get back where she belonged, Damascus wasn't sure where that was anymore. She only knew she couldn't quit looking at Roslyn. She just couldn't help herself, just like that animal that had crawled up in a house where it knew it didn't belong. Damascus thought a crazy thing, that maybe she was waiting for Roslyn to tell her what to do next.

When she continued to hang around, Aunt Ivy demanded, "What? What is it?"

Damascus didn't know what it was, but something had changed, and she suspected what it might be. She took a deep breath and answered in as loud a voice as she could eek out. "Nonnie was right. Everything she said about Roslyn Byrne was dead on."

Chapter Five

Roslyn

Jumping around after an alligator will tell you real quick what you've got in you and where your limits are. The house looked like a couple of drunks had been brawling, and my docking station with the iPod had gotten knocked over. Blaring *a cappella* gospel filled the house, a tenor yowling about 'Sweet Beulah Land,' but at least the alligator hadn't eaten up my kitties when all was said and done, and I was still on my feet.

Ivy Cain stood limply at my side on the porch. She looked like a matchstick set on fire-red hair flying free of the braid now.

"You said to call if I needed anything," I said.

While I went inside to step into some panties and turn off the tunes, she sent Damascus home. Then she refused to listen when I said I was embarrassed she'd been dragged from her bed. I swore that I was fine to straighten up, she didn't need to stay.

"It's too late to sleep now," she said, so I put on a pot of coffee and the two of us got busy setting the house right. Pretty soon I figured out she was about as worried over how I was going to take my first day on the island as I was sure she'd decided I was a loon.

"What did she mean, I'm everything Nonnie said? She's that woman at your store? What is she saying about me?" I'd waited to ask until Damascus was gone, mostly because I wanted a straight answer.

"Oh, who knows," Ivy said, waving a hand as she scooted the couch back into place. "Nonnie sits for Damascus when Urey's working or out nights. She's always saying stuff to try and scare Damascus into staying in the house. They didn't want her over here bothering you."

A little alarmed and slightly offended, I said, "Great. I must not have been scary enough. Obviously it didn't work."

That's when she came around to the foot of the stairs. She stood there staring at the scattered bones a moment before she looked up. "This your charm?" I stared at her, unsure if I'd heard her right. "No. Course it's not," she answered her own question. "We found them just like that. What is it?"

"It's a root." Ivy scooped the bones up with a small clatter that caused the hair on my arms to stand up.

"I'm sorry?"

"Hoodoo. Island magic."

I followed her back into the kitchen. She threw the whole thing into the trash, then went to wash her hands. When she turned to face me, she looked older than her years.

"Nonnie's paid you a visit," she explained. "Probably before Damascus even got out here, she'd already come and gone. I knew she would do this. I just didn't think it'd happen here, or tonight."

"Happen? What is going on?" I'd been foolish to think there was any place on earth I could hide my reputation. People had opinions about girls like me. They wanted to teach me lessons, remind me my sins would find me out.

"They're just bones, and you throw them out and don't let her bother you with that crap."

I half shouted, "She left a boney freaking curse in my house and let an alligator in on me, and I'm not supposed to let it bother me?"

"The alligator, I don't know about. You'd have to take it up with him. But the charm, it's called Throwing the Bones, a way of reading your future. It's nothing to hurt you. It could be a housewarming thing," Ivy said. But I could tell she didn't believe it. "It's harmless, swear to God. Like shaking a Magic Eight Ball when you were a kid. You did that, right? I use it all the time in my cleaning, just blessing this and blessing that. Nothing to it except people love thinking they've got something special, throwing a charm over them. You look at it that way, all right?"

I shuddered, wondering wildly how long it would seriously take me to pack. "Could you read them? Did you see what they said about me? Because if I was reading them, they'd say 'Get the hell out.' I never saw that on a Magic Eight Ball."

"All right, listen. She's Saltwater Geechee, same as Mama was. She's just got her ways, and one of them is that she thinks this house is hers. She's right, too." She saw my confusion and added, "Legally, the house is Urey's. But Nonnie, she's Delia's girl, my cousin."

"Delia. The woman who lived here before?" I guessed, tangled in the branches of the Trezevant family tree. I couldn't bring myself to say witch.

"That's right. It's a long story. But trust me, Nonnie's just protecting the house. It's nothing personal."

I was starting to feel nauseous, I was so over stimulated and exhausted. Ivy seemed to notice I was fading fast. She put out a little can of tea cakes I'd bought at the store and poured the coffee just like we were in her home.

I took a sip and burned my tongue. "The last time somebody threatened me with a dead chicken, it was headless, and my cousins were chasing me around my granny's house. I think I handled it better then," I grumbled.

"Good Lord, what a day," she said. She sat down hard across the table, nibbling on a cookie until she finally added, "Listen, you've probably been about every place in the world, and you could up and go from here, but my brother needs the rent, and I need my brother to get used to somebody else in this house so he'll finally sell the damn thing. I'll make sure nothing like this happens again. We'll get out of your hair, and you'll think you're the only soul on earth."

"Oh, I doubt that." I finished off my coffee and started to feel a little better.

Ivy looked exhausted. "Well, you'd get a better result if you'd turn that music down."

I was so surprised she could make a joke, and truly relieved she didn't seem to share the opinion of this Nonnie, I couldn't help but giggle at her face. "Sacred Harp music. They sing it on the mountain where my mama grew up."

"Sounds a lot like a Stomp, the way the people used to get together and sing here, the people I grew up with. Everybody's about gone now that would remember that. Do your harp people clap? There's a rhythm here for every song. They have a name for it. I forget."

We're not so different, she was saying. An olive branch. I tried to forget the bones. I wanted to like Ivy Cain. She was watching to see what I would do.

"They clap sometimes. I've been listening to it since the . . . accident. Looking for some meaning, like all sinners, I guess. Some assurance there's more to it, that life's not just random."

Without realizing it, I'd placed my hands over my belly. I had on an old pair of soft shorts and a T-shirt and although there was no physical evidence of my miscarriage, any woman could look at me and see the truth. But when Ivy looked at the soft roundness of my abdomen, she didn't say one word. Instead, she sat back in her chair and waited.

"I lost a baby." I took a deep breath, enough air to float my mania. "You probably know that."

"I'm sorry."

It wasn't the first time someone had said those words, but it was the first time I'd believed them. I looked hard at Ivy, a mother, another woman close to my age. She might as well have been an alien for all I knew about how to make friends. But I decided to trust the woman who could face alligators and hexes and religion and grief without batting an eye. She probably wouldn't have believed it, but I was watching her, too.

"Yeah, I haven't read what they put in the papers. Mama wouldn't let me. But I can guess they had a field day. Not every day a Sugar Plum Fairy tries to bury her baby with a garden spade."

Ivy lifted a thin, red brow. If her mama was a Saltwater Geechee, her daddy must surely have been a redheaded woodpecker. What a pair they must have made. Her grim smile gave me hope she wasn't completely scandalized. "You're sitting in my family's personal haunted house," she finally consented.

"What am I going to say?"

"You have a point." We sipped our coffee quietly until I sat my cup down and said, "Have you ever seen a ghost in here?"

"All the time. Except what I say is a ghost may just be me wishing. I see my mama here, mostly, the way I like to remember her. I guess that's a kind of ghost." Then I saw another, less pleasant thought take hold of Ivy, and she leaned forward. "Why? Did you see something?"

"Last night I thought I heard someone singing."

"Not Damascus? Or maybe Nonnie?"

"No, I know this voice. My Granny Byrne. She died a few months ago, and I've been hearing her for a while. But she was here in the house this time, and I was glad. I was hoping what I'd heard was true. That she was real. That this house was haunted." Ivy's shoulders relaxed. "Maybe it's the same as what you said, wishful thinking." I waited to see if she could understand, but she only went on looking at me with her soulful, blue eyes. "I know how that sounds. I mean, I know—now—it wasn't real. The sounds, the feelings, they were all in my head. Or maybe it was Damascus. She was out there. I don't know why I'm telling you this."

"Sounds like you want me to tell you it wasn't just your imagination getting the best of you. But I don't know." She cocked her head to the side as though she were listening, maybe checking to be sure she hadn't missed anything, then shook her head and focused on me again.

"Nonnie'd say it's the shell ring. It's west of the house. Delia always acted like she'd built the thing personally. She was half Indian on her Mama's side. They liked to talk about being Seminole, but those are pretty muddy waters."

Ivy looked anything but Seminole, with her strawberry hair and fair skin. The Trezevants were a true melting pot. "Delia's daddy was a black man. His son used to be tenement farmer here, Delia's half-brother, but he's an old man now."

"And she did this . . . hoodoo?"

"She got fixated on the idea of Annie Tommie, this real famous Seminole woman that was a witch doctor. There's paintings of her someplace. Delia, she liked thinking she was carrying on such as that. I don't know how much she really knew about what she was doing, and what all she just made up.

"So, you say you've been hearing your Granny." She shrugged. "I'm not surprised. This is a woman's house. The spirit of the place is such, the windows always open, right on the river where you can see what comes and goes, or sit and visit for a while, come and cure what ails you. It makes sense she'd find you here, don't you think? You'd hear her best in a house like this. I been talking to this house for years, myself."

"She'd like this house." I started to explain about Glenmary, but the words lodged in my throat. Instead, I said, "I don't really know how to do this girl talk thing." My voice was loaded with my need to speak of the last few weeks. The room was so still I didn't want to breathe.

"Whatever you've got, let it rip."

"You may not want me staying, once you hear."

"Fine. Don't tell me. Tell the house."

If her words hadn't convinced me entirely that she could handle my confession, the look in her eyes set loose a flood inside me. Whatever Ivy'd read in the papers, I wanted her to know the truth if I was going to stay here with her niece running around. I wanted that Nonnie woman to know. I didn't leave anything out, not the garden spade or the crochet squares. Not the pep pills or the way I'd let Mama handle everything, everything, until I didn't know how to handle anything anymore.

And when it was all spilled out, I swear I was surprised to find the truth didn't take up any space between us in that room. I stared at the floor as though I expected the facts to be piled there, suffering, horrific. But it was only the floor. Only the burnt smell of coffee and Ivy, not a hair out of place.

She let out a long slow breath and sat up, gathered the empty cups and went to refill them at the pot on the countertop before she turned to take a sip and hand my cup back to me. "You just had a life pass through you, that's all. It's what women got from Eve. The knowledge of the tree of life."

"I want to give it back." A terrible case of hiccups came on me, and I sat there, jerking like a drunk.

"We all do. We weren't meant to have it. That's the one thing Delia taught me, told me right here in this kitchen. She told me this one day when I was just a girl, a long time before I had my baby, but I remembered it. I still think on it." She had an earnest look on her face, like she'd been thinking about this for a long time, like maybe I was the first person she'd really found willing to listen to her ideas. "Man got to rule over the earth because he was made in God's image, but the Lord spared him the knowledge of the tree, the part he couldn't handle. It was Eve who took the holy burden of the tree for women. Not power, not giving life, not being able to sustain it or call it forth, just having it passing in and out and through us like window screens. You can't do a thing about it. What you have to do is just tell yourself you're not God, and be thankful for it. I've got a kid, nearly full grown, and, believe me, he's a mess. I tell myself that same thing every day. I say, 'Ivy honey, this is not the end of the world. It's just your little time on Earth. And it's hardly a blink.'"

The thin light at the window surprised me. Dawn was creeping over the island. Ivy noticed it, too, smoothing her hair back from her face with a deep sigh. "Lord, it's nearly five." She turned her back to me and looked out the window at the river. "I better get on out of here."

"I need to thank you," I said, feeling scattered. "I wish there was something I could do."

Ivy smiled. "Running around after a gator in your house all night's not enough for you?"

"No," I laughed, feeling jittery from too much coffee and honesty. "I mean I got you up in the middle of the night. You didn't have to come out here. Most people wouldn't."

She shrugged off my appreciation, put the cream back in the refrigerator. "Looks like it's going to be hot," she said. "I've got four houses today and then, Otis. I'll be dragging by this evening."

"Otis?"

"Otis Greene. I go over by the old folks home to look in on

him a couple days a week, take him a Baby Ruth and watch his show with him. It's a house they're in, not a facility, like a real home. Not a bad place at all. I clean for them once a week, and Will keeps up the yard in the summer.

"Otis is the man I told you about that farmed out here after Delia died," she explained. "Sweet old man. Ninety-two. He's outlived everybody I reckon he ever knew, except us. He's about the only one left to remember like we do."

"So he's who started the stories it was haunted?"

"Oh, he believed it. Still does. But he don't talk about it much anymore. He's crazy about the television and he won't miss his *Fantasy Island.*"

"So, he's Delia's . . . half-brother?"

"Yeah, I know. Everybody's related out here. It ain't a big place. Three or four families, the odd folk sprinkled in here and there. Most of them come here when the Indians were run off from places up and down the coast, slaves that hid out, mixed together. Now you cain't tell what all we might be, except this place. And it's changing so fast what all I knew about here's almost gone."

I could understand in a way. And I thought of Mama and Jackie. Maybe that's how Mama felt, watching Jackie get sicker and sicker, thinking about the part of her life he'd take with him, the part of her no one else would ever know. I'd seen the same desperation in her eyes that I saw in Ivy Cain's now.

"I could go for you," I offered without a thought in my head. "If that'd help today? I mean, if it would be okay."

With absolutely no qualifications, I was ready to commit to hours in a nursing home with strangers just to avoid hours alone with my own thoughts and a body that wouldn't cooperate.

"You want to go sit with some old man? That's how you want to spend your first day on vacation? Listen, you're just here a few months. You don't want to hear all our craziness. Put your feet up and rest."

I could tell she was uncomfortable with my offer to help. I made something up fast. "I tried that today. Didn't really work for me. Maybe I need to work out some absolution." I laughed awkwardly because it was so pathetically true. "Besides, I think I ought to hear the stories about this house if I'm going to stay here. Sounds like Otis is the one to tell me."

Ivy hesitated. She surprised me when she dumped the rest of her coffee down the sink and took her seat again.

"Listen, I don't have time to make this pretty, so I'm just going to lay it out. When I was just a little thing, we got turned out of the little farm where I was born on the south end of the island. Delia offered the upstairs here. Mama said it was the kindest thing anybody'd ever done for her, and she didn't care who it was coming from.

"Mama died, later. I got married and moved off. Nonnie left then, moved in the back off Cain's. We rent that to her, me and my husband. And then it was just Urey here, him and Fawn and Damascus. Fawn was the girl's mama. This was the first home Damascus knew."

I nodded, unsure why I needed to hear this before I could take her shift in a nursing home.

She rubbed her face with both hands and pushed her hair back from her forehead.

"Now, what you'll hear is how it was a mean marriage. When Fawn died, honey, I said it wasn't the cancer, it was out of pure spite."

"Oh, God," I said, unsure if I wanted to hear more.

"Mm-hm. That's the truth." Ivy made sure I was listening before she said, "Fawn ate about a week's worth of pills she'd squirreled away. She was always a weak thing, hanging on Urey, and blaming him when things didn't turn out her way. She was smiling on her way to hell because she'd made it so the law came after him like he'd up and killed her off."

"Oh. That's awful," I said, feeling slightly queasy. I thought of Urey Trezevant's dark features, his scowl, the tension in his joints. I remembered how he'd carried the rifle over his shoulder like he was headed for a hanging. "I didn't know. I'm sorry for all of you. For him."

"Don't. He wouldn't have it. My brother didn't kill his wife, but he blames himself all the same."

I understood. But I would've been lying if I said I didn't have my doubts. And I thought about that little girl looking down at me in the bathtub and cringed. Who had she been seeing when she pulled me out of that water?

Ivy's mouth tightened. "This house has a history, but the only thing people like to remember is what happened with Fawn. They like to talk about the bad, to make out like what went wrong was to blame for the way the house went to Urey instead of Nonnie. My point is, you want to talk about a bad reputation? It's why Damascus don't go to the public school over at Brunswick. There's a bus, you know. JB, my boy, he takes the ferry every day, back and forth. But there's such a story about this place and what happened, Urey's put in Damascus' head that those kids will just torment her. And I guess they would, at that."

She flicked a glance my way, but then lowered her eyes to her hands where they lay in her lap. "But I remember this house. It was my home. I think you know what that means."

I nodded and blinked hard. Chasing the alligator had been nothing compared to this night's conversation. I felt like I'd been through a war, but I was starting to understand that Ivy Cain was the woman to have with you in the trenches. She looked at me with her searching eyes.

"So, we've traded our sorrows, Roslyn. I won't judge yours if you won't judge mine." She let that sink in. "Now. You still want to do me a favor?"

"Of course. Tell me the name of the home again?" My mouth was so dry I had to run my tongue over my teeth.

"Just tell me if you're leaving," she said quietly. "'Cause if you are, I've got to call Verna and see if she can find us anybody else bat-ass crazy enough to rent this place."

I pushed myself up. "No. Don't do that. Just one thing first. What did Nonnie really say about me?"

Ivy rolled her eyes before she said, "That you talk to alligators. Listen to that." The occasional roar from the river wouldn't let me forget that we were surrounded. If Manny's Island was my sanctuary, the river was a moat filled with dragons. "She says you're calling them here, and they'll just keep on coming 'til you get what you came for."

I felt like I might bust out laughing, and I was afraid if I did that now, Ivy would know how unglued I'd truly become. I covered my lips with my fingertips as though I were considering the nature of the offense. "Seriously? That's what she said? Well, what in hell does that mean?"

I was thinking compared to what I was truly capable of, that wasn't even B-grade horror. And highly unbelievable since I never even saw an alligator in my life until tonight. Still, I figured, according to Mama, we were one step away from beasts on the Keller side. A loud roar from the river seemed to agree, closer by. Part of me kind of liked the idea he was calling to me, even as I glanced at the gun I'd propped in its place behind the door.

Ivy shrugged, back to making light of Nonnie's weird overtures.

You can fool a blind alligator, but this is not your house. The thought shook me.

Ivy waited for my answer with anxious eyes. Honestly, I didn't have one.

"All right," I sighed. "Let's see what the house has to say about it." I hobbled over and gave the trash a shake, then upended the can, sending the bones to the floor in a clatter. We peered at the bones to see if the conjure woman's house would have me. "Am I leaving?" I asked the ancient roof, the clapboard walls, and the tabby foundation.

I met Ivy's solemn gaze.

"My sources say no," I said, trying to smile. Those bones scared the hell out of me, but I had nowhere else to go. "I wish I could whisper to alligators, at least that'd make a good side show act. Look, I don't like being here anymore than she wants me. But to tell you the truth, since that's what we've been doing, right now I'm more afraid of going home."

Ivy frowned and raised a pale eyebrow, possibly seeing something I'd missed in my amateur reading. She cocked her head to the side to look at me a little closer, and her wide mouth, so like her brother's, tipped up into shaky smile to match mine.

"You'd better get some rest, sister. Damascus goes with me every week to Sunrise Hills. She's going to love this. And I sure hope you like Ricardo Montalban."

Chapter Six

Roslyn

When I got to the dock the sun was high, and Damascus sat on a half-rotten picnic bench, barefoot and holding a plate with plastic wrap covering a tall chocolate cake that was about to melt. She sprang straight up and headed for the dock. "Where's Aunt Ivy?"

"She's busy." Ivy must not have told her I'd be the one making the trip to Sunrise Hills this morning. I squared my shoulders under the girl's dark stare. "I'm going to visit somebody for her today."

"Really?" Damascus looked less suspicious but shifted to skeptical. "This'll be good."

We didn't talk while we waited for the ferry to dock, or over the roar of the engine once we were underway, just let the wind lift the hair off our sticky necks. But finally, I pointed at the cake. "Did you make that?" I had to holler.

Damascus wrinkled her nose up. She was ten, but sometimes she looked a lot younger. "No," she said. "Piggly Wiggly. Nonnie hits the bakery of a Saturday and buys up their sale stuff. Puts it out at the store. But she charges too much. It ain't any good." She shrugged a shoulder. "She's got a mountain piled up behind the store, just stale stuff not fit for anybody to eat, and that's just waste."

"You stole it?" It was clear she was completely unconcerned. "If it's no good, why take it?"

"You won't get nowhere with Mr. Otis if you don't speak to his sweet tooth first thing. He ain't picky, long as it's sugar. He's a hog for a Twinkie. If I can swipe one of them, it's a big deal to him, I reckon 'cause it might just be the last Twinkie he'll get."

She settled in for the rest of the ride, letting her eyes close. "Besides, you cain't steal cake. Nobody owns cake. If you don't have sense to know cake's meant to be eaten up, you ought not be making one."

She seemed convinced there was simply no argument against that logic, so I didn't bother.

"Well, thanks for bringing it, then," I said. "Thanks for last night, too."

She nodded and clutched her cake.

We rode the rest of the way in solemn silence. I wondered what she thought of last night after the things Nonnie had told her. Clearly, she believed every word. She'd said as much before she left the house. She'd seen that alligator in the house, and now there'd be no convincing her I hadn't called it there. But she didn't seem afraid of me. With her hacked-off haircut and dingy clothes, she was a far cry from the little ballerinas that watched me with wonder at the shows and when I visited the company's dance school. Damascus Trezevant was unlike any ten-year-old girl I'd ever known.

The car sat in the asphalt lot, and we had to open the doors and step back to wait while the sizzling hot air escaped before we climbed inside. Then we sighed at the blasting air conditioning. I followed the directions Ivy'd given that morning, and drove down a short, shady green lane as it rose upward from the water where Sunrise Hills and Mr. Otis waited. Usually, she walked it, she'd said. I wasn't sure I was up to that yet.

When I switched on the Sacred Harp music, Damascus groaned. "Good God, not again. You really like listening to this?"

That got my ire up. "If you don't like it, get out. And it's called Sacred Harp. My grandmother sang this music. I lived with her when I was little, and all my family and the people from her church, they'd sing once a month."

Damascus shook her head. "Sounds like a lot of hollerin' to me."

"You have to hear it live to appreciate it."

Damascus tucked her chin and grumbled, "You're not kidding."

We turned off the pavement onto a gravel drive. "I hope this is right."

"It's right. See, up there." Damascus held the cake plate tighter. "You're not going to play that stuff in here, are you? 'Cause you'll give somebody a stroke."

I cut the engine, and the music died.

Sunrise Hills nursing home wasn't so sunny—that was the first thing I noticed about the small, cedar shingled house that sat back under a scraggly group of trees, the yard overgrown with palmetto, the walk to the front door cracked and broken. The humid air, too far inland for a good breeze, was filled with no-see-ums. We stepped inside, into a large living room with paneled walls and shag carpet that was matted down so flat it was slick under my shoes. Everything was neat and clean, though. That room opened to a kitchen emitting lingering smells of breakfast.

A large black woman ambled over, the sound of her polyester pant legs swishing loudly, a nametag embroidered across her left breast announcing she was an employee. Sheree, it said. "How ya'll doing today? Hey there, you sweet thing," she said to Damascus. She made a fuss over the cake and took it off our hands, handing it back to another lady in the kitchen.

"Ivy sent me," I said, introducing myself. "She said to tell you I was here to visit with Otis Greene."

"All right, honey." Sheree nodded, making the tower of braids piled high atop her head wobble precariously. "Yeah, Ivy called about you. You're the ballerina? Well, how about that." She smiled widely and gestured for us to follow her, and it was hard to miss the shirt, so bright and busy with a sunflower design. You could feel the heat coming off the print.

The hallway wasn't empty. A skinny white man whose pot belly strained against his T-shirt shuffled past. He leaned heavily on a walker, giggled, a garbled sound, and reached out to pat Damascus on the shoulder with a clumsy, heavy hand. "Hey there, girl. You gonna give me a kiss?" he asked.

Damascus shook her head. Sheree spoke up in a loud voice, causing the man to let go. "Mr. Pinckney, now, you behave yourself." He waved at her and went back to his shuffling walk. Sheree was a jolly woman, and she had me by the arm. "That old fool's a flirt, the worst kind. You better watch out for him." Damascus shot a look back at the man, but he was headed in the other direction, and I thought she was relieved. It was the first sign of unease I'd seen in the girl.

We passed a tiny, ancient woman, this one white and very nearly bald, so wrinkled she looked like she might slip right out of her skin. She sat in a wheelchair outside the door to a room, cradling a well-worn baby doll in her thin arms.

"How's your baby doing this morning, Ms. Johnson?" Sheree asked in passing, and the old woman continued rocking and humming softly, smiling a toothless smile at us. "That's Ms. Mary Johnson. She's our sweetheart. Had eight kids, you know. Every one of 'em gone on to be with Jesus before that sweet soul. I guess she just don't know how to be in this world without a baby in her arms, 'eah?"

Finally, we reached a room at the end of the hall where Mr. Otis Greene sat up in his bed with a glazed look on his narrow, dark face. His eyes were like black marbles while he watched a small TV that sat atop his dresser. I wasn't sure whether he was fully clothed or not, since he had a sheet pulled up over his legs.

"Mr. Otis," Sheree said. "Mr. Otis?"

Nothing. Didn't even look over.

A family sitcom played a cheerful tune as it went off, and Mr. Otis stretched his scarecrow arms over his head, settling in as the next show came on the screen.

"Like this one, 'eah?" he said. I had the impression he would have been talking just the same had the room been empty. "Like that li'l guy there, here he come." He laughed, paused to watch his favorite part of the theme song, and then laughed again.

Sheree gave a little shrug. "Cain't get that old coot out of the bed for nothin'. He can do it. Don't let him fool you. Just give up." She shook her head and took on a softer more worried look as she leaned in toward him. She lifted the sheet to peer at his feet. They were wrapped in thick bandages, but his toes stuck out. "Diabetes," she said aside to us, then spoke to him. "How your feet feeling today, Mr. Otis?"

He didn't act as if he heard a word, and she patted his leg gently, tucking him back in and made to leave. "Ya'll have a good talk."

The last thing I'd expected was the awful hollow feeling in my chest when I looked at the small, old man, alone in his room. I had a terrible vision of Granny Byrne, curled up in the old bedstead in the hollow, waiting for us to come. I swiped the back of my hand hard across my eyes and cleared my throat, pulling myself together before Damascus could notice I was upset.

I said Mr. Otis's name a few times, but didn't get his attention. I was starting to think visiting wasn't going to turn out to be much. Lulled by the hum of the window unit pumping air conditioning into the room and the loud volume of the TV, Damascus and I nearly jumped out of her skin when Otis laughed out loud.

"Hey, hey!" he practically shouted, suddenly animated. He turned his eyes on Damascus. In a thick Geechee accent, he said, "He a funny man."

Mr. Otis worked his jaw a moment and studied Damascus until she started to breathe hard. Then she said, "Well, what are you looking at? Ivy sent us. Brung you a cake. Say hello or something."

He seemed to consider this a moment, his eyes gone wide at her tone. "Chocolate?"

She nodded, and he smiled, but then he cut those eyes around at me, and they went darker and harder.

"Hi, Mr. Otis. I'm Roslyn Byrne, Ivy's friend. I'm staying at the farm."

The shiny marble eyes bore into me. "Get on outta here," he finally said.

I tried to explain that Ivy had sent me, but he was having none of it.

"Ivy thought you might like telling me the stories about the house," I said over his low protests. "About Aunt Delia."

Damascus made a low noise. "Oh, you done it now."

Otis Greene screwed up his face and let out a bellow like a toddler throwing a fit, thrashing around with his fists in the air. I was too stunned to know what to do.

I was trying to calm him with no success. "What? Mr. Otis, I'm sorry. I don't know what I said, but everything's okay. It's okay."

Sheree came flying in.

"She asked about Aunt Delia," Damascus explained.

Sheree rolled her eyes and started patting at him and waving at me to vacate, which I gladly did. Damascus stayed in the room, and I wished I'd pulled her out with me so we could get out of there. Under Sheree's hands, Otis Greene didn't much settle down even with me out of sight.

"Ree-ah We!" He screeched some Geechee speech I couldn't understand, except that it was a serious accusation.

Mr. Pinckney was shuffling my way, wagging a finger. He might have seemed more threatening if it weren't for the pitiful way he dragged his left foot along and slowed down by the minute. By the time he got to the end of the hall, he wilted against me like a dish rag.

"What you about, girl? Mr. Otis don't deserve no trouble."

I looked the man in the eyes, hazy green as they were. "Mr. Pinckney, I'm not going to hurt him. We just brought him cake."

He grinned then, easier to convince than Otis. He had a different agenda, and the finger he'd been wagging, he now tapped on his cheek. I laughed and leaned in to kiss Mr. Pinckney's feather soft cheek. When his mouth puckered into a round 'O', I winked at him. "I could use a friend in this joint."

Damascus came shooting out of the room then to gawk at us. Mr. Pinckney was getting his thrills with one hand resting comfortably on my rump. Another staff member happened along to take Mr. Pinckney off my hands, and I apologized and apologized. The thin, dark nurse with wide eyes glared at me in disapproval like I'd seduced the wobbly old rooster. She silently escorted him back the way he'd come.

We stood there a moment while the rhythms of the nursing home returned to normal.

"You could have told me it would make him so upset to talk about the past," I said. Damascus didn't look upset. In fact, she looked amused.

One of the nurses I hadn't seen before, a thin, white woman with dishwater blonde hair brushed off her face, handed Damascus her now washed-clean cake plate. No 'thank you.' Our cue to get out.

"I'm sorry," I said to her glower. "I didn't know he'd get so upset."

"I said this was going to be good." Damascus grinned. She looked at the other woman. "She asked him to tell her about the house."

The woman looked at me with pure infuriation.

I grabbed Damascus' hand and marched her out of there. "Come on, Tattoo," I said through clenched teeth.

"What?"

"It means 'traitor' in alligator."

Chapter Seven

Roslyn

Damascus might have thought I was being dramatic, but betrayal was a theme in my life, usually with me doing the betraying. Betraying and burying. We were southern Appalachian beneath the slicked-up suburb exterior Mama had worked so hard to perfect. Superstition and pride were the bones that held me up.

The spring Mama and I left Glenmary, a Keller cousin of Granny's had a son killed in Korea. She was a colorless sort of person with a wrung out look, and she sat up at the fresh gravesite with Granny, ringing her hands over and over, refusing to go up to the house after the service. Granny Byrne's house was just up the hill from the church, and most always people ended up over there following a service or a singing. There would be dinner on the ground under her pecan trees.

That day the congregation had already done the singing, standing in the square as was customary, with Granny calling out the page from the Sacred Harp songbook, the "lesson" she called it. It was so loud and pretty. You couldn't hardly even be sad for a poor dead boy because every word was about the glories of heaven. It drowned out every thought you could have but the sound of itself. But even after the silence rang in my ears and everybody headed off for coffee or a smoke or a piece of pound cake, nothing could be said or done to convince Judith Ann that the thing was finished.

That night we'd all gone to sleep when I felt Granny Byrne moving in the house. I got up to see what was the matter. I was only nine, but I remember she said, "I don't believe Judith Ann is going to leave that boy."

She took down the little box from the windowsill and gave it to me. With the heavy box flashlight she kept on the carport and a post hole digger, we made our way the quarter of a mile to the cemetery. She hadn't noticed I was in my bare feet.

Granny's light showed Judith Ann Keller stretched out on the dirt where they'd buried my cousin, and I was horrified. But Granny called out in a friendly, sing-song voice, like we were just meeting up by some happy chance. And to my amazement, Judith Ann sat up and patted at her bosom and her hair like a woman faced with unexpected guests.

"Judith Ann, I hope you don't mind us coming by so late," Granny said.

"No, that's fine." Judith Ann looked goggle-eyed at us.

"I tell you," Granny said, "I believe I know what's got you so torn up. All these Byrnes carrying on, day and night. They are, without a doubt, the loudest bunch of people, dead or alive, ever was."

A little sound came from Judith Ann like a kitty cat makes, but Granny didn't turn a hair. "It's been the longest time I've been putting off bringing Robert up here for that very reason, him being a man that appreciated the peace and quiet, even though it's always made me worry he'd be put out with me for keeping him stuck up on the window like a violet. But today, it occurred to me, he and Henry were the same kind. Did you know, Robert never loved a thing more than he loved going out on the river with Henry?"

Judith Ann was staring at my Granny like she was speaking some unknown language that was hard to make out, like half of Henry's whole self hadn't been left scattered somewhere over Korea, and her cheeks jerked like she could smile. Granny handed me the flashlight to hold.

"When I thought about that," Granny said, "I just got myself up and put on my shoes."

She said her prayers had been answered, and Judith Ann sat there gawking at us. Nothing would make my Grandpa, ashes that he was, happier than sitting up there on that hill with Henry, just like they were in a little boat together, out for a day, fishing.

And all the while, Granny was sinking that post hole digger again and again, making a little pocket in the ground next to young cousin Henry Keller's fresh grave. When she was satisfied it was deep enough, she finished the job, putting the little box down and covering it up, same as I'd seen her put in a garden. She patted the dirt down, brushed her skirts, and told Judith Ann she thought the men might like their privacy to get settled in, so why didn't us girls just go have some coffee. Judith Ann wobbled back to the house with us. That was that. Nobody even cried. Of course, Grandpa'd been dead awhile, and I figured Judith Ann'd had her chance.

I had no idea what we'd done was wrong until Mama met us at the door, sick with worry that we'd disappeared in the middle of the night. In fact, I hadn't thought about Mama at all, but now I saw I should have.

"You'd rather lay by yourself for all eternity than let those people so much as bury their own dead without needing you to do it for them," she screeched at Granny. "You spent your whole life giving over and giving over to that bunch, and now you've given them Daddy, too."

The next morning I watched Granny Byrnes, the church, the mountain, and that little valley with the pretty house all disappear in the rear view.

Manny's Island definitely didn't have the corner on the market when it came to betrayal or haunting, either one.

Days melted into one another as I tried to make a place for myself in the conjure woman's house and form a routine, something I'd relied on as a dancer. I didn't know if alligator whisperers required such discipline, but it was the only way I knew to fill my time since I'd been blackballed at Sunrise Hills. I did my exercises and walked the river bank and fumed over just what made Otis Greene throw such a hissy. Volunteering would have given me something useful to do, and now here I was, choked up on this sandy shore like Jonah. I couldn't find the first remnant of any mystical past on the property, just a dusty little house with drafts and uneven floorboards.

My second week on the island rolled around, and there'd been no further curses and no sign of a single Trezevant, just as Ivy had promised. Keeping me company along the river were fiddler crabs and herons. I checked and saw the blind alligator in that low spot. I could find him out there sunning himself or half sunk like a log if I cared to sneak up and have a peek. I made a habit of passing that way on my walks, just to have something else alive to know I was there. I was calling him Spook. An alligator, I could name. When I went through lists of possibilities for my daughter, nothing seemed right.

I was thinking hard about that while I watched small boats carrying tourists. I heard the sound of dolphins passing, sending up soft, sputtering sighs, and I began to fall a little in love with the solitude of the island.

On an optimistic whim, I took the golf cart on the road around the island to get my bearings, but the ruts won out, and I went back to the house without making it half way round. I wanted to march up to Cain's and demand to know what those bones said about me. But I'd spent my life neglecting the matters of the spirit in favor of controlling the physical, and I worried I was going to have to pay for that. It must have been my imagination that made it seem the alligators grew louder, more insistent in their roaring, and I worried in a way I couldn't put to words that somehow it was my need they were echoing, an inherent damage inside me that was there long before I lost the baby.

When I'd worked up enough of a temper to try again and finally forced myself over to Cain's, I was disappointed to find a teenage girl behind the counter with ear buds ringing pop music so deafeningly loud I could've sung along. She rang up my groceries without a second glance at me, probably some kid from Brunswick who had no interest in the woman renting the conjure woman's house.

The thing was, too much time to think, and I was willing to bet old Jonah would have crawled right back in that whale's belly. I'd only managed to prove I was good for nothing. Ruined physically, my skill set now consisted of alligator wrestling and frightening women, children, and the elderly. I'd become the crazy woman in the haunted house filled with cats. When the third Monday of my self-imposed isolation therapy rolled around, I was primed for disaster, nearly jubilant, when I came across boot tracks along the water. I'd known Urey Trezevant was out there. My presence wouldn't change his habits; he'd made that clear the first day. And it gave me a charge, I admit. I knew, if I left the door open, he'd find his way inside same as that alligator.

I'd imagined coming down to the river to find him. But in truth, I'd been careful of the paths I took. I'd turned my lights out early and locked my doors. I'd kept the rifle ready. I was too busy communing with my own ghosts to be out speaking to any alligator or a brooding widower 'til all hours. The trouble was, I was a bigger fool than I was a coward, and sanctuary, as it turns out, can feel a lot like exile.

So when I saw those tracks, I thought they looked like an invitation. And I followed them, by God. I dragged the rifle with me, leaning on it like a walking stick, barrel to the ground. I'd probably clogged enough mud up in the end that I'd be lucky if it fired, but I figured I had about as good a chance at reasoning with one of those scaly bastards as I had of killing one.

When I saw Urey, I stood frozen beneath the wide sky, just at the edge of the water. He blended into the grey-green morning light, the brown sea grass and the slate color of the water, but there was nowhere for me to hide. If he'd looked up from his work, he would have easily seen me. I did not move for fear that would draw his attention. I knew, instinctively, that I was intruding on a private moment.

But I couldn't take my eyes from him. I watched Urey Trezevant standing knee deep in the river on a sand bar that could only be reached during low tide. With his strong arms and broad chest, bare and brown in the hot sun that sparked bronze lights off his hair, he raised a circular net and cast it into the water with one fluid motion. My breath caught in my throat. He was the same fierce figure, but there was grace in his skill.

I knew the lines of the human form. I'd spent my life in the pursuit of unattainable perfection. But the sight of this man was as purely beautiful as I'd ever seen in his imperfect struggle against the current. He braced his legs wide, pulled the net in slowly, deliberately, and repeated the action again and again in a gentle rhythm that seemed to me to be the purpose for which his body was created.

There was no sound except the rush of the water, the light breeze in the tall grass and an occasional sea bird's cries. It occurred to me then that I did not hear the alligators, and that Urey was fishing where they lived, seemingly without any of the fear he'd implanted in me. The heat began to warm the top of my head, so sweat trickled down my neck and followed the groove of my backbone. But I could not look away.

The cadence of his work settled in me in some carnal way I understood without explanation. Granny Byrne's soft alto floated to me on a rising wind, and rose up in the back of my own throat 'til I almost sang out. My breathing came into a rhythm with his, so it seemed for a moment, we were connected. I was flying, and falling and being dragged back again, the same as the current slipping through Urey's hands, and the hands of generations of hands and currents before us.

I don't know how long I stood there. Only when he pulled in his catch, and I saw the flash of silver scales, did the spell break. Instantly I was anxious to leave, a guilty witness to a man making love to a river. But he looked up then, straight at me. Even from that distance, too far away to read his expression, I knew I came as no more of a surprise to him than the fish that struggled in his net.

My fingers ached from holding so tight to the gun. At some point, I'd gone from leaning on it to clutching it in an awkward grip. I understood in a thousand certain ways that there were things in this world from which no weapon could protect me, and the man watching me from the water meant for me to know it. I took several breaths, waiting to see what he would do, until he dropped his gaze, gently lay the net out on the water again, and set loose what he'd caught.

The emptiness where my child had slept deep in my womb gaped wide, tender and hot, and a helpless paralysis dragged at my limbs. For all my thrashing around these last few days, in that moment I understood I was easy prey. I felt all my false confidence slip away, tested by the river. A poor catch, set loose for another day.

Without looking back at me, Urey bent his knees and sank below the surface, disappearing momentarily. When he rose, he gleamed with the light off the water, and I watched the muscles in his back as he walked the hidden length of the sand bar toward the riverbank several yards from where I stood. A twinge of desire shot through me, shocking and humiliating me. I looked away, completely at odds with myself.

I'd gone looking for distraction from my little black soul. But Urey Trezevant was a kind of punishment I wasn't prepared for. I didn't know why, when nothing else seemed to touch me, not even the cries of the ghost child I could never comfort, I wanted to cry every time I looked at him.

For what it's worth, I made it back to the house in record time. Those long walks and days of concentrated effort paid off. I didn't look back to see if he'd followed me. But I stood at the kitchen sink gulping down a glass of water like an idiot, worried what I would say for myself, if the day ever came when he turned up at my door.

So I blamed Urey's net and a bad case of stir-crazy when I tried to drown myself the next day. I found a canoe dragged up on the bank downstream from Urey's fishing hole. It looked like a fast way to ease what ailed me, to keep me out of his domain, get me away from the four walls of the house, and give me a badly needed taste of freedom.

The water was calm, and the day was quiet, the picture of serenity. I anticipated following the riverbank just far enough to reach a beach I'd seen on my jaunt in the cart. A simple journey any fool could manage, two hours there and back, and I'd have my lunch knowing I was not some fish in a net. The river was not a mystical boundary, holding me captive, and I was nobody's victim.

It didn't take much to push the boat onto the water and climb in. I tossed my cane on the floor of the boat. For a moment, it felt good to be buoyant. I found I could manage the paddle with ease and even laughed as I picked up speed, a sound so foreign lately that I startled myself. It was such a relief to let the river do all the work, to get carried away by something stronger than myself.

Wasn't that the thing with dance, the gift that had overtaken my life? I'd allowed that high, that sort of immortality, to dictate my decisions and worshipped at its self-satisfying throne. Right up 'til the end, I thought I was the one in charge, that if I just flew high enough and contorted myself into all the right shapes, I'd be the right to heal all wrongs. I believed in the pride my mama felt, that her mistake had made good, and in the faith my granny kept that I had a destiny greater than myself. I hoped somehow it would come together by my hand—or rather, my feet—and redeem us all. Granny's disappointment in a fallen daughter and her fears for an illegitimate grandchild would dissolve when I danced.

Paying attention to things like forgiveness and pride never occurred to me, just as I'd neglected to note currents and tides in the Little Damascus until I was headed out to sea in a hurry. I realized my mistake too late. I worked that paddle harder than I'd ever done anything in my life, but that boat had a mind of its own.

It went all cattywampus and careened every which way except the way I wanted to go. At one point I gave up entirely and jumped out, up to my chest in the water. I kept hold of the boat with one hand and kind of hopped along with my feet mired up on the silt bottom of the river, grabbing onto the rushes and yanking my way back to shore. When it was all over, I dragged the boat far enough up on solid ground to collapse in the mud, far from my destination, the sandy beach. I hadn't even left the Trezevant property.

I just wanted things back to normal, back to the way they were. I wanted it by sheer force of will. Except, I thought, I didn't. Not anymore. My knee throbbed. The voice I'd been hearing came from inside this time. She sang softly. *You're not going anywhere until you deal with me. Deal with the consequences of your choices.*

Right. Well, I wouldn't go out in that damn canoe again unless my life depended on it. No more than I'd go on another stage.

The thought stunned me so, I sat up gasping.

"I don't want to dance." I said the words aloud. It wasn't hard. They were simple words. I should have been able to say them many times before I ended up marooned, before I'd let them suck the life out of me.

There was no sound to draw attention to the presence in the water, so I don't know why I looked up in time to see the long, solid, reptilian body glide past where I'd stood only seconds before. I waited to be a meal, but the monster passed by in silence, leaving me with a pounding in my blood as I watched him drift out of sight. He was terrifying and marvelous. I understood in that moment every myth and legend ever spoken about the dark beast. Death had passed by, and I was its witness. Truth spoken over ancient water, was that the spell I'd cast?

I'd been careless, hadn't even brought the gun along, although if I had, it would be at the bottom of the river with my cane. Still, here, carelessness could cost your life. But instead of the panic I'd felt every minute since burying my daughter, I stood up calmly and turned toward the house, forgetting the canoe.

The voice inside laughed freely, like Granny Byrne, like a precocious girl I remembered. The song she sang was one I knew by heart. And I let her lead as I stumbled back to the house. I was crazy like that.

Later that night, when I heard the sweet, high melody rise up from the water, I closed my eyes and imagined the child of my heart, singing in the square. She was the lucky one.

I'd called Mama twice to report on my progress. Yes, it was peaceful. Yes, it was hot, and I did regret there was no air conditioning. No, I had not gone over to that resort to at least have a nice fish dinner. The truth was, I would have liked a fish dinner very much, but I just couldn't bring myself to face a room full of people, even if most of them were tourists who wouldn't look twice at me.

Staying at the conjure woman's house was having a strange effect, the opposite of what I'd expected. Instead of feeling better about rejoining the world after a nice respite on the river, I felt less and less inclined to venture out.

I became accustomed to my new routine, pleased with my complete lack of responsibility, and I paid very little notice to the passing of time. I marked my days by my walks, the rising and setting of the sun, and the mid-afternoon thunderstorms that drove me inside for a cool drink and a nap. I was living a life of such negligent sloth that when it rained for two days straight, it never occurred to me to worry about the river. Or anything else, for that matter.

Any other time, I might have turned Damascus away when she showed up like a wet rat on my porch, but I gladly threw a towel over her head and dragged her inside. *Another*, I cheered in my head. *Come in, little alligator girl!*

"Daddy said it's gonna flood out here," she said, perched on the hearth, dripping.

"I was born in a flood. The water's the first thing I heard." It was funny how I hadn't heard that story since I was a girl, and Granny Byrne or somebody in the family would tell it. Now I'd said it, there was an ache in my chest for that place.

Damascus' gaze was steady and straight forward, but not necessarily warm. I couldn't make out what the child thought of me. She was not threatening by any means, but she did not act like other children. She watched me like a wary animal. She was a small adult who was reserving her opinions.

"Did he send you?" I asked, watching for signs he'd told her about my spying. But, really, I didn't care.

"No."

"Does he know where you are this time?" I didn't want to get thrown out of my cocoon.

A crisp nod. God knew how she'd convinced him to let her come here. Tit for tat, I supposed. I'd hoarded in on his privacy, and Damascus was what it got me.

Without regard to me, she paced around the room, touching things, flipping through a magazine I'd left on a table. "Worst it got one time, there was about three inches of water in the house," she said. "There was fish swimming in the kitchen. I caught some and put them in the bathtub 'til I could get them back down to the river. We took the john boat all around the yard. It's funny, floating where you ought to walk. Like walking on the ceiling."

Somehow, her easy conversation felt like a trick, so I spoke carefully. "I bet."

"Did you take that canoe out yet?" She brought her eyes to my face. Her cool regard was puzzling.

"Canoes don't seem to be my thing." She looked like she was having trouble keeping from busting out laughing. She knew, of course. Good grief, what were they doing? Crawling all over this river? Not so alone, after all. "You saw that? Right. Well, I had to ditch it a ways down. But you know that. So is that why you're here? Did you think you might help me get it back before I end up on the roof waiting for a helicopter?"

She tossed her head a little and sighed deeply before she announced, rather loudly, "I don't really have time."

She didn't mention the alligator. Perhaps she hadn't seen that much.

"Petty theft got you slammed?" I laughed at my own joke.

She rolled her eyes. "First of all, probably, we're not going anywhere tonight if we don't want to swim. And second, you ain't the reason I'm out here. I have a garden." Her expression changed at mention of this. Clearly, she was much more concerned about the garden than our need for the canoe. "It's down by the river, just past the house. That's how come I seen you."

"A garden. Really?" I said, hoping I sounded only mildly

interested. My brain was waking up now I had some company, and I was surprised I was mildly interested in what she was saying. I wanted her to keep talking, and chances were she'd shut down fast if she thought I was more than half listening.

"Yeah. Pumpkins. It started a long time before you even got here. But you should know because I'll probably be here a lot," she said. "I have to keep an eye on things."

She sounded very serious. If the place flooded, it was nothing to me. But maybe it was something to her. "What can you do, if the water gets too high?"

She blinked solemn eyes at me. Her face was flushed. "It won't."

Apparently, that was all she was willing to share on the topic, so I excused myself to make a cup of tea. When I returned from the kitchen I brought two cups, but she refused.

"Did you know I used to live here?" she asked. She was standing at the foot of the stairs, her hand caressing the banister. "'Til I was five. That was my room right up there. Mama and Daddy slept down here."

"I did know that."

She kept her eyes cast down, nearly shut, hiding her thoughts. She settled herself on the wool rug where she brought a book from a shelf. We were quiet, with only the sound of the water falling on the roof, until the deep, eerie boom of an alligator's repetitious call began.

There was an answer from another of the river's depths, possibly more than one. The magnitude of their alien conversation nearly shook the walls. They were nearby, close enough to make me a little uneasy, and I moved to peer out the window into the yard, half expecting to see them lounging on the porch.

"How long does this racket go on?" I asked, not really expecting an answer.

Her small voice was like a bell, but it was a taunt. "Forever."

"Oh, well, it's amazing," I said, causing her to scowl. "No, I mean it. They scare the shit out of me, but it's powerful. You have to respect it."

She was listening to me now, and I had nothing else to say. I scrambled for a coherent thought. "My grandmother lived on a river when I was your age. Not like this one, though. It was different, in the mountains, no alligators. But catfish, we had those big as a truck." I laughed at the unexpected detail of the memories this place was turning over inside me, but Damascus looked like she'd heard her share of fish tales and hardly believed mine. "You'd like Tennessee," I finished. "Still one of my favorite places on Earth."

"Why didn't you go there now, if you like it so much?"

I laughed, confusing her, but it was so much like my own response to Ivy. "There's not much to go back to," I finally said. "Or so I hear. I haven't been since I was twelve. I started dancing after that."

"That's not really a reason."

She turned her attention back to the book in her lap. She flipped through the pages slowly, glanced at me a few times and then tapped the open page of the book with her fingertip. Seeing I was watching, she said, "You should read it."

When she fixed her gaze on me, her expression was guileless, but I felt as though I were being led down a path, and had the singular urge to toss out breadcrumbs, so as not to lose my way.

"Really? It's good? What is it?"

She explained it was a book all about alligators, and, not surprisingly, it had belonged to her father. She showed me his name scribbled on the front flap.

"Did you know," Damascus said, "alligator mamas sometimes eat their own babies?"

I made a sound she could take any way she wanted and didn't look at her. "I think I knew that. It's not on purpose, though."

"Tell that to the baby. There used to be these people that worshipped alligators. They believed gators were supposed to teach you how to live, after you died, in the afterlife. Made statues of them and everything."

I laughed a little. "Oh, my mama would love that. Who is

this? More Seminoles?"

"Egyptians, like the ones in the Bible. You know," she prompted, "them ones the Lord wiped out with frogs and burning bushes and stuff. You've heard of them?"

"I know who the Egyptians were."

"Well, don't you think that's something? I mean, Bible people sat around like a million years ago, just like us, listening to all this bellering. Trying to figure out what all the noise was about, thinking maybe they could hear a big secret about what was coming for them. Like they could cheat death, you know? If they were a step ahead or something. They talked to the alligators, the ones that had the gift." Then she cocked her head and asked, "They believed all kinds of shit in the Bible times, you know?"

"Oh. Really?"

"Yeah, like putting people's eyes out or stoning people for having sex and stuff."

"Well . . ."

"They did. You had to believe it all, too. Not just parts of it. That's what it says. All, or hell to you. You know what else?"

I waited, raising my brows. She looked like she was enjoying this part, getting to the point she'd been trying to make all along.

"They all thought they were so smart, building all those statues and making all that noise. Sacrifice this and pray, pray, pray. If you get frogs or killer bees or flesh-eating grasshoppers, too bad for you. Just say you believe, and your sucky life won't matter 'cause you're going straight to heaven once you slit your own wrists, right? But when they all died, the Egyptians and those gators, too, then what? Who knows what really happened to them then. There ain't nothing in this book that tells me that.

"I been trying to figure that out forever," she said. "Gators are still out there carrying on, and I'm still sitting in here having to hear it, but all them Egyptians, who remembers them? Who can prove they ain't just river slime now? So what's the point?"

The sounds on the river carried on just as she said, and the girl never took her eyes from my face while I weighed the options. "Maybe you have to speak Egyptian to understand gators."

Damascus finally blinked. "Hmph." She slapped the book shut and got to her feet, swinging the door open and leaving it that way, letting a fresh, cool breeze inside as she went to sit on the front step. Over her shoulder, she threw one last scrap of opinion, as though it weren't even really worth mentioning. "Or it's really just all about sex. People will make up anything to keep from telling a kid about sex. Daddy said they were arm-wrestling. I mean, please." I laughed.

I sat the iPod station up in the open window, cranked up the Sacred Harp, and took a chair to the porch. The water rolled off the roof, but the wind had died down. It was nice, like a waterfall. Damascus looked skeptical and leaned in the doorway to watch my routine.

"It's like those creepy monk songs or something," Damascus observed.

"Gregorian chants?"

"Is it one of those other religions like Catholics?"

"No, I don't think so. Not anymore, anyway." I laughed. "It's old though. They sang like this in Shakespeare's time. You know who that is?"

"Kind of sounds like the alligators, too. The Seminoles got a song just for alligators. It's different from singing to God, I guess. But the same, too."

"I guess it is."

She wasn't a convert yet, but her interest was piqued. It appeared alligators were a real interest to this kid. In a way, I had to agree with her; the song was universal in many ways. You could hear anything in it if you listened long enough.

While I went through a series of pliés, prances and fondues, I couldn't resist telling her some about Granny and the monthly singings in the small church house. She listened, trying to look bored.

"The whole inside of the church is wood, and there's hardly a stick of furniture except the chairs that make up the square for the singers. They do it like that on purpose for the sound. There's nothing like it when they really crank it up, either. It makes your bones hum, that's what I remember, like you're a tuning fork standing there. And when Granny would lead, she'd look lit up from the inside. Just the once, she let me stand with her, at the center. It liked to have blown me away."

So caught up in my own thoughts, I didn't notice she'd reached over and turned off the music on the porch until she said, "It about gives me a headache."

"Yeah? Well, I don't remember inviting you here." More hurt than was really called for, I looked away from her, disappointed she didn't get caught up the way I'd hoped. I supposed I'd assumed anyone would, given the right introduction.

She asked another question. "Why're you doing that?"

I started to answer, but chewed on the words for a minute, and realized with Damascus, I was going to have to tell the truth. "Because it's what I know to do. Because I want to get better and I figure if I start with the outside, maybe I'll figure out how to fix the inside." I didn't know where it was going to end anymore, and I was starting to be okay with that.

"Just stretching or bending over a little, that's going to make you better?"

I sighed, tired of dealing with her. "I want to get my strength back."

"So you can dance again?"

"No. I'm done with that," I said flatly.

"You going to work at Sunrise Hills, then?"

"No, I don't think they'd let me in the door after last time."

"Oh sure. They're desperate. They'll let any Joe Blow in off the street to keep those forgotten souls company. That's what Aunt Ivy calls them, forgotten souls. Mr. Otis will get used to you."

"And my Joe Blow qualifications. I don't know." I bent from the waist, swooping one arm down to the floor and bringing myself upright, bending from the waist so I leaned backward. She watched, cock-eyed.

"When you're aware, centered," I explained, "you have more control. Muscles lose their memory if you don't train them every day. You have to remind them of their business, or you wind up flat on your ass."

She snorted. "Like some people I know." I glanced up to see something in her eyes that made me pause. "Otis, he sits in that bed about all the time except to go to the toilet, I guess. That's why I bring him stuff he likes. If it was me in a place like that, I guess I'd live for chocolate cake."

"That's why you go?"

"Ivy makes me." She shrugged, then said with long-suffering pride, "And I let them touch me. They just love it, old people do. They like to get hugs and hold onto my hands and stuff. It's kind of gross. I don't like it, but you can't hardly say no." She gave a small shudder.

"Well, you could, actually." I was impressed. And sad to think this was how she found affection in her life. "And you could tell me why he got so upset the other day. What was he calling me?"

"He's old, I guess," she said. "Probably, he figures you're a haint. Ain't nobody else going to want to stay in this house."

"A haint?"

"A mean old ghost. And you know, maybe he just thought you were weird. I did. I thought maybe, when I heard that holy roller racket and all, you might be trying for a miracle or something. Like you might be one of those people that goes wild." She cut her eyes up at me. "You know about such as that?"

"I think you mean Pentecostals. I've heard about it. Never seen it myself. Have you been to a service like that?"

She shook her head. "Daddy don't hold with organized religions. Specially them holy rollers. That's what he calls them." She hesitated, then added, "People talk about you as it is. If they see you out here, doing this," she gestured at my exercises with one slender hand.

I laughed. "Better a holy roller than a haint. Might confuse them as to which side I'm playing for." She watched intently as I extended my arms overhead and stretched from the waist. I saw her gaze stop when she noticed the bone charm on the doorpost, but she didn't say anything about it.

A particularly loud bellow reached us then. "He's a serious one. Best pick up line I've heard in years," I joked, in hopes of lightening the mood. "I think the rain's letting up."

Damascus took one step backward so that she stood inside. Several times, she pushed the screen door with her toe so that it swung away from her and came back with a bounce, then finally stopped it wide open enough to allow her to reach outside.

She held the heavy book out toward me, and when I took it, let her hand drop to her side and door fall shut all the way. I felt certain her eyes would bore a hole through me. "I saw it in the paper," she said. "What happened to you. It said you was pregnant. You didn't want it? I mean, you got rid of it. That's what Nonnie says."

I let out a bark of annoyed laughter. "Ask your dad. He'll tell you every bit of what Nonnie's told you is ridiculous."

"He won't tell me any such thing. He won't say one word. It came on him like that when Mama died. He don't say nothing to me except do we got milk? Can I run that laundry? Don't give him no trouble. Don't expect him back early."

Damascus remembered this house, her room in it, her parents here. What else did she remember of that time? She was such a suspicious kid, I knew she'd put all her faith in alligators and hoodoo magic as surely as she'd lost faith in the adults in her life. She was expecting me to side-step the truth.

I swallowed hard. "No. I didn't want her. But I was going to have the baby. I did have her. She was stillborn. Do you know what that means?" I said, choking a little.

"Dead. I know." She nodded. "You cain't be no kind of ballerina with some kid to take care of. I get that. Some people can choose."

"No, that's not how it was, Damascus. I changed my mind. But it wasn't my choice to lose her." Oh, I doubted my own convictions.

"I didn't mean nothing bad. It's just, that's what brings alligators. Death. Like the book says. I know, 'cause I reckon I bring them, too." She surprised me when, with what seemed like genuine empathy, she said, "But I'm sorry."

"Sorry for what? What do you think that means, calling alligators?"

She didn't look at me, but past me, into the dark to where the river moved, swollen and dangerous. "People don't think about alligators much, but they've been here long as the earth. Everything sweet and good and soft don't last long. Did you ever notice? But alligators do. They just keep on going. They're just about dinosaurs. Did you know that?"

She raised her gaze to me then, and her eyes were dark and older than her years. "My grandmama's people said alligators been around so long because they live on broken hearts."

Oh, so that's what we were doing now, trading our granny wisdom. I saw where this was going and shook my head while Damascus furrowed her brow under her ridiculous bangs and tried hard to explain.

"She knew because she was alligator clan. You know what that makes me? Half damn alligator. You know what that means?"

I tried not to let her hear the hitch in my voice. "You're a survivor."

She nodded miserably. "The way I figure, I'm going to live forever."

I knew the burden of a blessing when I saw one, even if I didn't fully understand why this upset Damascus so badly.

I choked on my emotions. "Listen to me. Whatever's going on, you're too old to let people tell you tales. You're too smart for that. I say maybe some people call alligators, and maybe they don't. What does it matter? I don't think they depend on us or our hearts one bit. Those alligators are just doing what they've always done, what they'll keep right on doing. But if we can find some strength in that, well, good for us."

But she wasn't buying it, and, frankly, I wasn't doing much of a job selling it, either. In fact, Damascus seemed flat out disappointed in me. Frustrated, I cast about for a new angle. I'd been right. The rain seemed to be slacking off. "Your dad's going to be looking for you."

"He knows I'm here. He sent me. I'm supposed to say come to the clubhouse if you're scared." She hesitated until I looked up at her. "But nothing's going to happen to you."

"Because Nonnie says that, too?"

She shrugged. "'Cause it quit raining." I watched her close the door in my face. "I'm gonna sleep in my bed. I got pumpkins to watch over."

She meant the bed in the room upstairs, her old bed.

"Hey, Roslyn. What's her name, your baby?" she asked.

"I don't know."

Through the curtain, she stared out at me, blank-faced, and I saw her move through the living room, picking up both kittens along the way, to mount the stairs.

Chapter Eight

Roslyn

Come morning, the water had receded, leaving only puddles in low lying areas around the house.

Damascus slept in. During the sleepless hours of my night, I'd checked her, and again this morning. She slept as though she hadn't had rest in years, so I scouted about the property, down to the blueberry bushes to assess things. They were as full as they'd been before the rains, and I decided to go to the store in hopes of finding what we'd need for making jelly. It was one of the things I remembered doing with Granny Byrne in detail. Apparently, when I looked deep, I found fruit preserves.

Before going back inside for coffee, I discovered Damascus' patch. The pumpkin vines were safe atop their mounds. Truthfully, they didn't look like much to have been the basis for so much drama.

Near noon, I finally heard her stirring. She dashed outside and came dragging back ten minutes later, after convincing herself the pumpkins were undamaged. I didn't say a word. I scrambled the last two eggs in the house, and we had a silent brunch. I fed the kittens with the eye dropper while she watched. Like Damascus, they'd have to open their eyes soon. Lord, everything around here had trouble seeing clear.

I finally broke down and spoke. "If you want to add anything to the list I have for the store, it's on the counter."

She nodded agreement. But she didn't speak.

A half hour later, we sloshed across the sandy puddles toward the store. Damascus cut her eyes at my shorts, which revealed the long scars on either side of my right leg. When we rounded the end of the island and pulled up to park, there stood Nonnie out back watching us. She wore her long, grey-streaked hair pulled back so it hung in a tail between her shoulders, a pair of jeans and a cotton shirt, barefoot with strings of bright beads around her neck. She made me think of a peacock, and I was more than uncomfortable around her. But there was no avoiding the woman if I wanted to eat.

Damascus waved, but Nonnie only turned and went inside.

It seemed like a Trezevant family reunion was going on in that store. Ivy and a skinny, broad-shouldered teenaged boy who was obviously hers stood at the counter, arguing. Nonnie watched everything, me especially.

"Looks like this storm's washed up all sorts of things," Ivy said. "We were just saying, wonder if that girl at the house made out all right last night."

"Girls, actually. Damascus stayed with me." Stunned looks all around. "The water's already gone down a lot this morning. I have all these blueberries. We thought we might make jelly."

"Well," Ivy said, doubtfully, "Sure-Gel's on the back shelf."

Nonnie made wide eyes at Ivy. I grabbed a plastic grocery basket, hung it off my arm and left the lot of them to speculate. With the things I'd need piled up in my basket, I snagged the last dusty box of Sure-Gel off the shelf at the same time Nonnie was suddenly at my side.

"You getting settled in?"

I glared hard at her. "You mean your chicken bones aren't keeping you informed?"

"I don't need no bones to tell me what I already know. You might ought to take a good look, though. See what kind of woman you are."

I pulled myself up straight and pointed a finger at her. "I'd like to get this straight, whatever you think you're doing, my batteries, my cats, my life is none of your business."

She shrugged. I might as well have been talking to myself for the way she looked at me without the least bit of understanding or any shift in expression. No deal.

But her voice was smooth and dark as molasses. She took

her time with each word, the picture of customer service. "You finding what you need?"

I narrowed my eyes in that way that had intimidated all the girls in the company. "Lemon juice," I said flatly. She smiled. I didn't trust her.

She led me briskly down the back aisle until we found the small green, glass bottles. "Here," she said, pulling one down and putting it in my basket.

"I think it was you that spooked that poor little man at the nursing home," I said, "telling him something awful and plain false about me. Why would you do that? I'm no threat to you. I'll be gone soon enough. Take up your fight with Urey, not me."

Her high, clear brow was smooth, without concern. She answered with a steady gaze. "I ain't tell that ole Otis nothing 'bout you. He knows you're in her house. That's not my doing. That's yours. I ain't done nothing but try an' help you."

I snorted. "I don't need your help, thank you."

"You don't know what you need," she said, almost still smiling. She pursed her lips and gave me a look down her long nose. She wasn't any taller than me. We saw eye to eye, but I felt she grew a few inches when she spoke. "I know you. I seen you since I was a girl, though I ain't never laid eyes on you 'til this time."

Well, that settled it. "You're out of your mind." I took a few more steps back, but her next words stopped me.

"I can tell you what business you have here. I can hear that singing trailing you. You're not here to take up with Urey Trezevant or none of his, nor to pick a mess of berries, or sweeten up ole Otis Greene, neither. Oh, I expect they all look pretty good to you. Like you might could squash them all together and make something for yourself."

"You don't know anything about me."

"I know you come to name your baby is all, and you will."

I gasped and she shushed me, shaking her head as though I should know better than to think she was a threat. "It's you, don't know nothing 'bout me."

"I want you to leave me alone."

She took on a pained look. "You won't be able to help yourself, poor girl. No, you won't. But I'll be there. I sure will. You kept them bones. You believe, don't you? I could tell that about you right off."

She reached to pull something from her pocket, and I drew back, but she only held it out to me, palm up so I could see. It was a long black sliver of wood and what looked like dried leaves tied together with a red string. "Lightning split the tree," she said. "I gone out and got this for you after the storm last night. Very powerful protection, my best medicine, thunder medicine. The Seminole know it's the strongest kind for healing, for making war. You carry that. Keep it close."

She pressed the piece of scorched wood into my hand. I thought of the alligator moving past me in the water.

"Are you threatening me?" I said, but I could see that wasn't the case, even as she patted my hand with her cool, narrow fingers. There was a strange gleam in her eyes, but it wasn't malevolent.

I shivered. I should have given her back her whacked-out charm, but I'd heard what she said about naming my baby and I found myself giving her a nod.

I turned and walked away as fast as I could. But I put that splinter in my pocket, wondering what it would cost me.

I called, "Damascus, let's go," and I put my basket on the counter and dumped it all out for Ivy to ring up. I was shaken up, and all I knew for sure was that I needed out of there.

Ivy's boy walked out to help me load up the golf cart while Damascus hung around the ferry dock, poking sticks at crabs and watching a gopher turtle. He watched me from underneath the bill of a baseball cap pulled low over his eyes.

"JB, this is Roslyn Byrne," Ivy said. "She's the woman out at the farm."

"Ma'am," he said, nodding respectfully. His curiosity was obvious even before he said, "You look like a stiff wind could carry you off. You sure it's a good idea, staying all that way out by yourself? Uncle Urey said to see if you don't need anything."

"Thanks, I'm doing fine," I said. I might have been

offended if I didn't agree with him.

"Yeah, I figured you'd say that." Not necessarily a compliment, I gathered, but his tone was friendly. He was reserving judgment, not finished gathering facts. "I heard you run an alligator out by yourself. You must not be too bad off."

"I'll live."

"You need to eat," he suggested earnestly. "I flip burgers over the other side at the dock. Come by, and I'll set you up." His appraisal of my figure was frank, sizing me up for more than strength, until his eyes reached my face. I just smiled and watched his ears flame.

"I hear fried alligator tastes like chicken," I teased.

"Shoot," he said.

"JB, really. Go see about Damascus a minute, then we'll go," Ivy said.

He looked very much like his younger cousin with his dark eyes and the way he shrugged as he went to join the girl near the dock. I would start to think of that as the Trezevant dismissal.

"I told you. Nothing but raging hormones and appetite," Ivy said. "I heard what all went on with Otis."

"Well, Damascus is better than the nightly news. Did you know she's stealing cakes from the market?"

"'Course I know," Ivy said, lowering her voice. "I'd let her take money right out of the register if I thought it'd keep her showing up. That girl needs some other people in her life. Don't go blaming Damascus for tattling on you. Will was telling me. He was out to mow yesterday afternoon and heard about it all. I'm sorry. I asked Nonnie, and she swears she had nothing to do with it."

"You believe her?"

"I should've known Otis would get all tore up over you being in the house, but I never seen him do like that before. Urey really just let Damascus spend the night out there?" Ivy asked.

"Sent her out to bring me to the clubhouse if I was scared. I wasn't." Ivy tilted her head at me with a grin. I shrugged. "She holed up in her old bedroom." I let that sink in before adding, "She's got a little patch of pumpkins started on the river. Did you know about it?"

Ivy shook her head. "Pumpkins?" I nodded. "What on earth? Better than marijuana, I guess."

I thought of the bundle of leaves Nonnie had just given me and wondered if Ivy wasn't so far off the mark. But I didn't mention it. There was no reason. It was nonsense. And so we laughed. I was surprised at how good it felt and just as suddenly, felt a little shy of her.

I touched her arm briefly. "She's had some strange ideas put in her head. And she's pretty attached to that house." Damascus' voice carried back from the front of the store where she stood with her cousins, and I decided it wasn't the place to get into the details. Especially with Nonnie lurking.

"It's so nice since the storm cooled things off, I was thinking I'd head out to the shell ring for lunch," Ivy said. "This time of year, we don't get a day like this. Usually you'd fry up there this late in the summer, even under the trees. Today it ought to be real pretty. JB'll come with me if I promise him food, but he's not much good for gossip. You and Damascus want to come? We can visit a little more."

She didn't have to ask twice. There were some things I'd like to talk to her about. And she seemed surprised but pleased when JB opted to join us after all. He jumped behind the wheel of Ivy's cart. He was good-natured and jolly, unlike the rest of the Trezevant clan, and I warmed to him, watching him call out endless knock-knock jokes to Damascus, who was smiling coyly.

We rode in caravan, in two carts, bouncing along, sloshing through the low spots where water stood several inches deep, until Ivy pulled off the sandy road. I could see nothing different about the spot than any other all along the way, but I pulled to a stop while Ivy handed out the loot. Ivy toted the beer, and the kids carried grocery sacks full of a picnic, leaving my jelly supplies behind. Ivy reached under the seat of her cart and pulled out a small shovel, which she handed to me. "Think you can manage that and a little walk?"

"If it's not too far. What's this? Do you dig for something up there?"

She grinned. "Shell rings don't have plumbing."

A few yards off the road, the ground rose up in a steep incline. The mosquitoes buzzed, my knee was on fire, and I began to think I might regret my decision. Ivy turned and took my hand. "Use the shovel for leverage. It's not far. You'll make it."

I faltered once, but Ivy was right. I was surprised to find I was stronger than I thought. Before I knew it, we'd arrived on a kind of wide plateau. In front of us was the open water of the Atlantic, and as we turned we could see the Little Damascus River feeding into the bay on the other side of the island. The conjure woman's house was hidden underneath the canopy of live oaks.

The sun was warm on my head and shoulders, and sweat trickled down my spine. I felt as though I stood on top of the world. Ivy laid out food on a sheet, and Damascus explored the broad hillside of scrubby vegetation.

"You want something to drink?" Ivy called.

I started toward them, suddenly realizing I was thirsty. JB stretched his long legs out on the sheet. He gobbled up a ham sandwich, watching me with a mix of contentment and anticipation. I got the feeling he had something to say, but was waiting for his moment.

The beer was cold, and I drank too fast. I had the impression that the storm had swept through, leaving only this high place in its wake. Make friends, eat well, climb hard, breathe deep.

"This is the shell ring?" I asked.

JB squinted up at me. "I think it's the Indian dump." His tone suggested an old argument.

"It might have been a dump," Ivy intoned. "It might have been a place for rituals. It might have been anything. They haven't really decided."

"But you all have." I smiled. Damascus called to her cousin, and he sighed hard before getting to his feet.

"A man in demand," he said, hitching up his shorts. He grinned at me before he ambled off, all arms and legs and the promise of a man.

Ivy rolled her eyes at her offspring's clumsy attempt at charming the new woman. "Dump," she said, answering my question. She pulled hard on her beer and scanned the horizon and the scrub. "Urey loves it."

I ducked my head, drawing with my finger in the sandy dirt to hide my reaction to his name and all the feelings he stirred up inside me. Since the day I watched him in the river, I felt ridiculously exposed when I thought of him, as though he knew when I thought of him, or he could overhear this conversation.

"He says bury him up here after he's dead. But I'll be damned if I will, because it's a dump. That's what it is, and all it is. Of course, by then he won't have anything to say about it, will he? And somebody can finally do right by the fool man."

I drank my beer, too, and then ventured, "Maybe it's because it's a high place. Maybe he likes the view. You can see the whole river from up here. Feels like you could fly right off the edge and keep on going." Used to, I could fly, I thought. I closed my eyes a moment, remembering powerful legs, the leap, the full extension of my body, and the instant when it seemed I was soaring, that I'd never come down.

But I had. Grace, but not mercy. That was something else Granny used to say, how she'd understood her creator's plan. Our lives were granted to us out of grace, and the troubles we faced were meant to strengthen our souls. So if I believed that, then survival was a free gift, but now I had to live with what I'd become.

Ivy sighed and closed her eyes to the warm sun, sinking into a memory. "He'd stand up here and preach sermons on what this place is and isn't. Lord, and we'd have to listen. But I say it's a dump. Everybody leaves the same thing when they're gone, and this is what they left. Can't take it with you."

Some things you just have to let go. Too much homespun philosophy.

But I was glad for the hot sun and the burn on my cheeks. "You live here. Maybe it's one of those things you can't see for what it is up close. The kind of thing you can only truly appreciate from a distance. I think that's how it was for me and my mama with the mountain where she grew up. Well, for me anyway. There's something about an ancient place, the assurance that it never changes. Imagine the people who built this ring, how long ago they put this here, never knowing we'd sit here one day and wonder about them."

"That's not how it is here. An island shifts. It's not the same one minute to the next. They call it rolling over, like a dog. The water changes the coast every minute, little by little, 'til one day you look around, and it's nothing you recognize. This shell ring will be gone one day, too. It'll disappear, same as the people who put it here."

I thought about the family we'd left in Glenmary. I had no idea what had happened to any of them. For a moment, I looked out at the water, and it made me sad. But I'd drifted.

The sound of JB laughing brought me back to the moment, and I smiled.

Ivy said, "JB'd stay here forever, I think. Both those kids would. Scares me to death. I can't even imagine getting far enough away from Manny's Island to want to turn around and look back."

"Then maybe you should," I said absently. "Get away. There's no law against it."

"How far do you think that golf cart'll get me?" She leaned her head back, eyes shut, and inhaled deeply. When she opened her eyes, she looked far off over the water. "Besides, with things the way they are, it's tight month to month for us. I'll be taking on some more houses if I can get them this summer."

I offered to hire her to clean at the farm once a week, and she hesitated. "I appreciate it, but honey, you don't need me."

"I guess I offered to help," I confessed. "But also because I'd like the time to visit with you."

"You make it a habit to buy your friends?"

I snorted. "Would it work? I've tried everything else, and dancers don't make much money. Out of work dancers make less. We wait tables and get our asses pinched."

Her eyes crinkled in a reluctant smile. "So you felt right at home at Sunrise Hills."

"You'll see what I mean about making friends." Ivy laughed outright at that, and I felt the constant knot in my belly loosen a little more. "I'm going back," I said. "Whatever idea he's got about me, I think I could help him get out of that bed if he'd listen to me. And it pissed me off, too," I admitted. We laughed. "Okay, so nursing is probably not the way to go as my second career."

"I always thought I'd like to work in a hospital," she said. "Crazy, ain't it? I graduated high school, you know. I had a couple of classes at community college in Brunswick before Will and me got married. Sometimes I think if I could, I'd go back and finish up some of that and get a real job, not just picking up after people." She shrugged. "Maybe sometime I will."

"Maybe you will."

"Can't complain. We get by better than some. Nah, we won't leave," she said. "It's what we know. Where we are. But you go back and see Otis. He needs somebody to poke him with a stick."

I'd been a lot of places over the course of my career, and none of them had ever had the least influence aside from making me feel more alone, more lost. I'd been on Manny's Island one day, and Ivy Cain, who'd likely never been farther than fifty miles from the place she was born, was telling me what I'd never learned in all my experience.

I said, "So, how do you feel about canning? Maybe we could talk some more about what we're going to be when we grow up."

With a bemused smile, Ivy nodded.

We watched the kids chase one another while the sun climbed higher. "He's showing off like a little red rooster," Ivy said. "Are you impressed yet or should we wait 'til he decides to take his shirt off?"

We giggled and enjoyed the passing minutes, talking about boys we'd known and the stupid girlhood crushes that had broken our hearts.

When the kids joined us, they drank a liter of orange soda and polished off a box of graham crackers between them. We made more ham sandwiches and put them on paper plates with pickles and chips. JB wasted no time asking his questions. Apparently, he'd judged the time had come. "So, did you travel all over the world? Did you go to Russia, even? I bet you seen some things. I know some girls in school, now they're dancing. Make a pretty good living."

I raised an eyebrow at the insinuation. "Oh? Where?"

Ivy made a low noise of warning. "Off the highway, most likely. That's enough, JB."

JB grinned. He knew he was on thin ice with Ivy, but he had a way of teasing that let him get away with more than he should. Even I couldn't help smiling. He knew good and well the difference between legitimate dance and hoochie mamas climbing poles. He was measuring me in subtle ways. Maybe it was because everybody had been so careful around me since the accident, but I was grateful for JB's humor. I wondered how many emotional bombs he'd diffused in this family with that smile.

"I didn't make it to Russia, actually," I said. "And when you're in company, dancing professionally, you don't get out a lot. Mostly, it's long rehearsals and performances." There was the old twinge of disappointment that I'd traveled, but not experienced any of the places I'd been. "But I did dance in some of the major cities in the U.S., and Paris, once, at Christmas time. I sat in a midnight mass at Notre Dame."

That got me some points with the audience. I could see I'd impressed JB, but even as I said the words it felt like I was talking about someone else's life. I'd been sick from food poisoning in a tiny hotel room with two other girls the whole three days we were in the city, and the true memory was neither glamorous nor sophisticated. Still, I saw Ivy start to pack up with a pinched look on her face.

Damascus had already wandered off, collecting shells along the sloping sides of the hill. They'd seen a rabbit earlier, and she was looking for its warren. When we heard her yelp, all three of us jumped to our feet. She was only a few yards away, but I took up the rear, slower than the rest to reach her. Ivy and JB stopped just short of where she stood, but I saw what kept them away and pushed past, shovel in hand. I raised it as high as my shoulder, and, using all my weight for momentum, drove the sharp edge down hard. When the spade sunk into the sandy earth, I lost my balance and landed hard on my side.

"Holy shit," JB said.

The twitching tail of a coach whip snake continued to slap at my legs, but the head had been severed clean through. The group stood silent as Damascus stepped around me and went to her Aunt Ivy's side.

JB looked at me with something like true love stamped on his slack-jacked face. I'd never get rid of him now. Ivy and Damascus stared at me, open-mouthed. I smiled weakly and explained. "I had a granny that knew how to use a hoe."

Heavy on the grace. Not so free with the mercy.

The thunder medicine Nonnie had given me—good for healing, she'd said, and making war—was digging sharply into my thigh.

After that, the party was pretty much over. Things wrapped up quickly, and we made the trek down the hillside with JB at once attempting to act the gentleman, offering a steadying hand to me, then complaining that Ivy wouldn't let him bring the snake home to skin it. Ivy shut that down, barking out assignments for the day, sending JB off to help his daddy with the rental carts while she knocked out an extra cleaning on the south side of the island. He hunched his shoulders and looked back at me regretfully before stalking off in the direction of Cain's.

"Ms. Byrne, you need anything, you just holler," he said. He met my gaze squarely with respect. Clearly, slaying a serpent to protect the innocent meant something to JB Cain.

"Call me Roslyn," I said. He nodded and went along to his work. I liked his cocky walk. I could see the Trezevants in him, but his father must have been a charmer, and I understood how young Ivy had lost her way. I told her so as we parted, but she only shook her head and blushed a little.

Damascus, on the other hand, was not so impressed with

my heroics. She still looked wide-eyed, but I was puzzled by the way her mood soured. She had nothing to say until we were in the cart again, heading back to the conjure woman's house. I asked if she'd like to drive and waited until we were alone, trying to allow her some dignity over the whole thing when I asked if she was going to be okay.

She didn't answer right away. When she pulled up on the bank near her pumpkins, and we both climbed out, she said I deserved an answer, since I was the one who killed the snake. "It wasn't me screaming," she explained. "It was the rabbit you heard."

From her pocket, she pulled the head of the snake and dropped it at my feet. I gasped and jumped back, mortified at the sight of the bloody lump, jaws still wide in rigor.

"Anybody knows you've got to bury the head if you don't want bad luck. Don't feel too bad about it. He'd already got what he wanted."

Chapter Nine

Damascus

Roslyn Byrne made everybody act like idiots. That was the problem, Damascus decided, late in the afternoon following the picnic. She'd seen how JB looked at Roslyn. She'd heard her tell Aunt Ivy to leave the island. It was trouble, the things that woman did, the ways she was confusing people. Roslyn said she didn't believe broken hearts called alligators, but Damascus had seen those gators cruising the river, and she heard them carrying on all hours 'til it seemed like they'd never stop.

Damascus studied the veins in her arms and hands, and she was almost certain she was turning the most peculiar shade of chartreuse, like everything else since the storm. The rains brought more than flooded gullies and fish washed right up to the front door, confounded and gasping to death. She'd asked JB if he noticed the change, but he was too busy watching Roslyn like a puppy dog to notice something like Damascus' color.

After the trip to the shell ring, she'd run to check the pumpkins, certain they wouldn't be there. There was no way to know if they'd survived. It made her sick, worrying over them. And now she yanked at the ends of her stubby hair and sat on the steps of the first house, as out of place and suffocated as those poor fish.

Even before the flood, Damascus barely slept, sometimes not even waiting for dawn before she crept out to lie down beside the vines. But this night, she lay awake staring at the low ceiling in the loft until the first light of dawn, then crept down to the garden where she finally slept on the soggy ground. If the alligators wanted her broken heart, she'd gladly give it to them.

She said the words of protection over the pumpkins every night, sang to them in that spooky kind of tuneless chant just as she'd been taught, the same strange old Seminole blessing her daddy sang to her when she was little.

She'd grown pale and empty, so slight she thought she might disappear and leave her skin behind in a shimmery pile to be found on the riverbank. She was terrified Roslyn wouldn't get to talking to those alligators soon, that her mama's plan wouldn't work, that she'd miss the message, or that it wouldn't be there at all. What would she have then to convince Daddy to come home?

All morning, until the sun climbed high overhead, she read her mother's instructions over and over, so the fold in the paper threatened to tear. She was coming to a decision, and hard at work on the words she would need to convince her father that she would not leave this very spot until the job was done.

"Psst."

Damascus jumped, jerked her head around to see where the noise came from. Her eyes widened when she caught sight of Roslyn smiling, showing all her teeth in a way that made Damascus nervous, standing a few feet away in the side yard, crooking a finger toward her. Damascus got to her feet, ignoring the pounding in her head.

"Shhh. Come here. Don't make any noise," Roslyn urged. "You've got to see this."

When Damascus, barefoot, reached her side, Roslyn took her by the arm and drew her across the yard, down to the edge of the porch.

"Look, look," she whispered.

The kitties wobbled around on the porch, batting at a couple of balls of yellow yarn. Damascus couldn't help smiling at them and feeling good inside just to see their sweet faces and hear their little meowing sounds. "They're so little," she said. Damascus had looked in the sheds and under the house, but she'd not seen the first sign of the mama. Daddy said she wouldn't find a hair off that cat. It worried her because the babies were so small. But they'd seemed to know what to do, curling up together to stay warm and making screechy noises when they wanted milk from the dropper. To look at them now, she could see they weren't suffering. Their bellies were round, and they were playing hard, not a care in the world. Damascus had to admit, they were lucky their pot had been under Roslyn's counter.

Then she remembered Spook. "You better keep them inside."

Roslyn shrugged. "That's the plan."

"You still ain't going to run that Spook out?"

"I don't know. It's pretty small right now. Would it hurt anything to let it stay?"

"Only if you're a rat. Or a raccoon." Things that would eat pumpkins right off the vine.

"I think he's at a disadvantage, anyway. I wonder what happened to the little guy."

Damascus had noticed there were strange scars that furrowed the scaly face. Probably bite marks. Damascus imagined the baby alligator fighting for life, clamped in the jaws that were supposed to be protecting it.

"I was thinking about the kittens. Maybe we'll call one Casper," Roslyn teased, watching them play. "That other one can be Haint."

"That's stupid," Damascus said. She didn't know why she felt so sour about it. She felt upset and sour in general, and the more Roslyn tried, the worse it got. Damascus didn't like how she cared what Roslyn was doing, or what she thought. She would be gone in a few weeks. October was just around the corner. Just like all those dead Egyptians, being friends was pointless. "You're not good at naming things."

Damascus wished she could take it back as soon as she'd said it.

Roslyn used Damascus' shoulder as support to get to her feet. "You're right," Roslyn said. "So you're in charge. Whatever. I just thought you might like to see them."

She headed back to the house, and this time Damascus followed, feeling guilty and tender and turned inside out. She didn't know what was wrong with her.

They ate sandwiches like nothing had happened, but there were questions burning on Damascus' tongue, boiling under her green hide. And as the afternoon wore on into evening, Roslyn went through her exercises, fed the two kittens a bowl of milk and egg, which they figured out fast with their little pink tongues, and she invited Damascus to play a hand of Spades.

Roslyn beat her square at three hands. Then she gestured for Damascus to hold out her hands so that she could rub lotion over them. Surprising herself, Damascus allowed it.

She never let anyone touch her. But here she sat, with Roslyn's long white fingers gliding over her flesh in smooth, cool circles. She drew in her breath.

"What is this stuff?" she asked as Roslyn rubbed the remaining cream through her own fingers.

"Some French-milled something or other my mother sent me. Came today while we were gone." Roslyn didn't seem happy about it. She flipped the lid closed on the jar of lotion and tossed it into an open box next to her chair. "It's supposed to be good for muscle cramps."

Roslyn finished up and rubbed the rest of the lotion between her own fingers. Damascus settled, cross-legged on the porch beside Roslyn's box and poked around in there. It held framed photographs of Roslyn. Working up the nerve to confess her secrets, she absently rummaged through a few costumes, a pair of worn out ballet shoes with long tattered ribbons, papers that had names like *Giselle* and *The Sleeping Beauty* written on them, with lists of names, and Roslyn's right on top.

Roslyn leaned over to pull out a stack of old papers held together by a couple of rubber bands. She thumbed through them until she came to one that she pulled from the bunch. Reading whatever was on the page, a slow smile curled her lips, and she sighed softly.

"What's that?"

"I don't know." She looked up from the paper to Damascus. "I mean, my Grandpa wrote it. He wrote all these for my Granny Byrne. They're love poems."

"He wrote that much just about love?"

"Just about her," Roslyn said. "He published most of them over the years."

"Like a whole book?"

"No, newspapers, magazines, that sort of thing."

"It's enough for a book. I bet it'd be bigger than the alligator book," Damascus shrugged. "I don't know who'd want a whole book about nothing but love."

Roslyn's brow rose in consideration of the idea. "I would." Then she went back to reading the poem she'd separated from the rest. "But this one is different. I don't know why. I read it over and over, and I can't tell you why." She straightened the papers and snapped the rubber bands back in place before replacing the stack of papers in the box.

Damascus pulled a pair of the shoes out. Roslyn grabbed them, paused to look at them for only an instant, and shoved them back in the box, closing the cardboard flaps. "That's what mamas do, I guess. Load you down with crap you don't want. Keep your whole life in a box."

Damascus rubbed the remains of the cream into her elbows, then held her palms to her face to inhale deeply.

She peered out from behind her fingers, but kept her nose buried. Damascus felt her blood rushing in her ears. She'd never been this close to saying things out loud. She'd not known how badly she wanted to.

Roslyn looked down toward the river like she was enjoying the breeze while Damascus struggled to catch her breath. Keeping secrets takes a lot of work that you don't even know about until you try to tell it. Sometimes, Damascus was exhausted from it.

Still, she didn't know what to do with such freedom offered with an open hand. Choice. She was ready to bite that hand if it closed on her. The white arch of Roslyn's neck was beautiful as she let her head fall back to rest on the chair. Damascus was breathing so hard now she sounded like she'd been running a race. "My mama gave me them seeds to plant. She picked them out. Every one. She told me to grow them. I don't know why. It

don't make sense, and I know it, but I don't care. I just have to."
It came out in a rush. Her head felt light. The lavender was too
strong. But she was waiting to see if she'd been right about
Roslyn. If she knew about things like this.

Roslyn sat up in her chair. "All right, then. I guess that's
what you've got to do."

That was all she said, but Damascus knew then that Roslyn
would make sure it happened. She could look at her and tell.
And it was a relief like falling in bed after walking a hundred
miles.

Roslyn didn't ask any questions, either. She just said, "I've
got blueberries waiting to be washed. Your Aunt Ivy's going to
be here. Are you coming?"

Damascus clamped her jaw shut. "I got stuff to do."

She'd seen her daddy do it a thousand times when he didn't
mean to change his mind. She needed Roslyn to do this one
thing. "Daddy let me stay out here for the storm. He's never
done that before."

"Are you going to help me make this jelly or not?"

"He was all bent out of shape, asking did I want this, did I
want that, had I eaten good. It was plain embarrassing how he
paid Nonnie fifty dollars for all them cakes I took. He never paid
her before."

"Oh yeah? Who told him about that? More importantly,
what's he going to pay me?"

"I think he done it because of you, so you'd think good of
him."

"What?" Roslyn looked annoyed.

That wasn't what Damascus wanted. She'd meant to flatter
her.

"Just go talk to him. Make him let me stay here 'til I get
them growed."

Roslyn groaned.

"You're living in this house, ain't you? You're sitting on this
porch right here. You got some say. You got a canoe needs
dragging back. I can do that."

Roslyn'd killed a snake for her. She was keeping a blind

alligator and kittens that weren't good for nothing but eating up her milk and eggs. She was the kind to take things in. Only one other person Damascus knew to be that way, or used to be that way. But you wouldn't believe it if she told you since her daddy didn't waste a minute on anything but that owl anymore. Damascus figured she just had to get herself looking like one of them little things that needed took in. She had to show her empty belly and her wide eyes.

"I ain't got a mama. All I got's them pumpkins. I got something I can raise up. Something she wanted me to see, so I figure maybe I can see her a little bit, too. If them vines get eaten up, that's all." She saw the value of her bargain flash across Roslyn's face. She knew she'd won. Damascus jumped to her feet. Roslyn stopped her with a hand on her arm.

"Hang on, speedy. I'm going to be straight with you, because I think somebody needs to be. Honey, you're making a lot out of this, and I don't want to help you break your own heart."

Damascus pulled free and lit out across the yard to the river. She'd given all the answers she was going to for this day. She refused to think about what Roslyn said or let that kind of doubt take hold inside. There was no place for doubt in magic. No place at all.

Damascus stayed out on the riverbank until the sun was dipping lower in the sky, midges were thick in the air, and the willets dove and called over the water. She heard Aunt Ivy pull up the drive, but she didn't go in to say hello. She wanted nothing to do with that blueberry business. It was likely Aunt Ivy would try and haul her home to her daddy anyway, and Damascus wasn't giving her the chance to get a good hold on her. She still hadn't found those papers, but that didn't mean daddy had got rid of them.

She trailed along the worn path to the vines. They curled out of the ground, seemingly getting longer by the minute, as sure and certain as her mother's promise. The two pumpkins still attached had grown larger than you'd expect in such a short time.

The horizon turned a tender pink, and the sea breezes began shifting direction, the night air washing off the land and out to the water. The sounds of night things rustled in tall grasses. The forest seemed to breathe deeply as though it were waking. She couldn't help feeling hopeful for the first time in weeks when she thought of Spook, surviving by some animal instinct that told him to snap jaws shut just in time to snatch life—and any sneaky threat to the pumpkins—right out of thin air. With Roslyn's help, she thought she could do it. She could stay out here.

But nearby, a mournful wail startled Damascus. She stood, listening to the familiar sound. Again, the tremulous little quaver filled the mellow evening quiet. The whisper of wings moved overhead, and Damascus stopped short, nearly tripping over her own feet. She looked up into the branches of the oaks, searching for the bird, knowing that on the other end of Elder's circuitous flight, waiting to see what unlucky creature would be caught tonight, was her father.

Chapter Ten

Roslyn

"This is who you were," the note in Mama's box said. "Take a look. It wasn't so bad. But if it fits in a box, it wasn't everything. Love, Mama"

She was right. Probably, I was reading more into it than she'd intended. Everything about me wouldn't fit in that box. The best part, the only part worth anything, I'd left in another box, buried in Dalton.

Damascus had slept on the riverbank again, which meant I got no sleep. I'd propped myself up underneath one of the oaks near enough to keep an eye on her, with the rifle to keep me company. When dawn came, I snuck back to the house, lucky she hadn't noticed, sore and exhausted and in a bad temper. I couldn't keep this up and neither could she, but I had no idea how to keep her safe inside. And part of me resented that such a job had fallen to me. Who was I to be watching over some kid?

When the mail delivered the second package late that morning, I groaned and signed for it. Inside, I found another notecard and a new piece of mama's creepy pottery. "I call this one 'A Hole in the Head,'" the note read.

I realized I'd neglected calling home too long.

I yanked the thing out of the box, a rounded, squat blue jar the size of a fish bowl, poked full of holes. I put my fingers in the open places, testing it for some use, before I stuck my car keys in it and plopped it on the windowsill above the sink. The light from the window filtered through and cast the countertop in festive polka dots.

Time seemed to slip around me on this island, as though I

could step into the past as easily as I could be carried into the future, and Mama seemed far away in some other constant place. I'd put her on a shelf the same as her pottery, for when I could deal with her. But it was more than the packages that had soured my attitude.

It was the ordeal with the snake, and I'd been thinking about the day Granny Byrne died, when I'd answered Judith Ann Keller's nasty phone call. It seemed years ago, but in reality it had only been last spring, barely four months past.

With all that was going on with me that day, I'm still surprised I didn't feel the earth move when the call came. Judith Ann said she hated to be the one to have to do it, but she felt like Granny Byrne had always deserved better than my Mama, and it was a shame how we'd let that poor woman lay up for nearly a month by herself.

To be fair, no one had called to tell Mama what was going on. Judith Ann was only calling then because Granny Byrne had passed, not to try and help mend the rift. Mama was at fault for being stubborn, but she'd been unaware of Granny's illness, and the blame went both ways. Not the way Judith Ann wanted to call the score. They'd shut us out, all the same.

When I heard this, I could not think of Judith Ann as the sad woman lying prostrate over her son's grave. I wanted to go find that post hole digger and get Grandpa back from there. Instead, I had to call Mama, with news of death. And the life I hadn't been able to bring myself to tell her about yet.

I'd just come off the long run of Swan Queen, and I was this side of being put in a doctor's care. I knew I was pregnant by then, but I hadn't told a soul. In the strange way of these things, it occurred to me that if Granny was in heaven, she was the first to know my secret. She might have met the little soul of her great-grandbaby along the way. For the first time, my pregnancy seemed real.

Through tears in the parking lot, I'd managed to crawl into my car, fumble with the keys and crank the motor with the same determination I'd relied on to carry me through joint injuries, broken toes, and bouts of bulimia. But the SUV that collided with the driver's side door of my car was a force stronger than all my good intentions, and it surely changed my course.

When I came to in ICU, I couldn't bend my right leg. It was stabilized with straps and something firm.

Mama's was the first face I saw. Her cool hand fell across my forehead, and I took hold of her like a lifeline, trying to ignore how small the little bird bones of her hand felt. They buried Granny Byrne without us, and we'd never seen the grave.

I knew then I'd lost a gift I'd never get back, and my leg was only a reminder of my terrible fall. Ivory towers and pedestals have their dangers.

I'd gone home to Mama's, and she'd nursed me right alongside Jackie until I lost the baby. Then I'd come running down to the coast. It was like we hoped if we didn't go back to Tennessee, Granny and all those lost chances would still be there. The world had gone right on like nothing had changed, nothing was missing. And we'd denied the loss like so many other things, like Mama had pretended there'd never been a rift, just gone on talking like our memories from years ago had occurred only days before, although we hadn't seen Granny Byrne since the one summer we'd gone back when I was twelve. The summer I danced for the church, and Granny declared I had a gift, a responsibility to the one who'd seen fit to bestow it. I remembered that conversation now as the death knell of my childhood.

I wondered if it mattered if I ever made it back to Glenmary now? I didn't know if I could show my face there. If it was me or Judith Ann who was like that snake? Maybe I'd already gotten what I wanted and suffered the consequences.

I threw the snake head in the river. I'd had enough of burying things in the earth.

At dusk, blueberries bobbed in cold water, filling the kitchen sink. They boiled in an enormous pot on the stove. The air was thick with the tart aroma of warm fruit. My head swam with the memory of Granny Byrne's kitchen. My iPod charged on the counter, but the music lingered, as though coming in through the window, floating around me as thick as the sweet fruit. I hummed along, sometimes finding harmony with the voice inside, sometimes singing out on my own.

After the talk with Damascus, I'd watched her from the window as she worked all day, weeding, watering, even polishing the bright orange shells of her masterpieces. I'd tried calling Mama, missing her awful. But I got her voicemail so I left a short, impersonal message about the storm and the shell ring. I said I was about to put up some blueberries, imagining how she'd howl over the very thought of me sweating over a pressure cooker. I tried not to worry something had happened to Jackie.

Mama, the woman who had taught me how to hold myself apart from the world, from people, was now consumed by Jackie's increasing need.

She'd met Jackie Kennedy, owner of the Lincoln dealership in town, at a Christmas buffet at the bank. I don't think she'd had it in mind to look for love, but she surely appreciated a sweet man who could do the driving for a while, and in a nice Lincoln.

It wasn't long before I got used to Jackie being there in the evenings. He was older than her by a good ten years, but Mama said he reminded her of a kinder, gentler version of Burt Reynolds. He'd been married once, when he was a young man, but it hadn't lasted. He smoked, and Mama didn't like that, but he made sure to always do it outside so the smell wouldn't get in the furniture. And he was always smiling in his eyes. That was the thing most people noticed, including me, and they liked him for it.

I watched her pull out recipes she hadn't cooked in years: roasts, candied sweet potatoes, even the almond pound cake. He ate it all up, his moustache a little broom, and she enjoyed watching him. We all felt very satisfied, and it was a good time.

He might have asked her to marry him, but she never said yes. I never knew. Whatever the case, aside from the food, she did not change a thing for him, and he kept right on coming to sit in the house with us or take us for a movie or to the Sizzler.

He sat through my recitals and birthdays and holidays with

us, and we were glad. But it was still somehow just me and Mama. We were a pair, and the thing about pairs is that there's only room for two. Jackie must have come to terms with that early on, or I don't think she'd have ever allowed him in the house. But I was thankful she had him.

Granny and Mama and me, we all had our expectations. That was the thing about a house of women. But Jackie was a safe place to rest, a constant in our swirling world of estrogen. He was ever-present, predictable, readily found in his recliner, unflappable. I was grateful I'd seen that kind of love. I just didn't know if I'd ever find it for myself.

The splinter of charred wood from Nonnie was neatly tucked away in 'A Hole in the Head.' Something stopped me short of throwing Nonnie's charms out. I was gathering up every little bit of faith, hope and luck I could find. Maybe, I considered, I knew it was up to me to protect myself now. The little girl on the riverbank had figured that out long before me.

I was relieved ten minutes later when I looked out to see Ivy's cart pull up the drive. She'd finished up her extra housekeeping job and come to help me after all.

"Still hearing that singing?" she asked as I pulled the earbuds out of my ears.

"Every night. About dusk."

"At least she's a predictable ghost."

I laughed softly. I really liked Ivy Cain. I was glad to see her again, and not just because I needed help with blueberries.

I watched her notice Damascus, craning her neck as she walked up the steps. "What's she doing out there?" The screen door slapped shut behind her. "Is this about the pumpkins?" Ivy asked a moment later, beside me, peering out the window at Damascus' bright head in the late light. Her back to us, we could study her thin shoulders and the spiky hair.

"She's keeping watch. That's what she called it. I don't think she's going to leave," I explained. The words were barely out of my mouth before I heard the echo of that long ago night with

Judith Ann Keller.

"Well, what's she think she's going to do?" Ivy asked.

"She wants me to convince Urey to let her stay here so she's close enough to look over those pumpkins day and night, I guess."

"With you, or literally out there?"

"With me, and out there, I guess. I've sat watch over her the last two nights. She said until those pumpkins are done, or picked, or harvested, or whatever you call it, she's not leaving. Damn, I didn't even think she might mean she'd be out there *all* the time." Ivy looked confused, as anybody would. "It's got something to do with her mother," I explained. "Apparently, she left Damascus the seeds and some instructions. She's been hauling water, buckets of it, every day. Fertilizer, compost, you name it, she's doing it. This afternoon, she told me it takes a hundred and twenty days, start to finish once they're in the ground."

"And how long have they been there?"

"Ninety-two."

"Oh, good God. She's been doing this all summer and nobody's known about it?" Ivy groaned. "What in the world?"

"They're not hard to miss. They're huge, about the size of a real big beach ball. There's only two now. She's had to choose between them to keep them growing so big, and she's out there right now deciding which one she's got to cut off so the last one can take over. She says it's supposed to get about the size of the golf cart."

"But why?" Ivy looked thoroughly annoyed and let out a burst of air through her nose. "She's been doing good with her school work. She tests beyond grade level, did you know that?"

I shook my head, but couldn't say it surprised me.

"She needs a challenge," Ivy stated flatly. "More than I can give her in a couple hours a day when I'm bone tired and hardly able to keep my eyes from crossing. Another year, and she'll be running circles around me. She needs to get into school over in Brunswick where they can really teach her something. But I swear, she seems to be getting along pretty well."

I wanted to encourage her. It was obvious Ivy had her hands full. "She said she goes every week with you to see Mr. Otis."

Ivy's brows drew down. "Damascus took up with that a few months back. Now I see what was going on, and it didn't have much to do with me. It's this," she said, flipping a hand toward the girl and the pumpkins. "She's milking Otis for all he's worth on what to do for this patch. He give her a big old book of his on planting a good while back, but he ain't really saying nothing else. He could tell her any little thing she wanted to know, if he was willing. He just stays clammed up.

"Lord, I just didn't put it together 'cause I never guessed it would have to do with Fawn. Mm-mm. Sneaky child. I should have guessed, 'cause she's never had to do with a soul that wasn't getting her something she needed. Least of all me. She'd sidle away, any chance she got."

I touched her arm lightly, and she turned her worried eyes from the little girl on the riverbank to me. I said, "She asked me to talk Urey into letting her stay out here." Her eyes widened. "I'm still deciding what I can even say, but it's a deal I've made with her, and I need to do it."

"You don't mind?"

I was grateful for at least one person who didn't seem afraid of me, or suspicious that I might suddenly unzip my skin and expose my scaly true nature. "Well, it's not like she's cramping my style. And you know she's going to be here anyway, so I figure the best I can do is keep the peace."

"Make it so he thinks it's his idea. That's all that will do it." For most of the morning we contemplated how I would go about talking to Urey, which was not really so different than communing with alligators when you got right down to it. I felt as nervous. We agreed it would be best to let Damascus have her way in this case, since it would be safer to have her permanently on the riverbank rather than sneaking around at all hours in order to get there. Meanwhile, we worked and ate too many berries, and in the end I found myself relaxing and talking not of the pumpkin dilemma, but of course, of Granny Byrne.

"She loved teaching me things," I said. "Buttermilk biscuits. Fried chicken. Homemade applesauce was my favorite. And she canned everything out of the garden. She was so proud to put up those jars. And she'd say, 'See there what you made, Rosie. One day you'll have a family and a home, and you'll need to feed people something good.'"

"She'd be proud to see you now."

"No. She wouldn't. She loved that I danced. She's really the reason I did it, her and my Mama. But Granny Byrne was the one who told me the dancing was a gift, the purpose for my life. She said I was lucky because most people go through their lives never knowing what they were meant for. I'm glad she can't see me and my pathetic blueberries, feeling sorry for myself. No dancing. No family. No home. She'd have been disappointed."

"You could have those things." When I didn't answer, Ivy said, "Do you want to go back to it?"

I shook my head. "No. But I don't know what else I'd do. I don't know if I have a choice. I mean, I'm not stupid. It wouldn't be the same. I'm not the same. I can't do what I could before, I couldn't just go back to dancing with the company, that's over. Way over." I felt nauseous just saying it. "But you have no idea what I've invested, the years, hours and hours of work, the commitment it takes. And not just from me. Mama spent her money, all her time, making sure it would happen for me. What do I do about that now? Just say thanks and waltz off and do what? Go be a realtor or work at The Gap after they believed in me like that?"

Ivy looked wistful. "You think they'd want you to live your whole life out of obligation?"

"No, it's not like that," I said, struggling to put the weight of what I was feeling into words Ivy could understand. "You don't know where we came from. People from Glenmary just didn't go out and join the ballet. They didn't really go anywhere, except me and Mama."

Ivy pulled back her head and raised a brow. "Well, it don't sound like it's made you real happy. Sounds like an awful lot of pressure you're putting on yourself."

"I should be content with making bad jelly and moonlighting as the alligator lady? You're not," I snapped.

She frowned. "All right. That's fair. Is there something you think you'd actually like to do?"

I wrung out a wet towel and laid it over the edge of the sink to dry, and told her the first thought that came into my head. "Truthfully? I'd like to learn cast fishing."

Ivy blinked. "Like with a net? Like the old Geechee fellas do it? All the kids learn when they're little."

An idea sprang up. "JB can do it?"

Ivy nodded. "Sure he can. But why . . ."

I thought of Urey, saw evidence of him in his sister's face. But I was also thinking of Damascus and how helpless I felt to reach her. I only knew one person I'd seen get close. "Do you think he'd come show me sometime?"

"My guess is he'd beat a path out here to see you get in that river."

I laughed. "Great. So then what about you? What is it you want, Ivy?"

She screwed up her face and let out a hard breath like steam from a kettle before she could admit to it. "All right. I confess, I heard about a job at a pharmacy from a cousin," she said, "and I thought about taking it."

"Really?" I said, relieved to change the subject.

"I mean, running away and just . . . taking it."

"Oh."

She shook her head like it was nonsense. "It's not happening. It's all the way on the mainland, and I haven't had a car since we sold my old Bonneville near on six years ago. Even if I could, Will wouldn't go for it."

"I'm sorry. I'd offer you mine, if I thought you'd take it."

She looked into the sink, swirling the berries in the cold water with one hand and puckering her lips in consideration, not taking me up on the idea, but not rejecting me, either.

I reached for the pot on the windowsill that held the keys and put it on the countertop near her. I hadn't really meant to offer my car, but now I could see that maybe Ivy had been hoping I would, so I tried to work through the details. "I'd need the car back when I leave. I know it's not long." I felt queasy just thinking about leaving Manny's Island in that short time. "October's not that far off, but maybe you could work something out with your husband by then."

The light in her eyes shifted, and she shook her head with a tired smile of gratitude. "Honey, I've not done nothing but work it out with Will since 1995 when the stick turned blue." She looked around then, like she was noticing the room for the first time. "Ah, he's a good one. It ain't that. Will'd practically kill himself to make me happy."

"But he doesn't support what you want to do? Is the cleaning business that good, or is he funny about you leaving the island?"

"Neither. Will's always said we'd travel, soon as JB got up and grown. Will's got big plans to be shut of this place then and just take off, see all the things me and him should have done. He's been stashing money for years and got it all laid out, maps, pamphlets, I don't know what all. Our boy's not but a year from finishing high school. If I took up a new job, well, that might mean another reason to put off our plan. That's how he sees it. He cain't see the use.

"Really, it's me, I guess. I've got it in my mind that it would be good to live off this island awhile. Get a little place where we'd have something of our own, separate from all this. To tell you the truth, I think if we weren't around, Urey might let it go easier. Lord, the things I could tell you went on here."

"So, tell me. I'm sure not getting anywhere with Otis. And you were supposed to help me with that."

Her laughter bubbled up in a wonderful way, deep and sincere. "Maybe you and Otis just need to work something out," she teased.

All evening, until it was dark, we worked and talked, revealing little bits of our very different lives and learning what we had in common. Occasionally, we looked out on Damascus where she sat on the bank or hauled water in for her pumpkins. We ladled the hot fruit through a sieve to separate the pulp, and then poured the steaming liquid through a funnel, filling jars. I watched Ivy fasten the lid on the pressure cooker.

In Delia's strange, dark house, Ivy told me her mother had made out like they were the luckiest little family alive and expected them to believe it. She was proud to provide for them any way she could, fiercely determined to do it on her own. "And we pretended for her, because she wanted to believe she'd made a good place for us here. Right up 'til she died, we pretended. I guess that's some kind of love, a lie that big."

She turned to look at me then, and I knew she was going to tell me something important by the way she braced her hands on the counter.

"I married my Will that year, and we moved over to our place. I thought I'd do it different than my Mama. Have a husband, a daddy for my babies, get off this island and do something. He was something then, Will was. Just crazy how he could sing, and all the blood would rush right out of my head. He had some plans, too, and that's all I could see. I swear, to listen to him it was like he was spinning gold out of his ass. But once the new wore off, it was just keeping house and a man, too, not so different after all." She gave a small sigh and shook her head, refocusing on the memory.

"It's not that I regret it," she said. "God, no. I love my kid. Kids, really. JB's just about a grown man now, and Damascus is mine as much as she's Urey's. I'd take her and run if I thought Urey'd let me. She's with us about half the time as it is, so we've talked to him about it. I know how that sounds, but I love my brother."

I nodded encouragement. "I'm sure."

"And if you twist my arm, I'll admit it. I still love that fool man I married past the point a grown woman ought to." The tip of her nose had gone pink, and I couldn't help the twinge of envy in my chest. "It's just," she paused, her brow drawn down, struggling to explain, "I guess I didn't think that's all there'd be. Lately I look at Damascus and I think, maybe the two of us could both use a broader horizon, you know?"

"Maybe."

I couldn't say I knew what she meant, exactly. What I'd had with Stephan was nothing like that, nothing with any staying power. Forty-eight-year old Stephan Pillard wasn't a bad man, but he was a plain bad choice.

"You're a regular Evelyn Nesbit," Stephan would say, comparing me to the turn-of-the-century siren that inspired the Gibson Girl. I was flattered and infatuated with his brand of sophistication, but later I wondered if I shouldn't have paid more mind to Evelyn's fate. Hired out as an artist's model as a young girl to save her family from poverty, she'd known fame for her beauty as the Gibson Girl, but ended up a tragic figure, tangled in a crime of passion, and then struggled for happiness the rest of her life 'til she died alone. Not so romantic a compliment as Stephan made it sound.

The whole affair lasted less than four months. And by the time I reached my thirtieth birthday, Stephan was already going home to his wife as though I were a habit he'd kicked, like cigarettes or nail biting.

That's when I broke the second part of my promise to Granny Byrne: don't be like your Mama and let a man take your choices from you.

I'd kept that promise as long as I could. I recovered from two herniated disks and developed an allergy to chalk that brought on hives and made it impossible to dust my shoes before performances. Then, at the opening of this year's season, I faltered. It was a misstep blamed on infamous glass ankles. But I knew better.

For weeks I'd had no appetite, and what I did eat tasted all wrong, soured in my stomach. I felt dizzy. When I started for something across a room, I'd inevitably forget what it was by the time I'd taken my third step. There were whispers of a nervous breakdown. But it was not the manifestation of mental instability that had disrupted my carefully tended equilibrium. It was life; just not mine.

Losing the baby, I could now admit, shouldn't have been

such a surprise. After all, there wasn't enough substance between the two of us to have created a life. And part of me was not sorry; I could admit that, too, horrible as it was, because I'd have failed her.

"I understand things not turning out how you thought," I said to Ivy. We watched Damascus, clutching her knees to her chest, rocking herself.

Hold on, I thought.

We'd worked up a sweat over those blueberries when Ivy said, "She's like her mama that way. Not letting a soul close. When Fawn first got sick, she didn't tell any of us. Just like her. She didn't want help, wouldn't ask for it. I should have just come in and done something. But it didn't take long before it was obvious something had gone bad wrong. She wasn't more than skin and bones by late summer, and then Urey had to take her over to the emergency room in Brunswick one night. Her thigh bone had snapped clean in two. That's when we found out about the cancer. It had eaten her up by then. It was the worst, a sorry way to go." Distracted, she burned her thumb on one of the jars and turned to run it under cold water at the sink before putting it in her mouth. I grabbed ice cubes and wrapped them in a dishtowel for her.

"Thanks," she murmured, then continued her tale. "She wouldn't have any of that chemotherapy, she said. It was way past that by then, but even in the beginning they told her it would only be a matter of time. She didn't want to be laying up sick like that. She wanted to be playing with her baby. I guess she wanted what any of us would, and I didn't blame her. But Urey said it was because her people didn't hold with medicine. They stood on faith, he said, and he thought she'd just as well have killed her own self."

"I can't imagine."

"Urey was angry, Lord, was he. But not at Fawn, not really. It's always about control with Urey, and here this was, something he couldn't control. He couldn't beat that old cancer back with hard work or plain old stubbornness. And he wouldn't see Fawn after that.

"He was in the house, looking after Damascus, but he turned his back on Fawn. He just couldn't believe she'd lay there and die and leave the baby. He thought if he refused her, she'd come around, take the treatments, fight. He had us come, but he wouldn't go near that room. Not when she got real bad sick and couldn't get up out of the bed. Neither one of them would ever give up on a thing. Not when we had to start taking it turn about to bathe her and feed her and get her sheets cleaned up when she messed herself."

I was horrified for Urey, by him, imagining what the house must have felt like, but especially to a child.

"Her folks came down here then," Ivy went on. "Wanted to take her back home with them, but Fawn didn't want to go. She'd fallen out with them awhile back and said this was her home now, and she'd be here with Damascus and the rest of us long as she could. They blamed Urey, I reckon. It didn't matter. They'd always hated him and maybe should have. But you know, he did them one kindness after she was gone. He gave them the body.

"They buried her up with their people near Waycross somewhere. Urey's never been up there that I know of, nor Damascus neither. I believe that was part of the understanding they came to, how he'd stay away so long as they let him and Damascus be." Ivy shook her head.

"So she doesn't know them?"

"No, they died. One, the daddy, the year after Fawn. Her mama passed two years ago. Damascus never saw so much as a picture of those people. No phone call. No birthday cards. Nothing. Better off, too. Bunch of zealots. Made Fawn half crazy."

"Holy rollers," I said. A look of alarm flashed over Ivy's face. "Damascus called me one. Not me, exactly, but the Sacred Harp music. I listen to it to try and remember my grandmother's family. I told you before. I hear it, and I remember the people from her church, really, because we left there when I was little, and I always sort of missed it. It's silly, but that music calms me down."

"That ain't silly."

"I was only up there a short while, and then a few times growing up. It's just sort of a fixation, really. I shouldn't romanticize it like I do. But it seemed more real to me than anything has since, like I could take hold of it. I don't know. Maybe that's what those vines are about for her. A way to hold on until she can make sense of things." I shrugged. "Anyway, she said her daddy would hate the music because he hates holy rollers."

Ivy winced. "I sure hope she don't remember. It was an awful time when Fawn was wasting. We—me and Nonnie—we kept Damascus away."

At the mention of Nonnie, I must have tensed. Ivy raised her eyebrows.

"She's not what you'd think. Listen, that baby cried. She was nearly four. Got to throwing herself against the door one night and just bruised herself all up and down. Nonnie's the only one that could get hold of her in a lap and calm her down."

Ivy looked at me then. "That's when Nonnie had to take her back over to my house. It was Urey that packed her little things and sent them off. I remember watching him do it and thinking part of my brother just disappeared. This old gruff thing came and moved into his body, and it's walked around being him ever since.

"Those last two days, the morphine wasn't even touching the pain. When he told me to leave," she hesitated for only the space of a breath, "I worried what he meant to do, I won't lie. But Urey never could've done it like that, not even mad as he was. He'd have eaten them pills his own self, first.

"Fawn, though . . . I guess she came to take a different view on medicine there at the end." Ivy's face was blank, and her tone was quiet, as if she were recounting a recipe or a grocery list, not the assisted death of her sister-in-law. "Sweet boy," she whispered.

Steam escaped the pressure cooker, startling us. The jars

were ready. We worked quietly for the next hour until we had lined the counter with the jewel-toned jars. They were beautiful. When it was done and we stood on the porch before Ivy went home to feed her family, she grew very still. So still I worried she wouldn't draw another breath.

"I'm gonna take that job, Roslyn. I'm gonna go do that, and there's going to be some changes around here." She seemed to have stunned herself. "I done thought about it, and if I can get over there just two weeks so I can settle into the work, that's all it'd take. Then Will'd have to see it means something to me. I could do it, too. Lord, I sound just like Damascus, all of us at you for something. But . . . if you'd help me?"

"Anything," I said, realizing this was the reason she'd come here all along. She'd told me all about Urey and Fawn so I'd know what was at stake. She'd let me come to my own conclusions about Nonnie's ambitions. And she'd watched me, to see if I could understand. "But what'll you do? Just leave without saying anything? Won't Will come after you?"

Everything Nonnie had said to me in Cain's came rushing back, and my stomach clenched. But Ivy was talking again and I forced myself to focus while she laid out her plans.

"I've got a letter I'll leave. Will won't come, 'cause he won't know where to come to. Not at first. I'll send him whatever I'm making that I don't use up to keep myself, and I'll give him a call after I give him a day or two to settle down. He'll know I'm okay. He'll know what I'm doing, and he'll have some time to swallow how I've done it. That's best I think, so we don't end up saying all kind of stuff we cain't come back from."

I listened to her lay it out and imagined her writing that letter in secret, keeping it some place where no one would run across it too soon, pulling it out and going over and over it.

"Your family's big on leaving letters," I said, considering Damascus outside and thinking maybe I ought to take her something to drink. I didn't know if she'd had supper.

"A little space will be just what he needs to listen better. Right?" She looked up at me then. "It's just about set itself up without me having to lift a finger," she said. She seemed to wonder at the thought. "JB's working the marina, bringing in a little extra, and I've had this other girl covering houses with me. She'll be able to take on the regulars. They'll make out fine while I'm gone. They won't miss a single red cent. Did you ever have a thing happen to you where it seemed there was a hand involved, something larger than just your own doing?"

I snorted. "When Verna Oldham's involved, yeah."

Ivy gave a thin sounding laugh, both of us remembering that first night when she'd been afraid I was going to leave. Things had definitely changed.

"Only thing I couldn't work out was Otis," she said. "And then you showed up and I seen how you was. I figured that might be a good thing for the both of you, sending you to sit with him. And I'd have never dreamed that one would take up over here," she said, nodding toward the water. "Whatever the 'cause of it."

"It's no great mystery, Ivy. She thinks she's home."

The light was fading, and still she sat there, Little Damascus. And then I heard it again, the low, soft sound of a child, singing. I grabbed Ivy's arm.

"Tell me you hear that," I said.

She stared back at me and then looked out the window, narrowing her eyes. "Well, I'll be."

"You do hear it? It's not in my head?" I said and clasped my one hand to my chest, relieved.

"This is what you've been talking about?"

"Not all the time," I admitted. "Not at first. But lately." I followed her gaze out the window and felt silly when I saw the girl standing over her pumpkins. "It's Damascus? What is she doing?"

We stepped silently onto the porch where we could hear the song clearly.

"That's my mama's song," Ivy whispered. "A Seminole blessing. We sing it to all our kids."

"What is she saying?"

"It's a blessing, a protection prayer for the living and a way of sending love to the dead. The translation was lost a long time

ago, but the singer is responsible for giving the song meaning."
We listened until the girl's voice faded and silence fell again.
"Urey sang that to her when she was a baby. Lord, how does she
remember that?"

"How could she forget?" I asked, probably a stupid thing to
assume.

Ivy looked at me sharply at first, but then leaned in to give
me a hug before she left. I made a gesture, telling her to wait.

I ran inside and grabbed the clay globe off the windowsill. I
put the whole thing in Ivy's hand. "Take the keys. Take the
whole thing. Go," I said. And I imagined what it would have
been if Granny had awakened my mother that night when she
buried Grandpa. If she'd taken her by the hand and pulled her
along with us instead of the way she'd done it, burying us all on
that hillside. If she'd helped Mama like she helped Judith Ann. If
she'd put the power in Mama's hands instead of making her feel
she had to spend her life grabbing and snatching at it where she
could steal it. Mama'd been contorting herself, too, just in
different ways. Is that what we did to our daughters? Was that
what Fawn's seeds would do to Damascus? I supposed it was a
secret, the same as the words in Damascus' song.

"I never done nothing like this," Ivy said, breathless. "Just
took off without nobody. Something about you, Roslyn, when
I'm with you I think I can do all this stuff." She looked at me,
and her eyes crinkled.

"You've got ideas about me, Ivy, and I'm not like that." I
didn't say they were the ones changing me, the woman sitting
beside me, the girl on the river, the thing she was asking me to
do and how she was trusting me to do it. Ivy Cain was putting
me at the center of her square, believing I could lead.

"You'll leave here," she said. She didn't try to hide the
weariness in her voice. "In a few weeks' time, none of this or us
will even be a memory as strong as one of those old hymns. But
it means something to me, what you're doing."

"Maybe. But I'll know how to fish. That's marketable, right?
At least I'll be able to feed myself. And apparently they take any
Joe Blow at Sunrise Hills." Ivy frowned. "That's what Damascus

tells me."

Ivy watched her niece as the light faded. "I don't know what Fawn was thinking, never did. But that little one's just got to see it through now, whatever this is. Urey's going to have to understand that. I'll say something to him." She set her mouth in a hard line of determination. "How many days did you say?"

I took a quick deep breath and tried to match Ivy's composure. "A hundred and twenty from start to finish."

"I'll be back before then." She smiled.

I knew she felt relieved to reveal herself, to take action. But the weight of our secret filled the evening air with apprehension, and the risk dug its claw into our shoulders. She glanced down at the pottery in her hand, turning it over. The keys jingled inside. "What is this thing?"

"That right there is 'A Hole in the Head.'"

She pulled her lips inside her mouth and tried to hold back a giggle, both of us blinking at each other, good and unhinged. She took that holey globe with her when she went. She didn't have to tell me that come the morning, I wouldn't see her. Nobody would.

I forgot entirely about Nonnie's thunder medicine. It went with the woman who needed it.

Ivy must've done what she said for Damascus, because Urey didn't come tearing up my drive to drag Damascus off. But I was going to have to see the man soon. And he was going to have questions I wasn't sure I could answer.

That night, I finally called Mama again. This time she picked up, and I was happy to hear Jackie was fine, still puttering along. I told her about Mr. Otis and the rain storm and the shell ring. I left out Nonnie and the coachwhip snake, but said I'd made a friend in Ivy Cain. I said I was coming to terms with what life had dished up, and although I didn't have any idea how to come home yet, I was making blueberry jelly.

"Well, glory be," Mama said. "And have you cut that music

off yet?"

"No, and I don't have any plans to," I said. "But I know what I'm listening for now."

"Then I guess I'll have to take what I can get," she said. "You know, this makes it a whole lot easier telling you what's up."

"Did something happen?" I worried about Jackie.

"You could say that," Mama said. There was an upswing to her voice that made my ears perk up. "We've decided on doing us a little tour around the old festival stomping grounds."

"No," I said, unbelieving.

"Well, Jackie's decided, and I reckon I'm going with him because somebody's got to roll the juice." That's what Mama called his oxygen tank. "Going down to Jacksonville, and then going around a little after that."

"Going around where?"

"Florida. We expect we'd get back home about Labor Day, near close to when you'll get back. Hun, Jackie's got him an RV. You know how he's always been after me about one. I guess we'll be gypsies now."

I couldn't believe what I was hearing. I thought of a million reasons this was the worst idea I'd ever heard. But I wasn't saying a word, because it was the best idea, too. She had to go so we said goodbye. She had to go, and I knew it. I knew it.

"Mama, tell Jackie I love him."

I hung up, hearing the twang of mountain voices, low and sweet, a chorus of guardian angels. They followed her, too, and I wondered if she knew it. I prayed, like Damascus' lullaby, their song would reach a little grave in Dalton with no name and nobody to put flowers on it or sit a while. I pulled out a notepad from the kitchen drawer and wrote down two names: Ivy Jane. Just to get a list started. I'd have to wait and see what else came to me. I was out in deep waters now. I intended to cast my net wide.

Chapter Eleven

Roslyn

JB came the next morning and started my training in the art of cast fishing. He brought a carefully knotted net he'd made himself when he was younger, and I spent hours doggedly attempting to get the swing of the net while he visited with Damascus, who bloomed under his attention. The clench she'd been living in eased almost immediately with JB's cornball jokes and the way his big hand ruffled her hair.

I stood ankle deep in the cool river and watched her giggle and blush and felt proud as a peacock at having devised this plan to get the young man out to the farm. By evening, I was exhausted and sore, and still lacked any grace in my casting, but I felt my catch was bountiful. I was feeling less haunted, knowing it was Damascus I'd been hearing on the riverbank, and not some vestige of my guilt. I was further surprised to hear JB join the blessing just after dusk. I'd gone to the house when I heard the two voices rise on the evening breeze.

But when JB didn't show the second day, Damascus was worse than her prickly self. She pouted and growled, and I knew Ivy had gone. I braced myself for a hail of Trezevant fury and waited. But when Ivy Cain had been gone four days, and I hadn't heard a peep, I began to venture back out, daring to resume my routines beyond the house and yard and Damascus' patch.

Dawn hadn't even lifted her skirt when I crept out of the house and made my way past the pumpkins to the river, following the water until the path veered inland. I'd discovered a clear way leading from the house to the shell ring, which was not a quarter of a mile away if my guess was right. I'd gone there several times to stand on the lip of the shell ring and look down over the open water of the Atlantic and a shallow, flat beach that began at the base of the ledge some four or five feet below. Standing there, I felt unbound, like the air was charged up. I wanted to see that place at daybreak.

Granny's tunes were swelling in my ears, and I stretched out in all kinds of ways. My chest opened. My hips and spine vibrated. That sun came up, glinting and proud, and it was a joy. I hummed with the song in my memory, singing the words I knew. The sight of all that blue and the warm, smooth air, reminded me of that day long ago, the last time we'd gone to Glenmary. I was twelve when I danced for the congregation, and it seemed there was a light like this one in my belly. That day, it lifted me outside myself.

The crowded sanctuary immediately came to mind, the earnest faces of the congregation as they endured the close quarters, Granny Byrne beside me, fanning determinedly with her bulletin the day the anthropologists from the University of Indiana came to see The Sacred Harp for themselves.

I didn't know what kind of truce Mama and Granny must have called that we had returned to the fold that summer and been received as though we'd only walked out the door the day before. But I wasn't asking questions. It's hard to talk when you're holding your breath, after all.

I couldn't eat a bite of biscuits, even when Granny scowled at me. I'd pulled my cotton jumper over my head and jerked my hair up in a swinging ponytail that hung in heavy, dark waves nearly to my waist. "You've got your mama's ways," she said. "Byrne ways," she added firmly, taking my chin in her soft hand. She kissed my cheek and looked deep into my eyes. Brown in a sea of blue and green.

It was a mystery what that meant for me, those unnamed genes. A boy nobody ever talked about. But his eyes most certainly separated me from the rest and marked me as suspicious. I might see the world differently than the rest of my kith and kin, and who could know where that would lead? I knew I was loved, but at twelve, even though no one had ever said the first thing to make me feel this way, I imagined I had something to prove.

All I could think about were those men, sent to expose my Granny's quaint, strange ways, and how they would surely find the whole of Glenmary, Tennessee, backward and worth documenting as rock solid evidence that my family was ignorant, eccentric hillbillies. I was sick that I could think of no way to improve upon the mountain and the people from whom I desperately needed acceptance.

Within minutes of the welcome and announcements, I'd spotted the Yankee-white faces of the professors as they sneaked into seats at the back of the church to gawk at our square. I say white not because there was a colored person within twenty miles of us, way back in those hills, but because compared to the mix of farmer's tans and the miner's nearly translucent skin, it was easy to tell who didn't fit. The people there looked like they'd been dug right out of the earth.

We stood up for the opening hymn. Granny was leading, and she stood at the center of the square. I'd positioned myself at the end of the tenors. People were already taking a gander at me and Mama, citified prodigals most likely carrying in disease and the ways of the world on the soles of our shoes.

When the congregation began to sing, the sound rose up, strange and wonderful, always in the same fashion, naming the shape notes before we actually sang the verse. "Now with the poetry," Granny called, so we sang the song again with lyrics.

Some raised palms skyward, some shook their heads and called out personal praises, others smiled or cried softly. That steady beat grew stronger as the choir began to reach the third verse, and the men in the back scribbled furiously in note pads. My fears only escalated. It seemed that everything about us was backward and strange. I looked at the people I'd known all my life and saw them as they must have appeared to those professional men, as threadbare and simple as scarecrows. That was what they'd tell the world. I stood there among them, the ones who had loved me and my Mama, the granddaughter of their matriarch, and I was embarrassed. The only thing I could think was that there was only me to stop it.

Fast, before Mama could grab hold of me, I was beside Granny, arms raised, with a stomp and the swinging of my hips—this was not classical ballet. This was not Baptist in the least, but I was carried away on something more than even I had anticipated.

I was consumed by the song at the center of that hollow. I forgot those slack-jawed professors. I didn't notice if anyone around me was shocked. The soulful old tune filled my long-limbed body with purpose and freedom. I waved my arms like flags. The top of my head felt as warm as if I'd been out in the sun. When I opened my eyes, I saw Mama, eyes shining, her fingers steepled underneath her chin, the same way she looked at a lump of unformed clay, seeing promise where the rest of us just saw mud.

I remembered my legs trembling. But I'd stopped dancing at the burst of a flashcube from the back of the sanctuary. The song came to an end. "Well, my Lord," someone said. People turned to stare at the intrusion.

The research team stepped forward to where I'd remained up close to Granny. "You folks won't mind if we take a few photographs for the journals?" one of them asked.

I stood up straight while the guests, clearly atheists who weren't afraid of being struck dead for doing business in the church, tossed out a couple of twenties, payment for services rendered. I shifted uncomfortably.

"Well, sirs, this is my grandbaby, Roslyn Byrne." Granny stuck her chin out, daring anybody in that place to say the first word against me. "You make sure you put that in there. It's the Spirit's stood her up on her toes. And she's going places."

Her soft old arm came around my waist and pulled me close. Suddenly, the color of my eyes didn't matter. Later, she would chastise me, but for the moment, I was her own, and she was a balustrade against anyone who would tear me down.

I believed I'd turned everything around. Those men barely even remembered the music. They were printing up an article about me. And afterward, with Granny's pride carrying me along, I did not see the way the others looked at me. I believed I'd found a purpose for my life that was somewhat divine. It did not occur to me until too late how far it would take me from her. From me.

Now the truth is, we left there the next day, and not a thing changed in the cove. But I had. I'd learned to be ashamed. I lost my way when I stepped away from the square, when I believed I had to make excuses for the blood that was, or hide the peculiar ways of where I'd come from.

The longer I was on Manny's Island, the more I began to understand I'd spent the rest of my life trying to find a way back to that moment. I felt it in the song, a connection to a place and time and a girl I wished I could talk to before she sold her soul.

I sang for her.

It couldn't have shocked me more when the swoop of wings whooshed up my back and lifted the hair off my neck. A big bird came flying too close. I flipped around to see it was Urey walking up the beach. The last time I'd seen him, I'd run away. Today, I planted my feet firmly.

His forearm was extended and covered with a heavy leather gauntlet. He held a large barn owl whose white face was eerie in the soft light, wide eyes glaring at me, the both of them. With the earbuds in my ears, I hadn't heard them coming. But he'd heard me, the desperate howling of my song. I could see the disapproval in his face.

The bird resettled its wings, twitching on its perch. I jerked the cord around my neck, and the music was replaced with the sounds of the waking island and the water.

"What was that about?" I yelped.

Urey didn't answer, but turned his head as though he'd heard something I missed. He gave a sharp whistle, and the bird hunched its body, pushed off with its legs and disappeared into the scrub behind me. "Breakfast, I reckon," Urey said. He started toward me, but didn't climb to join me. He stood below, looking up. "Could be she mistook all that bellering for fighting words."

"Maybe she's right," I said, provoked. I'd been fighting a losing battle with myself, and I was more than willing to take a swing at Urey Trezevant.

He wasn't wearing the uniform from the resort. Instead, he had on a faded gray T-shirt and shorts that looked suspiciously like a pair of khakis cut off at the knees, with no shoes and, for the first time, no hat. The skin on his face and arms was tan from the sun and lightly blistered across the sharp planes of his face, giving him a hardened appearance. I was struck again by my reaction to the ease of his movement, surprisingly graceful for a man who otherwise seemed so rough. I didn't know if he meant to intimidate me with the owl now, but it was working.

"Ivy said something about you liking it here," I said stupidly. "You were helping preserve it or something. I should have thought. I didn't mean for anybody to hear me."

He squinted in the growing light. "Never would've took you for the holiness type."

"I'm not. Holy."

He shrugged, that fatalistic gesture I was beginning to expect from the man.

"Never would've took you for a conservationist," I fired back. "So don't tell me you don't care about history."

"History? Shit." He seemed to get a charge out of that. "Pile it up, or let that old river carry it off and lay it down someplace else, it's still the same earth." He pulled a shell out of the exposed embankment and placed it at my feet, a bleached curl like a ghost. I picked it up and dusted the smooth surface while he said, "People come and go, and it don't make much difference, really. All I done was keep Elder here a place to hunt in the meantime. Owl's not much but a flying stomach."

It felt ridiculous, looking down on him, but he made no move to climb the embankment, and I wasn't going to give up the high ground. "I don't believe you," I said. "Nobody that feels like that would work so hard to stay here."

Urey ran his hand through the short spikes of his hair so it stood on end. "You want to know my take on things, really—I don't care what you want to say it might've been, or what have you. I'm going to look for the thing that holds out. This shell ring, it's here, by God and that's something right there. That's what I'm going with."

This was truly the most words I'd heard the man string together at one time, and it did seem to me that he was speaking a truth at the heart of my own search. "Then we have something in common," I said. He might have agreed with me by the way he nodded, or not. "Anyway," I said, "that's all I'm trying to do. Hold out. I come from mountain people. We don't shift easily. But I'm finished for today. You and your flying stomach are welcome to it. I'm sure she's devoted."

I reached to swat at the unseen bugs that had found my legs in the warming air.

Urey shrugged. "She don't aim to please me any more than I do her."

"Of course not," I said, rolling my eyes. "Then what's the point?"

"I'll tell you if you swear not to come back up here every day doing that caterwauling, scaring off everything living for a mile."

I made a face of agreement. "Tell."

He cocked his head to regard me a moment, then simply said, "Watch."

He turned to cross the distance from where we stood to the edge of the pines and stood very still, lifting his face like an animal sniffing the wind. I wasn't surprised a moment later when Elder glided in to silently perch on Urey's offered arm. It seemed their hunt was on.

Neither man nor bird looked one another in the eye. They did not acknowledge one another at all, aside from the times I watched in the next thirty minutes as Urey walked around the shell ring, checking the air and the ground and then signaling the bird to take off after some invisible prey. Inevitably, the owl returned with something small and furry in her talons. I sat down with my legs drawn up to my chest just at the edge of the embankment, watching the demonstration. After three flights,

Urey turned back in my direction, looking satisfied. When he was close enough, I could see the eager look in his eye had relaxed to a soft blue, and the bird hopped to the ground to make breakfast out of her morning's work.

As if the demonstration might not have been enough, with something close to a smile, he answered my question. "The damn bird always comes back."

Urey let his hands hang off his hips, shoulders bunched, and looked at me with skeptical eyes. "Guess you know all about what Ivy's done."

I didn't bother trying to put on about it. I said I knew some. I had no reason to lie.

"Seems like she was out visiting you just before she lit out."

I shook my head and got to my feet, dusting the seat of my pants and intending to make a quick exit. "I don't know anything about where she's gone. The rest she told me in confidence, and if you want to know about it, you'll have to ask her." A flash of annoyance in the blue eyes was followed by a quick smile, but I knew it for what it was. He was showing his teeth.

"Will's about beside his self." He was having to shield his eyes now, to look up at me.

"He shouldn't worry," I said. "She's not leaving him, not like that."

Urey did smile then. The ankle strap on my sandal had worked loose, and he reached up to hook it back, then let his fingers wrap around my ankle and rest there. I was holding my breath like a silly girl, not a woman who's traveled the world. "They've been married fifteen years," he said. "And known each other since diapers. I guess he knows that."

Urey was looking at me so closely I felt the hairs rise on my arms. He was looking at me the way I'd seen Elder staring hard after her unseen prey.

I changed the subject. "Looks like I'll be going back over to Sunrise Hills this morning. Ivy asked me to." He scowled at this, but didn't let go. I thought he must have forgotten he had hold of me. "So, what is it with Otis Greene? How do I get him to give me the time of day?"

I don't know what I'd been expecting, but he shocked me when he ran that hand assuredly up the back of my leg to my knee where the strong, blunt fingers prodded and pressed. He sought out the weakness immediately and began to massage the tightly strung tendons, avoiding the tender areas. For a moment, I stiffened, but then took the weight off that leg and gave over to his attention. "Where'd you learn to do this?" I mumbled.

"You ain't the only one that's been places."

"Oh. You've been places?" I had the random thought that JB had said much the same to me on my first trip to this shell ring.

"A bit. Colorado mostly."

"You spend time there?"

"It's been a while."

"But Colorado, that's what makes you an expert masseuse? Let me guess. You worked in one of those spas at a ski resort. I can see it." Sarcasm aside, I couldn't help the way my voice caught in my throat a little.

"No. That'd be vet school. Large animal."

"Well." I was lost in the beauty of the man and the way he was touching me, firmly, unapologetically, intuitively. I thought I might faint and how humiliating it would be. "Moo, then." He laughed, and my heart ached. I thought I knew what Damascus would pay for that laugh. I looked out at the water to avoid meeting his eyes. "And you did this because there's so much demand for a large animal vet on this island?"

"Right up there with ballerinas."

That was as far as either of us were willing to go with that.

But he was still working on my leg. It felt so nice to have someone touch me that I was willing to allow it. Following the muscle down the outside of my calf with the deliberate pressure of his thumb, my eyes slid shut as he finished off and patted the top of my foot while I moaned quietly. "Checkers," he said.

"What?" I blinked at him in the full light now the sun had grown high in the morning sky.

"Long as you're winning, you'll get him out of that bed pretty quick."

Suddenly, I felt my face flaming. He was talking about Otis Greene. He hadn't missed a beat. And here I was, sweating through my shirt for reasons that had nothing to do with the rising humidity. "Great," I said. "Thanks."

He was looking at me now with a new focus. "You keep casting that net. You'll get better at it."

He'd been watching us. Of course he had. "You should come by. Make fun of me."

My breath seemed hung in my chest, waiting to see what he would say next. I could smell him this close, the warm cotton of his clothes and something male underneath. He grudgingly added, "Damascus don't take to just anybody the way she's took to you."

His breath on my face was warmer than the humid air. "It's not me, it's the house. The farm." And, I thought, it's you. She deserves a daddy, even if it's you.

"If she's got a mind to be out there, that's where she's going to be, whatever I might think about it," Urey said. "Same as my sister gone off like she done." He was bitter, but his eyes were deep wells. I couldn't let myself fall in. I couldn't understand how he could be the man I'd seen in the river, how he could touch me as he had, but close himself to the beautiful soul of his daughter.

The heart of the matter was dawning on me. "You're afraid." I swallowed hard. "Just like Damascus. Do you believe what Nonnie's saying?"

Urey stood still as a man made out of stone until he finally said, "I don't know about calling alligators, but you've got a way with my family. I ain't never heard nothing so loud as I been hearing you."

A sense of alarm was building inside.

"So much for education versus superstition," I snapped, and tried to throw him off. "What are you doing mowing lawns and scheduling fishing trips if you've got a degree, anyway?"

"It didn't suit me."

"Large animals or education?"

The smile only widened, but it didn't fool me. "I needed to

get home."

"Oh. And did you? Get home?" He flinched, barely noticeable, but I saw it, and it gave me a false sense of victory so I pushed harder. "I know this little girl who's just about to kill herself to convince me that house down there's your home."

"That house's got awful crowded for my taste." He tried to keep it light, make a joke at my expense. But I could see the tension in his jaw.

"Did you ever mean to move back there?" Maybe I should've known better. Part of me knew Urey was not the person I needed to say these words to, but I also knew I was speaking for Damascus now.

He leveled me with a cool stare. "Not so long as Ivy's got her say."

"What is that supposed to mean?" As far as I understood, Ivy certainly didn't want that house. "Ivy had to practically make a prison break to get off this island, and about half of that bondage is you, Urey. All she wants is a shot at making life better for her family, and that includes you."

When he only turned his head and looked after the bird, I said, "Do you know Ivy wants Damascus to go school in Brunswick? Did you know Damascus is scoring above her grade level on all her tests? She's smart, Urey. Or do you even care? If anybody ought to be supporting what Ivy's doing, it's you."

He climbed up the embankment to stand level with me on the path, and he let out a low whistle. The bird left the last of the carcass it had been devouring and came to rest obediently on the leather gauntlet covering Urey's outstretched arm. The bird always came back. She didn't love him. She was an opportunistic creature.

I put my hand on his arm when he turned to go. "No. You can't just walk off. You need to know what's going on." He shook his head with an ironic smile, and I dropped my hand. "What?"

He looked at me hard enough to hold me where I stood. "You're a hypocrite. Turning up here just long enough to make us your personal twelve-step program. I know exactly what's going on."

"This is about Damascus."

"You're fooling yourself, lady."

"When's the last time you even saw her? While you're sneaking around casting nets or prowling at night with predatory birds?"

"Well, that's none of your business, last I checked."

"It's none of my business that a neglected child spends more time with me than her own family? Listen, ya'll have got Nonnie whispering hoodoo in her ear to keep her away from me, and you're talking about alligators eating people alive to scare her into staying where you put her so you don't have to be bothered to watch. And even that's not stopping her. What do you think that's doing to her? Every time she steps outside, she must expect it's life or death, Urey."

"Good thing she's got you here a whole two months to set her straight on all us evil-doers, I guess."

"No. Not good. You want to know the truth, I can't hardly stand myself for getting involved in this. And she can't even hardly let herself like me, for God's sake. She's not coming to see me, you idiot."

"Oh, yeah? Why's that?"

"I'm not her mother."

For once, I could see there was something Urey Trezevant and I agreed upon, and it cut deep. His emotions were impossible to read, his eyes gone dark and hard. On the other hand, I felt entirely raw, as though I'd been turned inside out in that one moment. All my secret motivations made known. I had filled a need with Damascus. I'd been so willing to let her fill the place inside where I'd eaten out my own guts that I'd believed she was a ghost instead of seeing the flesh and blood child right under my nose.

With Urey, it was always this way, a book of revelations. He'd caught me neatly, and now he opened his hand, as though I should be grateful.

"You hear from Ivy, you'll let me know," he said. It wasn't a question. It was that famous Trezevant dismissal.

A few weeks ago, I'd have been relieved to scurry away, unable to bear my own pain and unwilling to confront his. But now I thought I saw what Nonnie had been saying, what the alligators were roaring about, as surely as I'd understood the Sacred Harp that morning in Glenmary, and I knew I had to speak for us all.

I steeled my bones and closed the distance of three steps that separated myself and Urey so I could lay my hand on his chest. I felt the strong, steady beat of his heart there and watched his hooded eyes flash surprise and heat. And, I thought, not a little fear. "You say you've been hearing something. That's true. There's a call cast over this water every night. I hear it too. Your daughter taught it to me."

I began to recite, haltingly at first and embarrassed because I was unsure of the forgotten language of the Seminoles, words that had only the meaning Damascus had given them. "Tell me," I said. "What is that? What is she saying?"

Urey dropped his head like he was embarrassed for me, but it didn't have the effect he'd hoped for. I cleared my throat with determination.

"You know this song. You sang it to her when she was a baby. You know exactly why she's doing this."

I started again, everything I could remember. I could see by the way his jaw worked and he looked out over the water, searching, that this was a language he knew very well. When I didn't stop, only grew louder until I was practically shouting, Urey grabbed my shoulders, to contain me or to push me away, I couldn't tell. The sharp-eyed bird startled and flew off in a flurry. I looked up at him, stripped and bare, just as I'd left him. And we stood there, surrounded by the regrets I'd raised.

In a flash, I remembered that day in front of the Glenmary congregation and the looks of horror on their faces at the thing I'd done out of love. That couldn't be what I felt for this man, but maybe in spite of him. When Urey looked at me that way now, the sounds of Damascus' song died in my throat.

"You don't know nothing about what's between me and mine. You need to shut up about it."

I turned and started down the path toward the house. I'd been a fool and humiliated myself, but I had an awful feeling Damascus would be the one to pay for it. He was watching me. I could feel his eyes on me. I concentrated hard on keeping my balance, cursing the limp as hot tears made it hard to see a clear way.

Later, I sat on the porch with my own ghosts. I'd called them up, too, and it was time to start a conversation. I could go around all day giving marching orders to Urey Trezevant, but I had my own baby who needed a name and her daddy who needed a blessing. I didn't know if I had it in me to produce either, but I was ready to try. I had to if I was ever going to be able to stand myself. I couldn't keep making the same mistakes.

I watched JB and Damascus on the riverbank and wondered what they talked about all that time. I didn't know what the initials stood for yet, but JB favored his uncle enough that I couldn't feel too surprised at how Damascus watched his every move like she was starving, and he was fresh out of the wrapper.

I watched JB haul water up the bank for Damascus twice after lunch, and that was enough to make me look the other way whenever I caught the glow of a cigarette butt. Frankly, I was surprised a boy his age kept showing up like he was doing for Damascus. But with Ivy leaving like she had, I guessed that left them both motherless in a way. And now here they were on my riverbank. Will Cain must hate my guts.

That's when I noticed the cast of my feet had somehow made its way from the hearth to the porch step, like it was ready to jump off. On the air, I caught the faint scent of rosemary. I prowled around the yard near the porch until I found it, an herb patch easily mistaken for high weeds. The rosemary stood as tall as my knee, growing from a thick, gnarly stalk. A scraggly patch of lavender stood next to the rosemary and huddled beneath them were others, separated and marked by half-buried bricks. I found mint, thyme, and several I didn't recognize with bitter, strange scents. Delia's herbs. I clasped my hands tight to my chest at the discovery.

"I'll be damned. This is where you've been hiding," I said, kneeling. I'd cast my first net, thrown bones and accusations, and wailed down vengeance in tongues. I was an outcast and a meddler. I supposed I deserved a proper conjure woman's garden.

Chapter Twelve

Damascus

Damascus and JB sat alongside the two pumpkins on the ridge above the river.

"Now that's something to look at, ain't it?" JB asked, although the answer was obvious. "Man alive. I cain't get over the size of them things. Good God, girl."

He tromped over to have a closer look, and Damascus couldn't help the pride that swelled inside her flat chest. JB knelt down to run a hand over one of the pumpkins, the smaller of the two. His hair was cut so short she could see his scalp, and she almost reached to trace the swirl at the crown of his head, it was such a pretty sight. But he turned to grin at her, still squatting.

"See. This right here proves it. You're smart. Daddy says you could sneak out of a state penitentiary." Damascus laughed. "So, I said I'd help you out, but then you've got to shoot straight. You're totally up to something, and I want to know what it is."

The older boy's approval made Damascus feel reckless, and she smiled a little at him, but she could see the worry in the corners of his eyes. She knelt beside him and fingered one of the prickly vines. She was choosing her words carefully. Telling some, keeping back some. "I've got to choose one and I just cain't do it," she admitted. "I been trying for a long time."

"Well, then don't do it. Keep'em both."

Damascus shook her head. She couldn't tell him about her Mama's letter, or all her reasons because she didn't understand them all herself. "If I don't do it, this is it. They won't grow much more. I've got to cut one off if the other one's going to get big as it's supposed to, and that's the whole point. I done all this to see that. And now I'm screwing up. I mighta donc waited too late."

JB thought a second. "Knock, knock," he said.

Damascus squinted at him, dumbfounded and kind of annoyed. He treated her like such a little kid sometimes. "Who's there?" she finally mumbled.

"Howie?"

"Howie who?"

"Howie gonna get rid of one of these pumpkins?"

He laughed at his own joke, but Damascus felt her mouth fill with saliva, and her head throbbed at the thought of cutting into that vine. JB must have seen how she was feeling. He sat down flat in the dirt, and let a long breath out like he was thinking seriously now. "You said you've got to choose? Does that mean you've got to be the one doing the choosing, or that it's just got to get done?"

Damascus hadn't considered that. Until now, there hadn't been another option. She shrugged, but the sickness in the pit of her stomach let up a little. JB made a face, pushing his lips out and nodding his head like it was interesting to ponder the possibilities. Damascus let it go. She'd have to think on it. Instead, she said, "What do you reckon they're gonna do about your mama?"

"Ah, Daddy was about crazy," he said, rolling his thin shoulders and cocking his head from side to side like he was resettling his bones. "'Til he talked to her yesterday. But he's settled down now. She's fine. Taking some kind of classes so she can work at the drugstore, he said. She ain't saying where she is just yet, but he said that's good for her. Give her a little independence she ain't never had. He don't seem too worried she'll stay gone, so I guess I ain't too worried, neither.

"Truth is, I don't know how they'd find her if they wanted to. Dad ain't got no car. Uncle Urey can't just up and leave his job right here in high season."

"Not in no season."

"Mama give up all her houses, did you know that?"

Damascus shook her head. JB pulled a stump of a

half-smoked cigarette out of his pocket and a lighter he flicked
expertly at the already burnt end. He drew on it so the tip lit up
orange, then blew smoke out between his teeth.

"Give'em to Jenny Hayes," he said, kind of choked up. "So
that's that. Guess I better see if I can get on some extra hours.
You like burgers? Might be they'd let me bring home whatever's
been thawed and leftover of an evening. We can eat 'em a lot this
fall."

Damascus watched him smoke. Along with helping Uncle
Will with the repairs on golf carts, JB was working his first job
across the bay on the mainland, slinging burgers at the marina.
Damascus nodded and poked at the leaves of her plant with a
stick. She'd made the mistake of stroking them once, expecting
the leaves to be soft and instead, found herself with a rash on her
palms, stinging between her fingers for days.

"Just how big is them things going to get?" he asked.

"They're Goliath Giant Pumpkins. I got this book. It says
sometimes they get to be like five hundred pounds and stuff."

"Good God! Are you serious? Bet you can make a shitload
of pies outta them."

Damascus giggled.

"That'd go good with burgers."

"No," she protested. But she was still laughing, not sure if
he meant it or not. Not sure she wouldn't like making a thousand
pies with JB.

"I mean, hell, just think." He'd almost finished the cigarette,
and he was wrinkling his brow, leaning in to think the idea over.
"Wonder if we could sell 'em? Maybe it'd work. We'd make us a
fortune. Unless you got other plans you want to tell me about?"

Damascus just clammed up. She couldn't help it.

"That woman up there," he said.

"Roslyn."

"Yeah. She don't mind you down here like this? She's not
like Nonnie says?"

"No, she is. She's just like that. But it ain't how you think.
She wants me here. She'll want you, too."

JB looked like he smelled something dead, but Damascus

knew as soon as she took him to the house, Roslyn would change that.

The cigarette still pinched between his fingers burnt him, and he dropped it with a quick intake of breath, stubbing it out with his toe. "You ain't gonna say nothing about that, are you buddy?"

Damascus glowed inside just like that tobacco and shook her head.

"I get it. Some things there just ain't nothing more to be said about, when you cain't do nothing to change it?" He was thinking of Aunt Ivy, Damascus knew, and they looked at one another with some kind of understanding growing between them. "All right," he said. "We better get on back, I guess. See what's what."

But JB didn't move, and she didn't go. Damascus guessed neither of them wanted to go back to the empty place where Ivy had left a black hole. Damascus had a hole exactly that size inside her. The size of a Mama. JB was a big, grown boy, off to college next fall. He was supposed to go visit the school in a couple of weeks. Now Damascus wondered if he'd really leave. JB loved Manny's Island, almost as much as Daddy.

He leaned back on his tailbone and dug a hand down inside his pocket until he came up with a pearl-handled pocket knife and flipped it open. He held it up for Damascus to see briefly, and she swallowed hard, thinking about blood oaths. But quick as a wink, JB flicked the blade between his thumb and the vine and cut the smaller pumpkin free.

Damascus gasped and grabbed her arms around herself like he'd just run that knife through her. Her eyes sprang wide, and after a moment, when she started to breathe again, she let them wander up to look at JB's face.

He waited silently, watching her, but he didn't look worried. He looked calm as anything, and Damascus started feeling that way, too.

He said, "Clean cut's the best kind."

Chapter Thirteen

Roslyn

By Friday, Ivy had been gone nearly a week without anybody mentioning they'd heard from her, and I still hadn't worked out how to handle Stephan yet. After several failed attempts at writing a letter, I'd decided it wasn't something I could put on paper. It was going to require a bigger gesture, one I'd have to ponder. So I concentrated on putting my newfound magic to use on the other man in my life. It was funny that a few weeks ago, it seemed like this summer would never end. Now the minutes felt like they zipped past, and I was running out of time. I needed one win before I left Manny's Island, even if it was just a round of checkers.

Sitting on the ferry across from Damascus, who had her own head full of pumpkin plans, I had a checkerboard in my lap. I'd found it upstairs in the house. Two pieces were missing, but Damascus said since the pieces were still evened out, it would play a fair game. All I had to do now was win. Even JB had agreed it was the best plan to get Otis Greene to sit up and take notice. Ivy's son told me this the evening before when he sat on the porch eating Vienna sausages and saltines with Damascus after rolling one of the enormous pumpkins up to the house.

I tried not to think too much about what I'd done to Urey. What had seemed like such a courageous act of bravery the day before was making me a little sick today. I had the sinking feeling that instead of calling him home, he'd use that old Seminole prayer as a good excuse to never come back to the house where Damascus waited. Only time would tell, and the pumpkin on the riverbank told us the season would soon be over.

Damascus had found herself an unlikely champion, anyway. She'd have followed that JB straight off a cliff, which is what really got my attention since following wasn't something I'd associated with Damascus in any form 'til that point.

At the moment, he only wanted her to follow him as far as the dock, where they'd take their mother lode of pumpkin pies to the mainland. He thought he could talk his boss at the marina café into letting him set up a table to sell the lot. I had to admire his ingenuity.

My checkerboard held a sprig of rosemary, tied with a ribbon around the box to dress up the gift. I leaned toward Damascus so she could hear me over the engine.

"You know, what you and JB could do," I suggested, "is branch out. Try other things too. So you'd have some variety and not just two hundred of the same pie."

"I don't know. JB only said about the pie."

"Yes," I said, encouragingly, "but you could surprise him with your own ideas."

She looked skeptical.

I tried to be more specific to give her a mind for the limitless ways she could prepare that giant pumpkin. "You could do bread. I know that recipe by heart." I saw her brows ease and rise slightly. "Or even soup. People love cold pumpkin puree in the summer. Put it in mason jars and sell it for picnics. You could probably find about five hundred ways to do up pumpkin."

"I hadn't thought of nothing like that."

"Well, maybe you haven't grown up eating as good as I did." She actually smiled at this. Encouraged, I said, "Did you know," I asked, fingering the bristles of the rosemary clipping, "there's an herb garden near the house?"

The scent rose up sharply pleasant, even in the windy conditions on the boat.

She shook her head. "I never seen it."

"It's mostly grown over. I never would have noticed it if I hadn't kept smelling it, but it's got a lot of good things still growing. You could put it to some use. Course, that's if you want. Pies are fine, if that's how you want to go."

"No," she said, decisively this time. "I think that's good. But I cain't say it's my idea if you're the one that told me it."

I laughed. "I don't mind."

She looked squint-eyed at me. "Is that what you're doing with Otis?"

Looking at the checkerboard, I admitted she was right. "It was your daddy's idea, that's true."

"That's a charmed patch you found. Aunt Ivy always grew one for her cleaning." She looked down at my hands. The fingertips were stained from pulling weeds and pinching back the overgrown herbs.

Damascus was on the right trail. I was going to play the part, be the woman he expected, the one who appeared from nowhere with just what he needed, like magic. If he believed it, there was more power in that than all my protests. I'd learned that much from Nonnie. I was the chicken bones in Otis' house.

This time when we walked into Sunrise Hills (and we had walked all the way from the ferry dock since Ivy'd taken my car), there wasn't a soul to greet us or run from us, either one. We were wilted and grouchy and without the usual offering of cake since Nonnie had decided to become aware of Damascus' thieving ways and cut her off. I looked around for the nurse I'd met before but saw no sign of her wide, dark presence, so we let ourselves in, heading down the hall for Otis Greene's room.

Better prepared this time, I sidestepped the letch at the turn in the hall, leaned to kiss Ms. Mary's babydoll, and swept into Otis' room just in time to catch the closing credits of *Fantasy Island.* I swiped up the remote from the bedside table and turned off the tube. The look of shock and offense that slapped itself on his face was enough to make me think twice. I didn't want to kill him from shock, but I'd seen Jackie do that same thing for years when Mama would come to drag him out of the house, and now I parroted her words to him.

"Daylight's burning, Otis Greene. Are you going to sit up in here and waste your days?"

For an instant, I believed he might start with the hollering all over again, so I darted forward to the edge of his bed and grabbed hold of his wiry forearm with enough force to let him know I didn't mean to put up with that mess this time.

"Hush up," I said. "Now I put up with that the last time because I'm new, and you didn't know what to expect, but I don't have time for that today. I'm not a haint or anything like it. I'm a woman without a whole lot of patience, and I've got business with you."

His dark eyes rolled in his head, wide and anxious, and I let loose of him, patting him for reassurance. "I'm not going to smother you with your pillow, Otis. Good grief. I expected better of you from all Urey Trezevant's told me. A man who's lived on and farmed these parts as long as you have ought to be made of sterner stuff.

"Here now. I brought you something." I held the box out for him to take. I could hear the raspy noise of his breathing, but he made no other sound and no sign of interest. So I sighed and went about setting the checkerboard on a side table where he could clearly see it. I pulled the sprig of rosemary free, ran it under my nose for a sniff and then held it out to him, casually, while I proceeded to open the curtains to shed some light on things. "I'm here to make a deal with you, Otis."

"Devil Ree-ah. We always do," he muttered.

Unperturbed, I went on without batting an eyelash. I'd heard Mama come at Jackie this way any number of times when she had to weasel something out of him. Then just as I let the words roll off my tongue, I thought of Elder's flight, her singular purpose. "What I've got for you is this. One game for every visit I make. One game for every question you answer. I'm only going to be here two more weeks, so it's not like a lifetime commitment. Not even for you." I jerked my head toward the checkerboard. "You're the best, so I'm told. Seems a shame, a mind like yours wasted on *Fantasy Island*."

He was a dark, polished stone.

"Ivy asked me to sit with you because she feels sorry for you. But I don't. I don't believe you'd want me to, either, Otis. I believe you'd give just about anything for somebody to come along and jerk a knot in your lazy, sympathy-cake fat tail. So, you're going to climb out of that bed, and you're going to like it."

He took the rosemary and held it stiffly in front of him. I caught sight of Damascus still lingering in the doorway, and when I said her name, she jumped. "Go see if you can find an extra couple of chairs to drag in here, would you? Once Otis here gets his starch back and jumps in that recliner, me and you are going to need some place to sit for this visit."

"Sure," she mumbled.

Now I focused all my attention on Otis. The room was bright, and the checkerboard was ready. He saw what I meant to happen. Slowly, he drew the rosemary under his nose and took a long sniff.

"That's from Delia's patch. It's the only charm I brought with me today so you tell me: Is it going to do the job?"

He lowered it to his lap, but made no move to speak or get out of bed. So I perched on the edge of the mattress near his feet. He didn't flinch, but he was looking at me with expectation. I'd come with Delia's calling card in hand, and he recognized the power in that. He was listening.

Without fanfare, I gave him what explanation I had for being there to bother him. Ivy's gone. I've come. And now you and me are going to get up from here.

With the high points covered—my short career and injury, my coming to the island, my ideas about my recovery and how I thought I could help him, we could help one another—I finished up.

"You're not afraid of me, are you, Otis? I bet you laughed real hard, running me off that last time. Now all there is to be seen is whether you're smart enough to know what's good for you."

I tapped my fingernails on the checkerboard and waited. For all my bluster, I wasn't sure I had much chance. But Otis Greene met my eyes with his wide, dark ones and gave the slightest nod. I could have been seeing things.

"Yeah?" I said. This time I was sure when he moved. "Well then, you've got to get over to that chair. Laid up like a kept woman might be all right for Ricardo, but I won't cream an old man at a square game of checkers while he's in his sick bed. That wouldn't be right."

Otis' bottom lip disappeared while he considered this with some reluctance. His gravelly old voice took me by surprise when he asked, "What you want from Otis, if he plays this game?"

"I don't want a thing." What would have been eyebrows shot up on his smooth, dark face. "Not for me. Damascus needs gardening advice. Like I said, one question for every game."

The look of a man who believes he's swindling his opponent came over his face. It was a bargain.

A quick glance at the clock told me I only had an hour before the next ferry left for the island. I reached for the faded brown blanket that covered his legs. If I'd been operating under the impression that he was a weak bird, he changed my mind quick when he sat straight up and snatched those covers back. I nearly took a head dive into his bed the grip was so steely.

He hollered, "Ain't got my pants on, girl!"

Seeing the life jump out of the bony body made me want to clap my hands. He'd been playing invalid, just like Ivy said, and doing a bang up job.

I put my hands on my hips and smiled at him. I felt energized in a way I hadn't expected. I'd never considered that there could be a reward on Mama's end of things with Jackie, only that she loved him and put up with his stubborn ways. Now I was seeing different. "The better to beat your ass, my dear," I said.

Damascus came round the doorframe trailing two straight back chairs from the kitchen table and the day nurse just in time to see Otis Greene throw modesty over.

It took all three of us to get Otis up on his skinny, naked legs and from the bed to the recliner, only a few steps away. The nurse, a girl named Trish, said, "I'm not sure he's up to this, really. It's been a good while since Mr. Otis took to a chair. Now, Mr. Otis, if you feel like your head's spinning, you tell somebody and we'll lay you right back down."

But I ignored her, and I leaned close to Otis Greene's large, drooping ear. Without forethought, I simply whispered the secrets of my gift of balance and grace. I told him all the way how to imagine in his mind a center inside himself, one that is strong and whole and sure like the sun.

"Come on, Otis," I urged him. "I need to get one thing right while I'm here. Just one thing. Now can you get in the damn chair so we don't both look a couple of losers?" I leaned in and whispered in his ear so that only Otis could hear. "Or are you just a skinny ass old burden like that nurse said?" He turned his face to look at me straight on, and I saw him strengthen his resolve.

He struggled against my grip, but then the words seemed to sink in. His eyes did not meet mine, but I felt his spine stiffen a little, and he drew himself up straighter. With great focus, he took the last step almost unassisted and settled into the chair heavily.

I didn't say a word. Let him think on that. The last thing I wanted from the man was gratitude. But secretly, I was wondering at what had just passed between us. It must have been the same for him as he watched me set up the checkers with his mouth in a tight line, as though I was suspect. The nurse drew the blanket over his lap for modesty, also glancing nervously at me, although we were all relieved to see he was wearing his shorts. I knew that look. She wasn't happy with a ballerina who would cuss an old man, and she was pretty sure that's what had just happened.

"I don't know what you must've said to him," she said, flushed in her face.

"Guess I'm just speaking a language he understands." I smiled at her, and she grew redder still before rushing out to tell the rest of the staff, no doubt.

I didn't care. In the first minutes, Otis was slow to make decisions, and I worried more than once that we'd run out of time, and Damascus wouldn't get to ask her question. Not once, however, did I fear he'd beat me. Now that was the miracle of it, because I'd never been great at checkers. I bluffed my way along, and I got lucky.

He sighed deeply and gave me a hateful look when I silently cleared the board and packed it away at the conclusion of the game. But when I suggested Damascus ask Otis' advice about the pumpkins, he listened with thoughtful eyes. She fumbled around to express her concerns. Since I hadn't informed her of my plan, she took a minute to get her feet under her.

Once they started talking, I could see my game had been no loss for Otis Greene.

He said, "Pumpkins. You give 'em plenty a' water?"

Damascus nodded, slightly offended. "Course I do." She shook her head. "I follow everything the book says, the one I got that tells how to grow them. I done every single thing. But maybe there's something you can tell me, since you know how it is here."

What she wanted was a live person to say she was doing things right. I imagined she wanted to hear, 'Girl, you're doing a fine job of it.'

Otis raised his eyes to Damascus and said, "Get you some high phosphate. That's what they needs now."

Damascus was thrilled. "I thought so! I read it, and I thought so." Watching her, I felt as though a bird were flying around inside my chest. "Hey, Otis?" she said.

A second question wasn't part of the bargain, and I held my breath, seeing his eyes narrow.

"What's your favorite way to eat pumpkin?"

But that was it. One question, and Otis chewed his lip a moment, cast a nervous glance at me, and promptly checked out for *Fantasy Island*, very deliberately turning away from her face. He was a player, all right. We left with that.

But it was enough, I kept thinking. For Damascus, it was all she needed, and one thing I was learning: Damascus knew how to stretch a little and make it last. She'd have given Jesus and his loaves and fishes a run for their money.

Trish was standing in the door as we left, and she touched

Damascus on the arm. "I like a good pumpkin bread, myself. With that cream cheese frosting."

"We can make that." She glanced at me.

"Sure. We'll find a recipe somewhere."

Trish piped up. "Oh, go on over there and use the computer. Just look up whatever you want."

Damascus scurried over and went to work. I don't know why, but it surprised me to see that she was so comfortable with the technology. She'd been such a wild thing in my mind up until now. But of course, she was really an average girl, and above average according to her aunt. The one who would know.

Over the weekend, JB was working at the marina and out with friends in the evening, to Damascus' great disappointment. So, we baked. The first loaves of pumpkin bread, a half dozen of them to be exact, came out pretty as a picture. We'd gotten most of the ingredients from a grocery in Brunswick that had more selection than Cain's, and less Nonnie. And Will Cain, who had come and gone without a word to me, had helped Damascus get the fertilizer she needed. No one had heard from Ivy as far as I knew. I asked Damascus, and she shrugged and acted funny, like it made her mad that I cared. So I dropped the subject.

On the other hand, Damascus was so proud of the pumpkin bread I thought she'd explode. There was enough pumpkin bread to feed a third world country, but I was most impressed with the change in the girl making it. Covered in flour, she was putting away ingredients when she said, "You ought to name that baby something good. Name her 'Sugar' or 'Cinnamon.' Name her 'Vanilla.'"

We ate our pumpkin bread dinner until we couldn't hold any more, then lined the remaining loaves up on the counter, wrapped them in wax paper and complimented one another on our skills.

On Monday, JB had the afternoon off from the marina. He'd started back to school this week, though, so we had to wait 'til the late afternoon when we picked him up at the ferry dock before we spent the rest of the evening boiling the remainder of the pumpkin, and then sending it through a hand-cranked processer. The pulp could then be put into gallon-size freezer bags and stored in the deep freeze on the back porch. What we'd used up to make the bread didn't even touch the sheer amount of pumpkin left over, and we marveled at the bright orange bounty.

"Did your Mama call?" I asked the gangly boy when Damascus was out with her vine. "Did anybody hear from her yet?"

"Daddy did. She's all right, I reckon."

"Oh?" I let out a hard breath of relief before I could help myself. The boy didn't even look at me. "So, she did call, then? I guess I hadn't heard."

I was confused as to why Damascus had held out on me. But she was upset with Ivy. Maybe she blamed me like the rest of them for her aunt's departure.

"Still ain't saying where she's at, exactly," JB explained. "Except it's supposed to be for our own good, what she's doing." His answer was clipped and unemotional, an answer he'd given many times in the last days, I was sure.

"No? Well, I'm glad she's okay. That's all that matters, right? I'm sure she knows what she's doing."

He shifted his shoulders around underneath the sweatshirt marked with the High Dunes logo. His seventeen-year-old body was broad and tall, equal to a man's, but he was still baby-faced. He was worried about his mother. He leaned back against the counter and knocked his cigarette pack against his palm, lifted an eyebrow in question, and I frowned.

He pulled a cigarette out with his lips. "I can go outside," he mumbled around it.

"Why? Do they kill you slower out there?" He gave me a lop-sided grin. "I know somebody I wish you could meet. He'd give you a drag on his oxygen tank."

JB took the cigarette out of his mouth and slid it behind his ear, wise enough to know I wasn't going to have him smoke it in my kitchen. "I figure cancer's going to get you some way or other. Might as well have a good time while you can. You know that, right? You can't never tell when your time's gonna come."

I supposed Damascus wasn't the only one who'd been affected by Fawn Trezevant's death. Clearly, JB looked at me as a fine example for his faulty reasoning. I was in no position to lecture on the sunny side of life. But the elephant in the room was the uncertainty of Ivy's plans, and that was eating at her son, possibly destroying some part of his innocence as surely as any disease.

I closed the last of the Ziplock bags full of pumpkin puree. "I don't know what we're supposed to do with all this now," I said weakly. "It's been fun, and I swear I've not seen Damascus this happy since I got here. That's because of you, JB. But we'll be sick to death of pumpkin in a week, and this is enough to last 'til kingdom come."

"Biggest pumpkin I ever saw." He was proud of his ingenuity, I could see. But there was a tension between us that had been growing all day.

"Well, it's nice of you to help Damascus. She trusts you. She's looking up to you, JB."

He shrugged, uncomfortable with the compliment. "Family does for one another." He helped me stack the last bags of pumpkin inside the deep freeze, but stopped in the back door instead of following me back inside the kitchen. He looked out toward the water and judged the light.

"You like it here?" he asked. "You figuring on still leaving? I guess you miss that dancing?"

"My lease is up next week." How could it be so soon? "But you know that. I don't know what I'll do then. Go back to Atlanta, probably."

It was getting close to sunset, and he seemed anxious to be on his way, but he stalled. "I thought maybe you'd take up over with the old folks. Last time I was there it was like night of the living dead, everybody half propped up, sleeping or moaning. Give me the creeps. But you really got it livened up. You ought to go into business yanking people out of beds."

I smiled at his constant vision for making a buck. "You're

sweet, but I think they've already got that market covered."

"They said you cussed ole Mr. Otis."

"I did not," I said sharply. But I couldn't help laughing a little when I saw the sly twist of JB's mouth. He was angling to get a rise out of me, and it had worked. I didn't know why he was still hanging around. He seemed to be working up the nerve to get down to it, and, in the next minute, he finally rubbed the back of his neck hard and let out a short, hard breath.

"Daddy said you might've put this idea in mama's head to take off from here. I want to know, did you?"

I knew sooner or later somebody would ask. I should have had a better answer prepared. "I gave her my car," I admitted. "JB, do you think I could have made your mama's plans for her?"

He rubbed the end of his nose. He filled the doorway, but he didn't have the awareness of his size to be truly intimidating, like his uncle. Still, when the boy sized me up with those Trezevant eyes, I felt my skin heat up. He'd grow into that intensity soon enough.

"No. I reckon she made her own plans," he said stiffly. "But maybe seeing you set up camp here, made her think of it. Like she could do the same as you. I reckon ya'll cooked up this idea to do a switch."

"JB."

"Well? What do you think? You like trying on my mama's life?"

I was stung by the bitterness in his tone, not that I could blame him. He'd only come to the same conclusion as Urey, the obvious one. I'd moved in here and then, without even realizing it, so much of Ivy's place on the island had fallen to me when she left. And I'd needed a place, bad enough to not think too much about the woman who'd abandoned the island to a stranger's care. But her son's eyes wouldn't let me avoid thinking about it now.

"She'll be back, JB. She didn't leave you. She's just got some things she needs to do for herself. There's more to her than this island. She wants you to have choices she didn't have."

He blinked hard at me, shoulders tense. I saw I'd said the wrong thing and felt worse. I wanted to say it wasn't my fault, what Ivy'd done. I wanted to tell him I had enough of my own problems to deal with, that I'd never asked to be put in the middle of his family's troubles.

Instead, in a quiet voice, I gave the young man who'd already surpassed his uncle and father in my book for having the spine to stand here and say all this to my face, my respect. "You go ahead. Say what you need to say to me, JB."

I didn't need to tell him twice. He didn't suffer from the Trezevant stoicism.

"Maybe you do fine for ole Mr. Otis," he said, avoiding my eyes, "even Damascus. I mean, by God, I like you. I sure do. You're out here smiting serpents, you got the lame walking and the dumb speaking. Since ya'll came up with this deal, seems like everybody's getting something out of it. You're keeping Uncle Urey run off, and that's probably doing a favor for everybody, anyways, 'til things get sorted out with Damascus. It's just . . ." He struggled to get the words out.

"What do you mean, sorted out with Damascus?"

He shuffled his feet and shoved his hands deep in his pockets, taking a few steps back 'til he was heading down the steps. "Look, all I'm saying is, I ain't got a thing against you, Roslyn. But just don't do too good a job saving her place, all right?"

I swallowed and shook my head. He gave a jerk of his chin that told me we had an understanding, then we both looked up at the sky. Outside where my authority ended, he lit up his cigarette. Between the limbs of the oaks, we could see the first stars peeking through, although it wasn't fully dark yet. We stood there like that long enough that the tension eased.

"So, get a life, huh? My own," I said, still studying the stars as more began to show through. There was logic in the patterns if you knew where to look, when it was dark enough to see them all. "I was thinking about that today, that I might try something," I said carefully. "I had an idea. I don't think there'd be any money in it. I'd probably have to go back to school."

He took a last long draw on the cigarette before he tossed it in the dirt and ground it with the heel of his boot. "What are you thinking?" He cocked his head, looking at me again. The wheels were turning and, although he looked ragged at the edges still, I appreciated maybe more than I should that he would still stand on the stoop and listen to me.

"I don't know, really. It's not clear yet. But this therapy, or whatever you want to call it that I've been playing at with Otis, it seems like it could work. Like I could develop something there." I wrapped my arms around myself, feeling vulnerable for having spoken out loud the inclination to build a life for myself, as if I deserved one. "I don't know what I'm talking about, I just wanted to tell you. I'm not trying to take over your mama's life, no more than she wants mine.

"All I've ever been good at was dance. I'm just making the rest up as I go and that's all it is at Sunrise Hills. Probably I'll give them all strokes. People will think I'm a washed up lunatic selling snake oil miracles."

I saw his teeth flash white in the gloomy evening light. He swatted at a mosquito. "Then you ain't got nothing to lose with that plan. Best I can tell, people already think that."

"I want to go back to Sunrise Hills tomorrow," Damascus said when we stepped back inside the kitchen. "I want to take some pumpkin bread to Trish." She'd come in and finished stirring the cream cheese frosting together and stood back to lick the mixing spoon clean. No telling how much of our conversation she'd overheard. Knowing Damascus, she could quote it forward and back.

I didn't say a word about the fact that she'd spent more time away from the vine on the riverbank than she had in days.

JB left for home with a couple of the loaves tucked under his arm, planning to sell them at the marina. "You shoulda grown a whole field of them things," he said. "Then just think what we coulda done."

Damascus grinned widely at him, but I was thankful there

were just the two pumpkins. JB had big plans.

But aside from a profit, we were making more than pumpkin bread, that was sure. We were making memories. Ones that Damascus would always carry with her and maybe pull out like I pulled out hymns or poems when she needed to remember being happy.

"You think you got room out there on the bank for me tonight?" I heard JB ask Damascus from where they sat on the front porch. I felt a flood of warmth toward both of them, their backs to me, shoulder to shoulder on the front steps.

From the dark estuary beyond my walls came the strange, high chirp of a night bird. It was then I realized how quiet the island had grown. It had been days since I'd caught a tune on the wind or heard voices humming a chorus with the water. The music no longer haunted me through the things around me, or through the child on the riverbank. Summer was fading into early autumn, the roaring alligators gone silent, their song of life now fully realized, growing in some dark, warm place, as forgotten as the pumpkin on the riverbank. In fact, last I'd heard the music, I was on top of the world with Urey.

I was not the only one growing worried in the silence, too aware of his absence. We watched the tree line and the river like we expected the worst.

Chapter Fourteen

Roslyn

"I'm nervouser and nervouser, the closer we get. Do you think it's any good?" Damascus asked. She was turning the loaf of pumpkin bread over in her hands as we walked up the drive to Sunrise Hills.

"You never worried about the crap you brought before."

"Ha-ha. Well, that wasn't nothing to do with me."

"Sure it was. And they ate it up because you cared enough to bring it with you."

"Well, I shouldn't have. That stuff was gross."

"Maybe not. But they'll love this bread. You grew it, and you chose to share it. When people bring food like that, it's always good. This is your bounty."

She considered this for the last few steps before we reached the door, then said, "I'm glad you kind of get it." She sighed, and let us in as though we were facing a firing squad.

I smiled at her, but it was sad that she believed I was the only one who would understand. I wanted to ask her more about Urey, like what he did with himself when he wasn't working, why he never spent any time with her, and what she'd said to convince him to allow her to stay with me. I guess I thought if I could find him, I'd maybe try to appease him or lure him. Well, luring wasn't really high on my list of late, but I could still attend to an ego. I'd had enough practice at that with Stephan. I knew how to flatter a man's pride. But any time he came up, Damascus shot out of there faster than I could catch her.

I told myself to leave well-enough alone and tend to my own business like I should've done in the first place.

We walked into Sunrise Hills smelling like sugar and spice and every head in the place lifted up. Damascus shouldn't have worried. Starting with Trish and right down to Ms. Mary, the whole place went crazy for that bread. They slapped the cream cheese on it and carried on like it was their last meal. Even Otis, who refused to get out of bed, claiming he only played checkers on Wednesdays, gobbled his up and grumbled thanks.

"I put that high phosphate on, like you said to," Damascus said, tossing his napkin in the trash for him.

"Today ain't a question day," he said. His eyes dared me to force him.

"Mr. Otis," I said, "I don't know why you keep acting like I'm going to put some kind of hex on you or poison your cranapple juice. Now I wish you'd stop it. Is somebody telling you crazy things?" When he only blinked, solemnly, silent as a stone, I folded my arms across my chest. "Fine, then. Boo."

Mr. Otis mumbled his pet name for me under his breath, but I was no closer to knowing the word, while never mistaking the menacing meaning.

"Mr. Otis, she cain't even get the canoe downriver on low tide," Damascus explained. I was surprised to hear her come to my defense, even if it was only because she'd seen how harmless I truly was. "She ain't gonna do nothing to you that you cain't handle, long as you don't let her start in playing her music."

"Oh, well, thanks," I said. I didn't say a word about the song she sang each night. Damascus seemed to think it was her secret. And she had a little spring in her step now.

She shuffled around until I said we'd better go, since it wasn't a Wednesday. But Damascus surprised me when she said, "I ain't ever asked nobody for nothing, Mr. Otis. I ain't about to start now. But that pumpkin bread—" She actually smiled at him. "It's good, ain't it? Not like that shit I've been bringing. You can go on and gobble up my bread, even if you're mean as a snake. Don't worry. I got plenty more where that came from."

She walked right out, high on generosity, Otis staring after her, his stingy hands clinching the emptiness she'd left behind.

"You're glad to see us, aren't you, Otis?" I teased. "If I'm a haint, at least I keep you from going stale in here. I bet you never thought you'd be here. Well, me either. I never dreamed in my wildest nightmares that my sole purpose in life would be to get your bony ass in a chair every day."

He made a sound like a fart with his lips. But I saw his lips twitch with good humor. It was a little victory that went a long way.

Back at the house, I pulled up thyme and oregano, and we baked a casserole with the kitties winding around our feet. All afternoon, we made muffins and soup and tweaked the other recipes Damascus had gotten from the computer at Sunrise Hills. When the sun sank low, I made a pot of coffee, and we sat at the table together again, this time nibbling on ham sandwiches and croissants. I'd given up trying to make Damascus like the Sacred Harp music and turned it off so there was nothing but the sound of us in the kitchen. I told Damascus about the dinner on the grounds after every singing.

"Tables so laden with everything to eat that you thought you'd died and gone to heaven," I said. "Dishes served up with sweating glasses of sweet tea in the company of saints, ordinary people you'd known all your life, or strangers, all brought together to fill up on goodness."

"We're never going to use up all that pumpkin," Damascus said wearily, but smiling. "Too bad we don't got no saints around here."

I laughed. "JB's going to need a wheelbarrow to carry this stuff off." Truly, we had a mountain of food.

We had a mountain of pumpkin shell, too, still piled high in the wheelbarrow JB had forgotten to haul off, and the smell of it wafting into the kitchen. With the kitchen clean and my back aching after a day on my feet, I stepped out the back door and frowned at it. "Look at all this," I sighed.

We couldn't simply dump it. There was too much. It was way too heavy to haul far enough unless I wanted to unload half and make two trips, which would have been a rotten mess. And the stench was getting overpowering already. We'd have to haul it all the way out to the compost pile at the back of the property.

Then another thought occurred to me.

"Hey, Damascus?" I called. She leaned out the door, hanging on the frame. "Does that book of yours say anything about alligators eating scraps?"

We heaved the wheelbarrow onto its wheels and pushed it down to the slough. Skulking in the shallow water, Spook lurked just beneath the surface. Keeping our distance, we tossed the chunks a few at a time into the wetland and watched to see what would happen. The alligator jerked its head toward the startling sound and hissed, then lunged to gulp down one of the peelings faster than seemed possible.

"Good Lord," I muttered. The thing had grown quite a lot more than you'd expect in a short time. It worried me a little.

"Yeah, you ain't supposed to feed them."

"Well, why didn't you say so before!" I squawked. But we'd already emptied our load, and it was hard to be mad when Damascus' face glowed. We hurried up and dragged the wheelbarrow back to the house sort of giddy from the taste of danger.

We collapsed on the porch and I laughed. "What a day."

October loomed before us, only days away, but I didn't mention it and neither did Damascus. Besides, it hardly seemed I was going anywhere. The Trezevants had all neatly disappeared. "Do you think," I asked, hesitantly, "you ought to be starting on some school work? Maybe you could bring some of your workbooks here? You don't want to get behind. People might say your daddy's neglecting your education."

"Who said that? That neglect thing?" she snapped.

"Nobody. I was just thinking . . . JB's back in school now. You should be working on your education, too. Besides, you sit out there with that pumpkin all day. What else do you have to do?" Damascus scowled but said nothing. "Or did you ever think about maybe starting school in Brunswick? Ivy says she thinks you're really smart, Damascus. You could think about it. I could take you over one day to look around, maybe?"

"I don't need to see nothing. I ain't going to school nowhere except here." She looked at me hard, but I didn't flinch.

"I'll bring my workbooks if you want."

I put up a hand in a sign of surrender. "Fine. I'm just saying, looks like you'd want to see what you're missing, that's all."

Damascus sat on the top step and cocked her head in the funny, birdlike manner to which I'd grown accustomed. "Do you think they'd come to dinner, if we asked them?"

"Who?"

"JB and Uncle Will. Daddy."

"Oh." The conversation had veered off in a direction I hadn't anticipated. I hadn't thought of this at all. I'd been content with our little cocoon. The thought of a house full of men made me slightly uneasy. But a direct invitation from his daughter might change the score with Urey and my ears perked at the possibility of damage control without too much cost to my pride. "I don't know."

"I just was thinking, we can sell some of this stuff, but while you were saying all that about dinner on the grounds, about how people come together and eat and then they feel just like family. It's kinda true. Kinda like how it felt to take stuff to Sunrise Hills. Like they sort of give a crap about me there. But Daddy . . . and them, they're my family and I don't never feel like it." She hesitated, but I didn't want to interrupt so I waited to see if she could work out what she was trying so hard to say. "I done all this, grew them pumpkins for some reason or another I ain't figured out yet. Maybe that's what she meant, do you think? I just wondered, that's all."

"Well," I said, knowing there was no way I could turn her down now. "I don't see what it could hurt to ask." Oh God, was that a lie. "They might come. JB would."

I didn't want to blow it. She'd shown so little interest in her family before this and I'd watched Ivy standing at my kitchen window, aching over this little girl. This little ghost girl. Now that she was finding her own way of reaching for the people who loved her, how could I be a stumbling block? Had I not spent weeks doing this same thing, looking to the women in my life for a wisdom that passed my understanding, praying they had something to offer me?

"Yeah, I know JB would be here. He'd go straight to hell if they was serving up snake on a stick, long as he could fill his tank," she said. "But we cain't do it during the week or Saturday neither, 'cause he's working. And he's going off with some boy on Sunday, fishing. What about this food? Can it wait a entire week to be eaten?"

"I don't see why not. Some of it, at least. We can freeze the bread and this other stuff and it'll keep just fine. The rest we'll just make new. My calendar's open."

"You're not going? It's October next week."

"I know it. No, I think I'll wait. At least until you bring the pumpkin in. I think it will be fine, don't you?" She nodded, looking down so I couldn't see her eyes. I didn't want to put the idea in her head that I would stay any longer than that, but I couldn't simply disappear. I'd quibble with whoever wanted to argue about the lease later. "All right. Well, we'll need to get our menu planned and clean up around here, anyway."

"Yeah, okay." Damascus brow furrowed, then brightened with a thought. "Uncle Will likes meat," she declared. "All kinds. When I was staying with them, they ate meat every night." She was very serious about this, and I nodded. "Might be he's pretty pissed at you 'cause of Aunt Ivy. But he shouldn't be, and somebody ought to tell him so."

"Kind of like what you did with Otis?" I cocked an eyebrow, amused.

"Otis? He's just afraid. You get it, don't you? When you don't think you've got nothing to give people, you'd just as soon they leave you alone." She shifted in her chair, bringing one foot up to the seat so she was holding onto her knee. "I didn't know that 'til today."

Honestly, I was taken aback by the child's bright and simple insight, but I was careful not to embarrass her by being impressed. "You mean you don't know everything?" I teased.

She made a rude gesture, then got serious. "I figured it out because of the pumpkin. That one we cut up. I seen what was in there and it ain't nothing but pumpkin. So then I thought, how come I'm growing these big old things if all they are is big old stupid pumpkins? Nobody needs that. What in hell'd my mama give me them seeds for in the first place?"

She didn't look exactly upset, and I hoped this was a good sign for the time to come when the other pumpkin was full grown. I hoped her expectations weren't so lofty. "I don't know. Do you?"

"I think," she said, "it's just what she had. Them seeds, that was just all she could do for me. She didn't have no time. She didn't have no pretty things to give me or nothing, and I was so little none of that would've mattered anyways. I'd have just broke it probably or losed it. She couldn't teach me no cooking like your granny done, or singing or nothing like that. But a little kid likes seeds. They like to put 'em in a cup and watch 'em grow on a window. That's about magic, right there. And she probably figured I'd do that, and then I'd see something come right out of nothing. I'd have something then, something her and me kind of made together."

She looked to me to see if I understood her. "I think that's pretty smart."

"Yeah. So that's why I'm doing it. So we can make a life together, a big, gigantic, bright-as-can-be, good-for-nothing-but-the-hell-of-it life. Even if it's just a pumpkin one, that's got to be better than nothing, right? I thought maybe Daddy could see that. How something good could still come from here."

Her last word wasn't clear, and I wasn't sure if she said 'here.' Or 'her.' We sat in silence for a little while and just let all that sink in.

"I'll tell JB and them to come," Damascus finally said, stretching to stand up from the step. "But you tell Daddy. He might be back."

It was the swing of a pendulum from maturity beyond her years to a little girl's deal to get what she most wanted. She had no idea what I'd done or that I was likely the last person her daddy would listen to since that misguided serenade at the shell ring. She wouldn't meet my eye, her need was so ripe. For some, her pumpkins would be enough. But for all her astuteness, she wasn't sure if enough would satisfy her daddy.

"Back? He's gone somewhere?"

She shrugged. "I seen Lloyd Hayes working his shift over at the boathouse yesterday, and I ain't seen him. Have you?" I said no, I hadn't, and asked if he'd disappeared like this before, feeling the heat crawl up my back. "I guess. Used to be he'd be gone soon as he got off. I'd wait around 'til it started to get dark, and if he didn't come dragging in, I'd know he'd lit out, and I'd go over and stay with her, you know." She made no attempt to say Ivy's name.

"Where does he go?"

"He don't tell me." Her eyes sparked. "He don't tell nobody. What's the point? Daddy don't answer to nobody anyhow, so he keeps his business to his self. Once, it was a woman. I know 'cause he smelled like her when he come back in. But it ain't been like that except the one time. All the others, he'd just take that owl and not show his face 'til Monday of a morning when he'd show up to work looking like a woolly booger. But he ain't done it in a while." Now she raised her eyes to meet mine. "I reckon he's gone to bring her back here. He'll put his nose to the ground like a ole bloodhound, and she won't have no chance."

"I think your aunt can handle him."

I couldn't understand why the thought of having Ivy back upset her. But at the moment, I was preoccupied for reasons of my own.

After our conversation at the shell ring, it hadn't occurred to me once that Urey might go looking for Ivy. I'd been too preoccupied with whether he'd show up here. My inflated sense of self may have ruined everything. Now I realized I'd taken for granted that he'd stay put on this island. I'd been so focused on Damascus, I'd certainly never considered that rather than stepping up, he'd go dragging Ivy back on his child's behalf. I remembered the day that alligator had cruised past me in the river, not even slowing down for a look at me. I should have been paying attention to that feeling.

My stomach curdled.

"Like I said, it can't hurt to ask." I sounded more confident than I felt.

I knew better. I'd asked for this table and now I had it. But what else could I say? I wasn't sure even Delia's herbs could sweeten a Trezevant family reunion to anybody's taste.

While Damascus made her plans all afternoon, chattering—and I mean chattering—to the nurses at Sunrise Hills, Otis Greene was miraculously out of bed in the recliner, and expecting me to do something to entertain him. He seemed agitated I was there, and swatted at my attempts to touch him.

"He gets that way," Sheree had confirmed gravely. "Neck just tightens up on him, gets a crick real bad."

I narrowed my eyes at Otis. "If you'll let me, I can show you what to do so that when this happens, you can take care of it."

His grizzled old brows drew down, almost meeting between his eyes, and he chewed his lip a moment before grunting. I took that as a yes and went to work on him. I'd done this for Jackie a million times, careful to seek out the tender spots, easing his head forward, then to the side opposite the pain, rotating his arms, lifting his shoulders. Otis was surprisingly cooperative, and by the time we left, the grimace had lessened, if not become a smile. At least he looked more comfortable.

The next time we showed up, Otis was in the chair, waiting for his game of checkers. I won again, barely, and afterward he graciously answered Damascus' pumpkin question. This time she only wanted to know what was his favorite way to eat it.

Before we left, I asked him, "How's the neck? Are you doing what I told you?"

"Got a pain in my hip, like to kill me," he said.

Without giving him the opportunity to resist, I'd taken him through a few of the exercises from my therapy, seated and making modifications where necessary. To my amazement, I felt confident, and, with guidance, Otis seemed to reap the rewards, even though he was still so distrustful.

But during the time I'd been visiting Sunrise Hills, the seed of my idea had begun to send out shoots. It took new and more involved shape every morning when I pushed my body further through the healing movements that were now as familiar as any choreography I'd ever danced. I recognized it as the same pure expression of the girl I was that day I danced in Glenmary. The Seminoles would have called it a healing dance. They'd have been right, too. I was healing myself, the same way I'd tried all my life to heal my family. And now I was finding the gift I'd been working so hard to deny was changing lives in ways I'd never imagined. And, stranger still, might just be the thing to save me.

Now if I could only convince the Trezevants that they needed to break bread together, I might have earned a little of my soul back. I owed Damascus that much. And as much as I hated to admit it, the only way to pay this debt was with a pride-swallowing apology.

Damascus headed to the house and her pumpkin, watching me with big, dark eyes, like I might not come back from High Dunes. She'd loaded me up with samples of her wares for Urey to taste. Lord, it was getting hard to make up a contrite attitude when I looked at that girl. By the time I'd walked across the manicured lawns and down the pretty boardwalk along the river to find Urey, all I wanted was to shove pumpkin bread down his gullet 'til he choked.

People in nice golf T-shirts at the resort told me he'd been in for work, but no one knew where he kept himself after hours. They looked at me sideways, probably trying to put together what they'd read about me with all their suspicions about the woman on the other side of the overgrowth that separated their world from the wilder side of Manny's Island. I smiled and showed my teeth. I gave into my limp just a little more than necessary so I lurched along, long skirt swinging with my braid, and tried to deny the urge to offer them a poison pumpkin muffin.

At least Damascus had been wrong about Urey being gone from his job. Fatherhood was a different story. I breathed a sigh of relief, hoping that meant he hadn't been tormenting Ivy.

In any case, when I pushed the door open on the boathouse at dusk, he wasn't there. It was like a cave so I pulled a few blinds and let some light in so I could find my way to the desk. It was neatly arranged with a blotter covered in appointments for fishing charters, a mason jar where pencils stood ready, a lamp, a clock radio and a phone.

I was uneasy. Now that I stood there, bribes in hand, I had second thoughts about being alone with him. I felt silly with my basket of meddling.

Grabbing a pencil and pulling a few drawers open, meaning to scratch off a note and leave the food, I quickly forgot my manners and gave into the urge to prowl around. I wanted to learn something more of Urey Trezevant, even the most trivial detail. You didn't have to poke around in his place of work to know he was a man with a preoccupation for this island, the sea, the land, the creatures that called it home. That's not what I was after. I was looking for the thing Urey kept up on his shelf.

But there was nothing beyond the fishing nets, tackle, boating gadgets, maps, the leather gauntlets he used with Elder. Nothing personal. There were shells collected in a bowl, and I saw he'd been using them to knot one of his nets. Of course, he made his own. I touched the coarse fibers and the smooth, cool shells and the memory of him standing in the river came to me clearly. But there was something I wasn't seeing, something I was missing every time I let myself remember that day. It disturbed me and kept me going back in my mind, even as I'd thrown my own net over and again, as though I could solve some mystery about the man by standing in that water.

But today, the net was only a net. The smell of seawater rose faintly from the equipment, and there was nothing romantic or revealing about that.

I ran my fingertips across the print on the calendar, knowing his hand had recorded the words. The quick flash of the memory of his fingers came to me, warmer than I'd expected, closing around my ankle. A man whose hands go straight for the weak spots on a woman is a dangerous thing, but

I was so tired of putting on a brave front, and it would be so easy to let Urey Trezevant work on all the places where I was torn up. I was drawn to his misery because it meant I could wallow in my own. I liked the way he wore his injustices like nobility on this scrap of sand, and, if I let myself, it wasn't hard to imagine climbing up on that shell ring and crowning myself princess, right beside him.

I could use that. I could call him. Stretch myself out on the water and wait 'til he was tangled in my arms, his fingers wrapped in the knots of my hair. We would sink so deep no tide could turn us. In water that dark, we'd forget all our ancient songs.

The thought tempted me.

Feverishly, I searched for paper to leave a note, trying to remember the rhythm of a perfect cast, pushing aside receipts and glossy pamphlets for High Dunes fishing, boating, and shelling tours. But just then, the yellowed edge of an old photograph caught my eye. I sat down in the hard, leather chair behind the desk. With trembling fingers, I pulled the picture from beneath the shuffle of disorganized business papers where it floated, out of place, meant to startle. Meant to stop everything, stop time.

The picture was of a young woman in a thin summer nightgown. Her pale hair fell across her bare, freckled shoulders and hid her face. She looked down on the sleeping toddler in her arms. The long, dark lashes of the baby girl fell innocently on soft, round cheeks, and her pink lips turned up in a secret smile.

For a long time, I stared at the picture. I'd never really been curious about Fawn Trezevant, and it was strange to see this image of her, for that's plainly who it was that I looking at, and still, she was hardly there at all. It was the baby I couldn't look away from. She was just as I'd imagined her, my own daughter, not the little lost beggar child roaming this island, but the baby I never sang to or told my stories to, or bathed or tickled or pushed high on a swing. I'd never waded in the cold water of the Cumberland with her or planted a seed or watched the moon come up or the sun go down or taught her the magic of a pirouette or a single thing. And I never would.

But she had taught me everything about myself.

I'd been sitting there too long. The light had shifted. I picked up the photograph and flipped it over absently. On the back, in neat, swirling penmanship, someone had written, 'Little Damascus Dreaming.'

And I knew, she was dreaming, still. Silently longing for her father's presence at her bountiful table.

So I left the photograph on the desk, along with the gifts she'd sent and a simple note.

> *If you want to know what she's dreaming, she's trying to tell you. With the seeds her mama left, she's made a place for you at her table.*
>
> *Saturday. 7pm.*
>
> *Sorry about the song. It was never mine to sing. I know that now. I'm staying in the house until she brings the pumpkin in. If you have a problem with it, come run me out.*
>
> *— R*

Chapter Fifteen

Roslyn

Without a word, JB took up watch over Damascus on the riverbank again that evening. I just looked out and found him there beside her, as was becoming his habit. I felt rung out after my time at the boathouse and slept all night for the first time in months, in a dreamless state. When I woke I felt as if I might have missed days or even years. But I knew the date. October first. It felt late.

In reality, it was early, not even eight o'clock when the biggest box arrived. When I called to say I'd gotten it, Mama answered on the first ring. She was anxious to hear what I thought of the latest sculpture she'd sent, but full of news of her own.

Jackie's big dream of life on wheels had been thrown a curve after the transmission in the RV went to hell in Tampa. After only two festivals, he and Mama were packing it in for Georgia.

"It was big times while it lasted," Mama said over the phone. She didn't sound too torn up about it. "I guess we'll be heading past you on our way home a little bit sooner than we thought."

"When?" My chest tightened. I knew it was time to leave the island, but I didn't want to do it with Mama and Jackie, and I'd made a promise to Damascus that I meant to keep.

"This Saturday. We can swing by and drive back together."

If I hadn't known better, I'd have asked where she learned to sabotage an RV. She wanted me to come back to Dalton and that house with her. She was afraid to be alone with Jackie, and the time I'd spent there had birthed a dream for her: just the two of us again.

"No. I'm not ready yet. It's not me," I added quickly. "It's the family. I mean, there's Damascus. The pumpkin hasn't been harvested. She's got another week at least with that thing, and I can't just go. Not until that's finished. She'd be so upset."

"Oh." I heard a thousand disappointments in Mama's voice. She could do that with one word. "Hasn't school started back down there?"

I rubbed my forehead where a little tension headache was kicking in. "Yeah. Ivy, the aunt, she home schools Damascus. But Ivy's out of town on a personal matter. Anyway, I've got some workbooks for Damascus here. It's fine."

Mama's tone turned stiff. "Well, these people can't expect you to put your life on hold while they work out their business, Roslyn."

Lord, how many times had I heard those words. "Nobody's taking advantage of me, Mama. I'm just finishing up what I started here," I said, but I didn't tell her about Sunrise Hills or my plans there. "Look, I really appreciate you offering to come by for me, but I'm good now. Really. I'll manage just fine on my own. I'll call you when I know I'm leaving. It'll just be a week or two at the most."

She wasn't thrilled about it, but she didn't push me. I was thankful for that, at least.

I knew it hurt her feelings that I was being so stand-offish, but I needed to get back on my feet on my own steam. So I let her help me with Damascus. She knew about little girls.

"It looks like I'm making this dinner," I said. "And I need your help." I told her about Damascus' plan.

"Well, it's just a chuck roast," she said. I could hear the confusion, and then the weariness in her voice as she realized I truly wasn't going to come home with her, that I was choosing to stay with a bunch of strangers. "Brown it in your pot first, then fill it with water to cover it. There's nothing to it, really. You just simmer the hound out of it for about three hours, throw in an onion, potatoes and some carrots for the fourth hour. Five hours if it's a big roast. Salt and pepper it real good."

"That's it?"

"That's how I do it." She paused before saying, "Sounds like you've got close with that girl." It was a question, really. Did I know what I was doing? Was I being smart? Was I using that child to avoid my own?

"She's took over, is what. But she's a good girl. She misses her mama, is all. And now Ivy's left," I added. "She's gone somewhere to work as a pharmacy tech, I guess. Verna knows. She helped set her up some little apartment, I think."

"My Lord. Well, I'm not surprised."

"She's left everybody here in kind of a lurch. I'm just trying to stay out of the way and keep up with Damascus."

"Mm. What's her daddy think about all that?"

Trust Mama to get right to the point. Don't get mixed up with another man who's got nothing to give.

"He's not around enough for anybody to know, really." I tried to keep the annoyance out of my voice. "Did I tell you, I've got an alligator in my ditch?"

Mama laughed, but I knew she was shaking her head. "It's not your ditch, and you're not bringing that thing home," she said. "But that don't worry me so much as the other."

I felt the burden of her disapproval, but didn't back down. Not this time. It was harder than I thought. Part of me wanted to give in, pack my bags and be waiting in the parking lot Saturday for that big Lincoln to roll in and take me away.

"Did you get my box? What do you think?" she asked.

"It just came this morning. I'll open it when we hang up."

I took a deep breath, laying my hands flat on the top of the box. It was going to take scissors. Whatever was inside this time was heavy.

"All right, then. I guess we'll be home when you get there," Mama said.

It was as close as she could bring herself to telling me to take the time I needed.

"Give Jackie a hug," I said, then added, "Really, that's all there is to the roast?" I'd eaten that roast my whole life, like it was a gourmet specialty the way it melted in my mouth. "Water and a pot?"

"And time."

I should have guessed. Most things, it turned out, were that simple. Like love. Or naming a regret. Like letting go.

I was thinking a lot about time, in fact, in those two days before the Feast of Damascus. That's what JB had started calling Damascus' plans for a family dinner. I didn't open Mama's box right away like I said I would, but left it for later knowing, whatever was in there, Mama's gifts always required a reaction, and it seemed best to face it at the end of the day. Instead, I spent the morning back at Sunrise Hills, rocking Ms. Mary's Lovey baby. She'd come to join us for Otis' exercises and surprised us all when she demonstrated a perfect, petite little waltz around the room. Evidently, she'd been quite the cotillion queen in her day. These memories were clear and concise. But then she'd lapse into talking of her children as though she'd just seen them, some of them dead before her. In her mind, time had become obsolete.

Listening to the nurses, most of them lifelong residents of the coast, recollect life on the island during their youth, I began to recall a cadence, a rhythm not unlike my own heartbeat. They talked of weaving sweetgrass baskets with their mothers and grandmothers. They recalled their wedding days and the days they buried husbands and parents and children.

Underneath it all was the magic of our bodies in motion, a celebration. And once Sheree started an old gospel hymn, they all joined in a low, mumbling sort of way that grew up into an actual harmony with a rhythm we picked up quick and sure. A ring shout, they called it. I told them about the Sacred Harp, and Damascus moaned and rolled her eyes.

"Not this, again. If I was God, I'd smote anybody that made that kind of racket. Shut up, I'd say. Go praise somebody else."

Only Otis agreed with her. The cock in the henhouse sat up in his chair by the window like a shriveled old king, showing off a little with his new strength, waiting for his game of checkers. He was lucid for longer periods now. But today something was different.

"Otis, you know you're going to have to keep this up on your own. Find somebody else to insult and do all the work for you."

"I let you win," he said. His gravelly old voice had become dear to me.

"Otis! You're looking me in the eye," I said, realizing what was different. "Aren't you still afraid I might put a hex on you?"

He didn't smile, but he looked at me in earnest. "Willie was wrong, saying them things. He's just smartin' over his gal running off."

My mouth fell open. "Willie? Will Cain? He's the one who had you all worked up about me?"

Otis chewed his tongue rather than confirming anything, but it made sense. I should have thought of it before. If I'd been Will Cain, I might have done the same for a little satisfaction. Well, that would certainly make dinner interesting.

"Them pumpkins woulda grown all by themselves," Otis said. "Old man wouldn't be in this chair. That girl wouldn't be looking bright and speaking up."

Gratitude was unexpected, and undeserved, I felt. I didn't know how to accept it when it was me who had changed these last weeks. I couldn't tell Otis Greene what it had done for me, watching his struggles and his small achievements, or how his advice to Damascus had given her confidence not only to nurture her crop, but herself. I felt I had very little to do with any of it. I'd been an observer and reluctant participant. And somehow, dignity was a gift we'd given one another.

"Oh, Otis. So, you're going to miss me, then?" I didn't touch him. He wasn't the kind to show affection that way. "I'm not a Ree-ah We anymore? Tell me what that means. Come on."

He lifted his chin and looked down his nose at me. In his best Ricardo Montalban, he slipped away into Fantasy Island again and said, "Ha-ha! Smiles, everyone! Smiles!"

While he and Damascus finished an episode of *Fantasy Island*, I asked Trish if I could use the computer. I wanted to do a search and see what turned up based on the things I'd been doing in my therapy and the modifications I was making for Otis. Immediately, the screen filled with information and sites about movement therapies. I was engrossed for the next half-hour. I couldn't believe I'd never even heard of some of this stuff. But then, I'd never looked far beyond myself for many reasons before. The one that caught my eye was called Benevolent Ballet. I was scribbling on the back of a paper plate, the only thing handy, when someone passed behind me and made a sound of interest.

"You've created a couple of monsters," Sheree said to me as she leaned in over my shoulder to see what I was looking at. "He won't be happy until he's beat every one of us at that checkerboard. Drags one or the other of us in here every day, and if we don't let him win, he's the biggest old baby, Lord."

Then she stopped talking long enough to read what was on the screen. "Benevolent Ballet. Hm. Would you look at that. Never heard of such a thing."

"Me either," I said. "I never would have put the two words together myself." I chuckled. But I scrolled down the page and took the contact information down.

"This ain't what you've been doing with Mr. Otis?"

"No. That's called Ambivalent Visiting," I said. "And it doesn't get you sued for liable. If I want to do this, I have to get some training and insurance. Maybe it's some kind of certification, I don't know. Maybe."

"Sounds like a plan," Sheree said, moving her massive self past me into the kitchen. She'd picked back up with the humming, the old hymn so familiar it made my eyes tear up.

I could feel my heart flutter at the thought. There it was in front of me. A future.

Trish caught my arm before we left. "Don't pay any attention to what all Will Cain's been saying. We know you've done Otis a world of good. We ran Will out this morning. Otis gets confused, but we told him Will's just blowing smoke over

Ivy taking off and you being the one to give her the car and all."

I shut my mouth and listened to her, trying to put the pieces together. Will Cain had been telling tales on me, not Nonnie. For a split second, I was furious and indignant. And then I realized he had every right to be angry with me.

Trish slipped a piece of stationary into my hand with an address and time on it. "I don't know if this will interest you," she said, "But I heard what you said before about the singings. Is this the same thing?"

I read the information. It said there was an all-day singing this Saturday at Bethany Baptist, just north of Brunswick. Dinner on the grounds to follow.

I felt my heart lurch. "You've got to be kidding me. They have this here?"

There was a phone number listed.

Trish explained, "I called my neighbor after I heard what you were saying, and she said it was Sacred Harp. She's done it for years and tried to drag me off to one of these things, but I've never gone."

I tucked the paper into my back pocket. I felt a tremor running through me. It was the certain knowledge of the fullness of time.

"I'll tell her to look for you, if you want," Trish said.

"No," I said. "I don't think I can make it." I told her all the same things I'd just said on the phone about not leaving Damascus right now, but I was thinking about it.

"It's just for the afternoon, honey."

"Well, I know. But thank you anyway."

I knew already I wanted to do it. I wouldn't follow that Lincoln back to Dalton, but I might just get myself a cab and go someplace in Brunswick to hear those voices again. Could they really be there as I remembered?

I carried that note home, and it felt like it might explode in my pocket any minute, announcing to the world that Roslyn Byrne was about to just kill her poor mama.

Damascus went straight for her pumpkin, oblivious to the way I was preoccupied. I sent her to the riverbank with a couple of the math workbooks and a pencil. I knew she'd fly through that work without even having to think about the problems. Ivy was right. Damascus needed to be challenged. She was too smart to just be sitting up in the house. I smiled to think I'd just used Mama's old way of talking about the Kellers wasting time and lazing about Granny Byrne's, letting somebody else do all the work. It wasn't quite right, the comparison of Damascus and those sorry relatives, but it was still a shame on both counts.

Clutching Mama's box, I crept across the yard, wanting some privacy, careful of Spook, keeping an eye out. The package was heavy as lead. Cannonballs. Steel girders.

"Why couldn't you just send seeds like normal, weirdo mothers?" I grumbled. Maybe she'd sent me a lead balloon to hold me down. It felt that way.

I sat down hard with my back to a loblolly pine and pulled the flaps back, having cut through all the tape first with a pair of dull scissors, and then my paring knife. Inside the layers of bubble wrap I found a familiar lump wrapped in newspaper, the way she'd sent all her pottery pieces. I tore back the paper, exposing the clay, painted a very glossy, chili-pepper color.

I knew the glaze was one of her favorites. She loved to brush it on, a dull brown, then fire it in the kiln and pull it out a day later, flaming red. I laughed, turning the hefty, hollow pot over in my hands.

"I guess I know what this is."

There was no mistaking the engorged breasts, the wholly rounded hips, the swollen, nearly obscene genitalia. In all the years she'd been sculpting, Mama had given me any number of bizarre and irreverent pieces, but when it came to her muse, the thing she created over and over again, never satisfied she'd captured the essence of the dream in her mind, Mama only ever said one thing when I asked for these pieces. "They're not ready for you, Roslyn."

But today, Mama surprised me. Now I held her in my hands, the goddess in all her unrelenting glory, and I could hardly see her for the tears that welled up in my eyes. On the note card in the bottom of the box, Mama had written this:

Maybe it's time you were ready.

And at the bottom of the box, I found the annual with the anthropologist's report on the Sacred Harp Singers from Glenmary, TN.

In all my life, I'd never seen it. How strange, I now thought, that I'd not looked it up or cared enough to see the words in print that had shaped my decisions and brought me to this place.

My heart pounded like it would beat its way through my breastbone while I searched through the pages for the report. The book's spine creaked, having sat on a shelf for probably all the years since it was published, having hardly been opened at all. For all I knew, I was the only person to ever read that report.

Saliva filled my mouth, and I felt chilled. When I found the page, I scanned down the very formal report with its clinical terms and dry rendering of the professional observation of the defining moment of my life. Only when I reached the last paragraph and turned the page, slightly stunned to find the report had concluded, did I realize I hadn't understood a word of it. I found no meaning in the phrases or jargon. I saw no evidence of the place and people I had loved so dearly. But Mama had highlighted one sentence about a 'young woman, who gyrated freely in an unnerving display of perceived spiritual ecstasy.'

I closed the book, leaned back against the ancient oak and stared at Mama's muse in all her flaming, imperfect glory.

Some native, maybe the same people who had built the shell ring, could have planted the strong tree at my back hundreds of years ago, never knowing a silly woman would sit underneath it one day and finally understand no one else could give her song meaning.

Chapter Sixteen

Damascus

All the good things she'd made, all that work, ruined! A raccoon had raided the porch pantry overnight. Who knew how the thing had gotten in, except somehow it must have wormed its skinny arm behind the turn lock and popped the door open. Now cellophane wrappers and tin foil were strewn over the back yard, and there wasn't anything to do except clean up what was left.

Damascus had already filled one trash bag, and now she sat on the back step, fuming. "This is a stupid idea. Nobody's even going to come, anyway," she yelled. "What you said before, about how I cain't watch all the time, then what about God? What good is He if He cain't even keep an eye on a damn raccoon?"

"What about Him? I don't know, Damascus," Roslyn said, frustrated. She might have even been mad. She had her own trash bag stuffed full. "What do you want from me? I am not the person people go to for spiritual advice." But she looked at Damascus hard, and Damascus just sat there expecting something more. "Do you mean does He watch?"

Damascus nodded.

"Of course He does."

"So He doesn't give a shit. He just lets bad things happen."

What Damascus was asking to know was a simple thing, but it seemed like the most complicated thing in the world to explain in words.

Roslyn sat down cross-legged beside her on the ground, in the middle of the mess the raccoon had made. "The way I see it," she said, "God is not like a person or even a thing, really.

People go around making God into whatever they want or need. But when you get down to it, I believe what my Granny Byrne said. God is love and love is about changing, becoming something more."

"So God's always changing?"

"That's what's confusing. I think God is both. Changing and the same, all the time, forever. We just can't understand it because everything in this world has a beginning and an end. Everything that lives, dies. We can't do anything but grab onto things while we can and try and squeeze something good out. We're not like God that way. But other ways we are."

"I'm like God?"

"Well, like you're becoming something better because you grew those pumpkins. They're a live thing, so they won't last—none of us will. But you won't forget your pumpkins, will you?"

She shook her head.

"You'll know a lot of things you didn't know before. And maybe you'll teach your children about those seeds. That way there'll always be new pumpkins. And it will go on like that."

"So I'm like your pumpkin."

Roslyn made a sound in her throat, but then nodded her head. "That's exactly what you are."

"Then you'll end. You'll go. So what's the point? I think God is a waste of time."

She took Damascus' hand.

"You knew that. And you're not going to be by yourself. Your Aunt Ivy's coming home. You need to stick with her, Damascus. She's got some big plans for you."

"I don't want her plans."

"Those beautiful things you made with your pumpkin, it's awful what happened, them getting eaten up like that, and not because they were eaten but because you didn't get to do the giving. They were a promise, weren't they? And now you feel like it's broken. I know how that feels, Damascus. I have broken so many promises. But that's how it is a lot with the gifts we have in this life. Your Aunt Ivy, she's trying to find a way to use her gifts. That's why she's left. It's what I'm trying to figure out."

"That's why you go see Otis? 'Cause you broke a promise?'"

Roslyn nodded. "I guess I hope even if we don't get it perfect, it's not a waste of time."

"Tell that to the pumpkin bread."

"That bread's just lost to the appetite of life. You can't get it back. You can't save it. But it's served its purpose. That's another thing Granny Byrne taught me. That appetite happened to be a raccoon this time, but the raccoon is serving a purpose, too. Maybe a nice snack for Spook one day."

Damascus made a face. "That explains a lot, actually." She let her breath out, feeling deflated but also like she'd just figured out some secret in a universe where suddenly she wasn't at the center anymore. The things that were failing all around her, just possibly they weren't her fault. At least not all of them, anyway.

"God, why'd it take you so long to get this smart? If you'd started out the summer telling me all this kind of shit, we'd have been a whole lot better off."

Roslyn laughed at that. "No kidding."

Then Damascus tilted her chin up and said, "Daddy's lost that way. When Mama died, he got lost to the appetite."

Roslyn did something then that Damascus hadn't expected and hadn't seen her do all the weeks she'd been on Manny's Island. She leaned her pretty head over so it lay on Damascus', and then she cried. A long time later, when she looked up at Damascus and smiled a messy smile, Damascus wiped Roslyn's face with the edge of her T-shirt. The little green thing inside her let go and disappeared, far inside where it was swallowed by the strongest feeling Damascus had ever known.

Damn it. She'd gone and loved Roslyn Byrne.

Chapter Seventeen

Roslyn

My back and legs ached from standing in the kitchen and cleaning all afternoon, but I found that by the time the vegetables were tender and the smell of roasted beef filled the conjure woman's house, ready for a family that had not sat down at a table in the place for more than twenty years, I had known how to do it all along. It was a new body I was living in, not the streamlined, waif-like figure of a girl but more muscular, rounded in places and calloused in others. Like the house had changed, it seemed my own skin fit the woman I had become, and I was starting to like her.

But I didn't think she was going to be enough. Damascus had no idea how much I'd cost her already—an aunt, a father, the protection of an owl that had been keeping that pumpkin safe.

Damascus set the table and then paced the front porch, back and forth across the yard to the remaining pumpkin, watching the drive for her uncle and cousin. And Urey. I had no idea if he'd gotten the invitation. There'd been no response.

Everything was ready when Damascus came rushing into the kitchen, flushed, with her bangs standing up where she'd been sweating and pushing them off her face. "Rolls!" she hollered, like she'd announced a bomb threat. "We ain't got no rolls! You cain't have people over and not sit out rolls in one of them little wood baskets with a towel. Them kind you get out of a paper box and slap butter on so they brown up real quick. Aunt Ivy's always got those, and they get eaten up so fast she sometimes has to make a whole 'nother slew of them. How'd we

183

forget that? They're gonna be here!"

I was standing at the sink, my mouth hanging open, patting the air to try and slow her down. "Nobody's going to care, honey."

"Yes, they will!" she insisted. "We ain't got half we planned already, 'cause of that butt-face raccoon. If we ain't got rolls, it's just going to be stupid. The whole thing's going to be shit!"

"Okay. Look. You've got time to run down to Cain's and get them before anybody gets here. They've got them at the store?"

"I don't know!" she wailed.

"And you've got to stop with the mouth. People don't want to come sit and eat with somebody who's cussing them every other breath, all right? So get it out of your system now, and put a lid on it."

I waited, and she scowled.

"Shit, shit, shit, shit, shit!" she said, her voice rising until she was out of breath.

"Good. Are you done?"

She nodded and almost cracked a smile as she bent in half, leaning her hands on her knees like she'd run a mile.

"Then go see about rolls. All you can do is see. That's all anybody can ask." I tried to reason with her. Maybe it was a good thing, an errand, so she'd have something to do with all this nervous energy. She was wearing a path through the yard as it was. "If they don't have rolls at their own store, then they can't fault you for not providing them at dinner."

Her eyes flew wide, and she stood up straight. "I cain't go. You go."

"Me?" I hadn't even brushed my hair all day that I could remember. I needed to get myself ready. I'd never met Will Cain and, although I doubted being clean and presentable would help my case with him, it was all I could think to do. "Why do I have to go?"

"Because you said I'm hostess, so I have to greet them. I've got to greet, Roslyn!"

"Shit," I muttered, pulling off the apron at my waist. She

made a face at me. "Fine," I amended. I went tearing through the house, trying to straighten myself quickly in the mirror and changing my blouse while Damascus hopped from foot to foot.

"So, if they get here, just give them drinks," I said, stopping at the front door.

"I know. You already told me all that." She was pushing me out the door. "Get three of them packs. They eat lots. No, get four," she said, alternately grabbing and pushing.

I tore out of the drive in the golf cart on two wheels and gave a sigh of relief to be away from all that pre-teen angst. What if I just didn't make it back, I wondered? Just took a little drive around the island and managed a flat tire so the whole thing was practically over by the time I hobbled back in? But I couldn't abandon Damascus like that, and I had to face up to the fact that I wanted this dinner to go well as badly as she did.

I pulled up to the front of Cain's and braced myself for another confrontation with Nonnie. It would be short, I promised myself. She wouldn't have time to get too weird on me.

The rolls were stacked high and deep on the bread shelf, and I yanked out six packs, just to appease Damascus, and flung them on the counter. Nonnie came out from the back office and made her way toward me at her leisure.

"I'm in a hurry," I said.

She made that noise of disregard in the back of her throat. "You always is. What you doin', now? Trying to drag those poor men in that house?"

"I am not dragging anybody anywhere." How she knew about my dinner plans was another mystery of the world. "Damascus is making dinner. They're her family. And it's none of your business. I don't want to hear any kind of hare-brained ideas about it, either. It's not my house to argue about."

The ridge of her brow rose. "High and mighty."

"How much?" I asked, shoving the rolls toward her.

She rang up the groceries and took my money. I snatched the plastic bags and turned to leave. She followed me out the door and caught up with me before I could get the golf cart turned around. I had no choice but to stop or run her down.

She held out her hand and shook it a little. She wanted me to take something from her. Against my better judgment, I reached out, palm open. I didn't have time for this. I had to get back to dinner and Damascus. It was important to her, and she'd had enough people fail to come through for her in her short ten years. I didn't want to be another one.

"I don't care nothing about that house," Nonnie said.

I thought about what Ivy had told me about Nonnie taking Damascus away when Fawn was dying. Her hand was warm, not cold as I'd expected, and she covered mine with her other one so she held me there in her grasp. A shiver ran through me.

"Seminoles, my mother's people, they're all animal tribes," Nonnie said. "A tribe comes down through your mama. They say Alligator tribe disappeared a long time ago when all the women died off, but Delia always believed she come from alligator, her and Ivy's mama, too. When the Seminole was moved off from their lands, some hid, some come here. That's how come Delia said her mama come here. She was Alligator tribe, a medicine woman, and the ring was her place, sacred ground. Same as it was Delia's. Same as it's mine."

"You mean the shell ring?" I'd been trying so hard to find Delia's presence in the house, but that was not her place. There never had been anything special about the house itself. She'd given it to Ivy because it wasn't the inheritance she meant for Nonnie. What she had for Nonnie was not bound by four walls.

I looked into the small, dark woman's eyes, and was met with that same knowing gaze that inexplicably drew me to her. Curses or blessings, I could never be sure with Nonnie. I was starting to think it might be because, at the source, they weren't as different as I liked to believe.

"Rattler gives high power. Give luck," she said.

I opened my hand, almost expecting it to be empty. There was no weight to the thing she'd given me. But I held in my palm the caramel-colored tail of a rattlesnake. I recognized it immediately because I'd played with them as a child in Glenmary, where the snakes were abundant.

"That'll sing along with the music."

I pulled away from the strange little woman, taking my rolls and my rattler with me, peeling out of the lot.

I thought of the bone charm and the thunder medicine. Could I believe she'd only meant to help me? No, I didn't. I knew Nonnie had her own agenda, and it was wrapped up in getting back into that house. I just couldn't see how I played any role in that. But the rattler-tail in my hand was another sign that Nonnie had other ideas. I shoved it in my pocket and took the rolls round the back of the house to the kitchen door where I stopped to lean on the house and catch my breath.

Inside, I could see the little hostess, face tense with concentration, pouring out sweet tea into sweating glasses. JB stood at the counter, comfortable in the familiar surroundings and bragging on the spread. At one end of the table sat a rust colored man with blue eyes, still wearing his work coveralls. My first look at Will Cain. There was no sign of Urey. My heart shrank. I wanted to get back in the cart and leave before Damascus could work it all out and realize it was my fault, the person she'd put her faith in. And here, all I had were brown-and-serve rolls.

If it weren't for Will Cain looking up and seeing me standing there, I might have just gone ahead and fed myself to Spook. When I came inside, his mouth spread in a genuine smile that went all the way to his eyes. He didn't look like a guilty man. Well, that could wait, anyway.

The chair at the end of the table sat empty, and we all tried not to look at it.

"Well, at least there's one we've been waiting for," Will said, leaning back in his chair real easy. "It's a good thing you got here when you did. I's about to gnaw my own arm off having to sit around with that roast smelling so good." All of this was said with charm piled high on top and a wink like a cherry. It was impossible not to like him right away. "Come on in here. Folks, let's eat!"

And I knew then exactly what had gotten Ivy Cain in trouble. I liked him despite myself. Despite the fact that I knew his cheer was false, and he'd likely throttle me with my crock pot cord, afterward.

Damascus was anxious and glancing at the back door every few minutes. Lord, I did not know where she got such a font of hope.

Everyone complimented her over and again. At first she grumbled excuses or explanations for things she didn't think had turned out perfectly. Lumps in the mashed potatoes, or a wilted edge of the salad lettuce.

"I like it lumpy," JB said. "I like it wilted. If you'd been eating his cooking, you'd believe me." He made a face over Will's cooking, and everybody laughed a little uncomfortably. He'd brought Ivy into the room. But the moment passed.

Will and JB kept going on about how good everything was, and I was having a hard time imagining Will having the capacity for spite. After a while, Damascus quit looking at me in a panic and started to simply say thank you.

I nodded and approved until I hoped she was convinced of her success.

I could have kissed JB when he left the room to bring in more tea and swung his long leg over that seat, to be nearer to her. He teased her and filled the gap at the table without missing a beat. "I done filled one plate and cleaned it, too," he announced. "I believe I'm going to need me another."

He made good on his word. Damascus adored him.

"You know what?" he said. "The kids over at the marina are talking about you."

I saw her draw up tight, but JB was smiling, and she couldn't help her natural curiosity. She had to know what he thought about everything. "What are they saying?"

"They got a name for you, calling you Miracle Grow. How's that?" He laughed heartily, eyes crinkled. "They want to see the girl that growed a giant pumpkin. Shoot. I told 'em what you done. They just about don't believe me, neither, that all that food come from one pumpkin. And then I said, hell yeah! And she's got another, bigger than the first!" He slapped his knee and laughed, poking another forkful of food in his face. "They figure you're just about a legend in our own time, little Damascus. They want to see what you got over here."

I saw her eyes flash with pleasure before she narrowed them. "You ain't selling tickets for nobody to come over to this farm and stare at me and my pumpkin like we was freaks, JB Cain."

JB's eyes went wide this time. "No, no. That ain't what I was thinking at all."

I relaxed. I'd been worried that's where he was headed, too.

"Don't you know this place is sacred? No, ain't nobody stepping foot on this ground if they know what's good for them. No, I told 'em, this old place is full of magic, the kind that can see clear through a soul. It takes a pure heart and a haunted riverbank to grow pumpkins such as that, and I guess that says all there is to say about you. Oh, they're scared shitless of this place, all right. But they're about in love with you, girl."

We all sat there, breathless when he'd finished. JB, the entrepreneur, the dream weaver. That snake charmer had done in five minutes what none of us had dreamed possible. And I saw the perfection of Ivy's practicality and Will's spin doctor genius, come together in the wonder on Damascus' face. By God, she'd just grown herself a new life.

Inside, I cheered, and hoped later she might go with JB to the marina. She might listen to Ivy and enroll in school. And I couldn't help feeling the ghost of Fawn Trezevant must be watching us all, us seed doubters.

To my great relief, the remainder of the conversation was all about the plans for next season's pumpkins and ideas for playing up the legend of Little Damascus' haunted farm, how to make a buck every which way. Urey's absence was nearly forgotten; Ivy wasn't mentioned at all.

"Pumpkin pie!" Will exclaimed when it was time for dessert. He exclaimed a lot. "I been waiting on this thing a week. Load me up."

Damascus cut him a large slice and slapped a huge dollop of whipped cream on top.

We all ate until our ribs creaked and the evening grew dim,

but there was no sign of Urey. When JB suggested he and Damascus take the canoe out for sunset on the water, her eyes swiveled to mine and then to the dirty dishes. I waved her off and they were out the door so fast they made a breeze.

"Thank you for coming, Uncle Will," she said so fast it came out like one word. She couldn't get away from Urey's absence and back to her pumpkin fast enough.

I didn't waste time, either, but got up and cleared away his place setting with a great clatter, wondering how this was going to go now that Will had the floor without witnesses.

"Whoa," he said.

"He should have been here." I wasn't apologizing for once. "You have no idea how big a deal this was to her. I grew up without my daddy. I was lucky. I had a stepfather who loved me. What does she have? This was dinner. Dinner! How hard would it have been to come sit here for thirty minutes and eat with her?"

When Will spoke, it was softly. "I guess I have some idea. Seeing as she ain't never even said my name out loud on more than maybe five occasions I can recall. And she's eaten at my own table nearly half her life."

I let out a frustrated breath. "Well. Maybe you do. But if you knew, he should have. He should have been here."

Will didn't make any attempt to excuse his brother-in-law. But I wished he could have explained him. The sweet exterior of the man was true to the bone. He stood beside me and dried every dish, took out scraps, and hummed under his breath while doing it. Finally, the guilt pushed me to hang my own neck.

"I know you think I told her to leave. And I admit it. I did. She took my car, too. And I don't regret it, I'm just saying I had something to do with it, and I won't blame you for being angry. You made it hard enough for me with Otis Greene."

"Yep. I did that."

"It took me a while to figure out what was going on there. I don't know what you told him, but you had him acting like I might shrink his manhood."

Instead of being contrite, Will looked proud of himself.

"That's just about the gist of it. Pretty shifty of me, wasn't it? You didn't deserve that. I did go back out there and straighten Otis out. He'd already figured it out, anyway."

"I know." I wished I could be angry with him, but part of me had enjoyed the challenge. In a way, Will Cain had done me a favor not unlike the one I'd done for his wife, making me fight for what I wanted.

"I was trying to do the right thing, if it matters. I thought she deserved a chance."

He laughed some at my relief, but raised an eyebrow.

"Yeah, well, a day or two after she left, I was getting pretty worked up. I might not have been so nice about it then. But you ain't got nothing to feel bad about. I blame myself."

"She worried you'd be angry. It wasn't easy for her to make that call. I was starting to think I was going to have to blow the whistle." He frowned at me, and I sat down in a chair across from him.

"She shouldn't have put you in that position."

"I put myself there. I don't know where she is, exactly. But we have a mutual friend who helped her find the place. The realtor who told me about this house. Ivy said she'd only be gone a few weeks. She said she'd call you once she was settled in. I had to wait to give her time. She was hoping it would help you understand if there was some distance."

"The woman's a pistol. Ah, Ivy knows I cain't see things but one way when they get fixed in my head, and she needed this thing at the hospital. What is it? Drugstore person?"

"Yes. She really wants this for herself, but she was worried about going out on a limb. We kind of understood that about each other."

His shoulders dropped.

"Not that you wouldn't understand."

"Well, I wouldn't have," he admitted wryly. "She done it 'cause I ain't got sense to listen the first time she told me about it, just blew her off. If you ain't guessed it yet, Ivy didn't marry me 'cause I'm the brightest bulb." He laughed at himself, and I refilled his tea. "But Ivy knows how to work this old boy. She's done all right. I have, too, come to that. Me and JB are going over to Brunswick tomorrow to see the little place she's got rented. A duplex she said, nicer than the house we got now. Got a pool."

"You're moving now?" I was truly surprised.

"Urey'll shit a brick."

"Urey deserves to shit a brick." I believed it. But I also felt like a hypocrite. He'd called that one.

"Yeah, I guess it looks that way." Will chewed on the edge of his thumbnail, then added, "It's not that big a deal. We're going to see how it goes. Rent for a while. Be easier for me to play over there, anyhow."

"Oh," I said, feeling uncertain. I'd been so involved in their lives the last few weeks, but it wasn't really any of my business at this point. There was one obvious problem that I couldn't ignore. "I'm glad. For both of you. But what's going to happen to Damascus if you go? Urey's been gone for weeks, and she doesn't even know where."

"Yep, yep. Ivy's been working on that, too. You leave out pretty soon, don't you?"

"I should already be gone. I was waiting for the pumpkins."

That was all Will said. Then he sort of shuffled around the kitchen like he felt too big for the space and didn't know what else to do with himself. Finally, I turned and put on a pot of coffee. That's when he sidled toward the back door, and I thought he meant to leave early.

But instead, he said, "You play?"

"An instrument? No."

"Sing?"

"Like a coon dog."

He laughed. "Well, then, that'll do just fine. You mind if I sit on your porch a while and fiddle?"

Delighted, I nodded. "Only if you're loud and fast."

He let out a little whoop and banged outside like a boy on his way to a party. "Gonna see my girl, tomorrow!" he called back. I decided Ivy Cain had no idea what a lucky woman she was. But I knew a way for Will to tell her.

I went to the bedroom and pulled out the box Mama'd sent with all the memorabilia. From outside the window, I could hear Will tuning up his fiddle while I shuffled through page after page of Grandpa Byrne's poems until I came to the one I wanted. It was his best, I thought. I brought the aged paper to my lips and kissed it softly before taking it outside to where Will sat on the front step. I held it toward him so he looked up and took the paper.

"What's this?"

"Peace offering."

He turned it over and then read the first few lines before his face brightened, and he looked back at me. "This is good stuff. Did you write it?"

"My grandpa. About fifty years ago."

"He could've made a nice living writing lyrics."

"He did all right in wallpaper." Will looked confused, and I laughed and waved it away. "Could you use it?"

His face went blank. "Seriously? Like, you've got this stuff copyrighted, right? I mean, I cain't pay you for it or nothing."

"No, that's not what I meant. I don't want money. I want you to sing it. He wrote poems, and they were published, most of them. But he was frustrated, I think. Not many people ever saw his work. After he died, my Granny kept his poems. They were dear to her. I didn't even know about them until recently. When I read his poems, at first I felt like I was intruding on something private between the two of them. But the more I read them, the more I realized how wrong it was to just put them away. He put all these feelings and thoughts on paper because he wanted people to always know how he loved her."

Will squinted up at me. "You ought to publish them for him. One of them do-it-yourself places. Mail it in and they send it back all bound up nice."

My hands clenched the paper in my hands tight involuntarily. "I don't know. I'd have to think about it. Maybe, though. Thanks for the idea."

It was a wonderful idea, honestly. I didn't know why I hadn't thought to do it myself, except when I considered mailing

the poems to a stranger, it made me nervous. I didn't know if I
could do it. But Mama had given them to me, and maybe they
weren't my gift. Maybe they were his, and now hers. I could do it
for her.

Will said, "Cool."

My fingers relaxed, as if they knew something I did not. As
if the poetry recognized this man. "This one . . . I thought
something about it was different. I couldn't put my finger on it.
I'd pull it out every time and read it again, and it just wasn't like
the others. I didn't know why until tonight. I think it's a song.
They sang together, in a choir. They sang all the time. I think this
was his song for her, and it needs somebody to sing it who can
understand that kind of love. Can you put music to it?"

Will Cain blinked at me and looked doubtful, like he might
not be up to the task. But he went back to reading the lyrics,
shaking his head over the impossible weight of expectation. I
knew how he felt.

I said, "I don't really think it's a hit or anything, but you
could play it for Ivy."

He looked up at me with a lopsided grin. "Only song I ever
play's for Ivy."

The tune came in starts and stops, carrying back to me as I
cleaned up the kitchen. It was a real song, not something I'd
imagined, just like the path I was taking at Sunrise Hills was a
real service, a career, and friendship. I looked out the window
over the sink but saw no sign of Damascus and JB returning with
the canoe. The sun was still at least an hour from setting. The
days were long at the end of summer. But the first weeks of
October were always warm on Manny's Island. The slap of the
screen door made me jump and turn with a start. Urey stood
there, hollow-eyed and grim. His clothes looked like he'd slept in
them, and he hadn't shaved in at least two days. We stared at one
another for a long time, and I waited for him to say something,
make some excuse, but he didn't. I turned my back and finished
rinsing out the sink. All the anger and guilt that had been

smothered by Will's music now grew hot as coals in my chest.

He walked to the cabinet, took down a glass, reached past me to fill it at the tap and then sat down heavily at the table. The empty pie tin still sat there, crumbs and pieces of crust stuck to the sides. I turned to look at him as he reached to pick up one of these and pop it in his mouth. Furious at his nerve, I swiped a hand hard and fast over the table and sent the pan flying. It hit the wall with an enormous clatter.

Urey chewed and eye-balled me while I glared at him. "That's a real mess you made," he finally said.

Seething, I spat, "You don't get to eat that. You don't deserve a bite of anything she's made."

He scooted back in his chair, looking exhausted, but didn't say anything. One of the cats had wandered in and rubbed against his leg. I picked it up and tossed it in the hall before I leveled him again with a cold stare.

"She worked so hard. All she wanted was for you to come sit in a chair. Why can you not do one single thing for her?"

With such sudden force that I leapt back against the sink apron, bruising the small of my back, he brought his fist down on the table.

"Oh, that's perfect," I said, my teeth rattling like I was freezing. "Take offense. You know I'm right."

"What do you want?" he bellowed.

"I don't want anything from you. She does. Damascus does. You don't even use her name."

"I give her what I had. She's took care of."

I made a rude noise.

"Lady, you're mad 'cause I ain't shown up at your table, nothing to do with my child. You think I ain't seen you up there at that ring every morning, looking out for me?"

I couldn't deny it, but I wasn't going to let him derail this argument. "I'm not talking about me. This is about your little girl, and she's about to die to get you to show one sign you give a damn she's even alive. She's so starved for love, she's trying to grow it right out of the ground, and that's your fault. You're responsible for that."

"Damn right I am." Immediately, he looked sorry he'd said it. Not guilty. Wretched. He hung his head, face blazing, but his shoulder hunched, and in that moment I saw a terrible possibility I'd never considered.

"It was you," I said. He was shaking his head in denial, but it was unconvincing. "The seeds came from you. The letter. Oh God. You wrote it. You signed it from Fawn."

"She wanted her mama," he said, eyes swimming. He chewed on his lip, trying to keep control. "I couldn't give her what she wanted." I saw him struggle with his temper until he shoved the chair back and stood up. "Well, I give her what I could. I shouldn't have come here."

I thought of Damascus' face tonight when she realized what JB was telling her, that she didn't have to be defined by the past. That she had the power to be her own person, to say what her life would be and who she would be in it. Urey being here now would destroy that fragile hope.

But I also thought of the man who'd kept that picture of a mother and her child. There'd been no place for him in that image. The two of them filled the whole frame.

I had the feeling he would leave, and I'd never see him again. It seemed I'd been feeling that way since the day I met him. He was leaving in increments, and I was aware of every second of his living and dying. I shuddered because I thought now it might be because Urey welcomed it. He was always looking to his end, watching it, keeping it in clear view on the horizon beyond the shell ring.

I stepped between him and the door. This was no kind of love, but I'd known we'd end up here since the day I laid eyes on Urey Trezevant. We were bound to one another through the little girl on the riverbank.

"Where have you been?" I said softly. It was clear to both of us that I did not mean only for the last few days. Sometimes you stand in a place with a person and know that life could have delivered you to another shore and you would have known one other in a different way. So many decisions in my life had brought me here to stand with Urey. What if I'd made different choices, better ones? What if he'd never met Fawn, or he'd finished vet school? Would we be happy people, content somewhere, living lives that never brought us to this island or this kitchen? If we'd found one another some morning on some high place, could we have still heard that ancient song?

He shook his head at my question. He'd been so many places, I knew, and it took him a minute to work up the words, but I waited. I would have waited all night. "I don't know," he said. "Wandering." He raised his eyes to look into mine. "You know what Ivy's after? She sent me papers. I ain't no kind of daddy, I know that. But I'm here. She knows she's got a daddy that ain't gonna leave her. Damn if I'd let her think I don't want her."

Everything that had happened to me came rushing in on me when I heard the sob in his voice.

"Do you know what it's like," I said, "to have just this one chance to do something that really matters and blow it? Completely blow it because you're so screwed up? You're so selfish that it's done before you even know it? It's over. And you can never go back or change it?"

His breathing was heavy, and I could feel it warm on my face, his nostrils flaring, but I didn't back off. This was our song, one we both knew. I let the tension go out of my arm because I wasn't holding him there by physical force anymore.

"I'm sorry," I said. "Urey, I'm sorry for it all." My voice faltered and I had to swallow a sob before I could finish. "She's been here every day, with nothing but those pumpkins. And you think she feels wanted because you won't sign a paper to let someone who loves her take care of her? You don't understand that your pride is no kind of love?"

He was shaking with the effort to keep from tearing past me, but my own pain propelled me forward.

"My baby, she never took a breath," I said. "Can you imagine? I loved her so much, and she never even breathed the same air as me. That's how little chance I had. We weren't even on the same planet. All I can give her now is a name, and really I don't believe it matters. She doesn't need anything from me. If I name her, it's like it makes it worse, because it's only for me.

"But Damascus, she's not some angel baby. She's here. She's out there! Right where you put her! Tell her what you did for her. Give her that." I was begging him now. I'd have gotten on my knees if I'd thought it would help. "She deserves to know, Urey. If you gave her those seeds, you have to tell her the truth. Whatever you decide about Ivy, you have to tell her what you did for her."

Silence fell, and it was too heavy. It was obvious there was nowhere else to go with this conversation, so I stepped back.

I reached for the glass of water he'd left on the table and drank it in one long swallow. He turned to look at me then, wide mouth tense and brows drawn down over those fierce blue eyes, and he crossed the space that separated us, moving to stand too close, lowering his head so I thought for an instant that he meant to kiss me. But he only made a low sound of frustration.

I thought of the kids outside. Urey's body lightly pressed against mine, with the edge of the table at my back. I was dizzy with the smell of his skin, his breath warm on my face. My anger faded, replaced with something more disorienting. It would have been so easy to go this way, forget everything for a few minutes of comfort.

That's all it would be. What he was really asking for.

"What if I said you're not the only one leaving this island?" he said. "What if I never sign those papers? What about I quit my job and just take Damascus and walk off from here? With you."

"Don't do that." The idea had played out in my dreams since that morning on the shell ring. I was human. I'd imagined finding a way to keep Damascus, keep this life, and Urey suddenly changing, discovering peace of mind and a way back from his demons. But when it came down to it, I realized with the clarity of a punch in the gut that what I felt for Urey Trezevant wasn't hate, wasn't love, or even compassion. It was pity.

"Hush," I said. I pulled him close, his head to my shoulder. Will's fiddle had picked up a beautiful melody, repeating a chorus. I knew the words. My grandfather's love song. I smoothed the curls at Urey's neck like a little boy.

"You don't know me. All I ever done was hurt things," he said, then laughed softly, without humor.

In my mind, I saw him with Elder, pointing to the hidden prey, giving the sharp whistle that sent her flying into action. He believed he was an agent of death, and so he'd taken up his place as henchman for that owl.

"That's not true. I know Damascus, and she's part of you. You didn't hurt me the day you helped my leg. You didn't hurt Damascus when you wrote that letter. Ivy told me about the animals, how you took things in all the time when you were younger. You've got a choice, Urey. You can do the right thing now."

I forced myself to be still. My breath came short and shallow. In a rush, I said, "I buried my baby like I was hiding a sin. I was ashamed of her. You poisoned the mother of your child because it was mercy." I knew I was right. Ivy couldn't believe he'd done it, but I could look at the man before me and know. He couldn't give anything to Damascus because of what Fawn had asked of him. "Urey. Which one of us deserves to be forgiven?"

I worked up my courage and reached for one of his hands, hanging at his side. The fingers were large and calloused, warm and strong. In a surprisingly intimate gesture, he let them twine with mine, but they were strong, possessive.

"Ros-lyn." Just the way he said my name, so hopelessly, made me want to open myself to him. "People use each other. They do it to live, and they do it to die."

I let out a ragged sound because I did not want to believe him, but he stifled anything more, putting his mouth over mine. His kiss was deep and urgent, and I shivered with all the adrenaline of the day's events. I let myself lean into him, but it was like trying to hold onto a ghost. I was caught up by something transcendent, far from the dark, cool kitchen with the whirring of the table fan. My thoughts ran to the Seminoles, the people who'd built that shell ring, living lives, raising families, loving one another and this island.

But in my mind, a harsh wind blew over them, and they disappeared as smoke, one by one, until there was nothing but the ring. I saw their faces fade into the blue sky and the wide water, and Urey's was among them.

Only when I opened my eyes to the sound of a quick step outside on the shale path did I remember where we were. Urey felt me tense. He must have realized at the same moment that our visitor was not coming round the front, but marching up to the back, already pushing in through the door.

Chapter Eighteen

Roslyn

The four walls of the house could have fallen down and me standing there, a woman in the middle of a structural collapse.

He did not look back at me when he took Damascus by the forearm, and I stood motionless, listening to the screen door slam, listening to their voices in the yard. I did not move until they took on an alarming volume and turned to protest and yelling and the noises of a physical conflict. When Damascus let out a wail, it shook me from my stupor, and I shot through the house.

The Cains and Urey all stood in the side yard, their long arms and large hands hanging helpless at their sides, their faces stark as they watched little Damascus' fury. In the dying light of the day, she was a wild, dark figure, swinging a long wide arc with the oar from the canoe, destroying the bottle tree. The colored glass splintered and crashed around her like sparks. Urey called incoherent things at the child, trying to stop her, but not once did she let up. I rushed down the steps and across the dirt yard, awkward but compelled by an urgent need to shield her from the inevitable, until I tripped. I hit the ground hard, but I wanted to dissolve into the sandy earth, taking all the confusion and hurt and disloyalty with me, so it would never touch Damascus.

I heard Will and JB rush toward me. They reached to help me up, and I pushed them away. "Stop it. There's nothing wrong with me. I can get up on my feet by myself. I've been doing it all my damn life. Somebody go help her!"

The awful crashing had stopped, and I checked a busted lip carefully, wiping blood from my chin, while I sat up, turning to

Damascus, then to Urey. They didn't even see me. They looked stunned, resolute.

Damascus dropped the oar and stood heaving, her narrow shoulders crestfallen with exhaustion, and she turned her eyes on my face. They were hollow, black holes in a skeleton face in the growing shadows, emptied of the hard-won trust we'd been building over the last weeks. I was struck dumb by the resemblance to Urey.

"You're just like her. You just care about yourself," she yelled, but she'd forgotten me. This was all for him. "You think I don't remember, that I don't know, but I do. Everybody knows. They feel sorry for me 'cause she wanted to die. She didn't want me, and I hate her. I hate all of you because you're liars! You're not leaving me, Daddy. Because I'm leaving you."

All apologies backed up in my throat, powerless. I felt small and broken on the ground, right back where I'd started, watching the child I loved slip away.

"Go away, Roslyn Byrne! Nobody wants you here! They don't want neither of us."

As quick and fleet as any wild thing, she took off through the brush, disappearing as completely as her father had ever done.

She'd gone to Nonnie, the only refuge left. What I didn't understand until Will Cain got the call from Nonnie was that the papers had already been signed.

"Ivy did it all by mail," Will explained. "She figured Urey'd take it better that way, and she wouldn't be so likely to cave if he tried to push buttons. But he's not fighting her this time. He signed the guardianship papers yesterday. Up and quit his job, too. Says he's not sticking around anymore, and to hell with all of it. I guess he feels like he did his time after Fawn, and it's best to make a clean break of it."

I'd heard JB say that to Damascus on several occasions. Clean breaks weren't always what they were cracked up to be, and I was an expert.

"Oh, God in heaven. That's what he just told her? That's what set her off in the yard?" He'd given her up. That's what he'd been trying to tell me. Will nodded.

All this time I'd been trying to get him to do right by his daughter. This is what he thought I meant? Did he think I knew about Ivy's plan? He must have. He thought giving over guardianship was the best thing for Damascus, giving her a mother again. Even if he was right, I felt hollow. This was what Urey did, I realized. He did the hard thing no one else was willing to do, because it was right. I remembered Ivy saying this, and how the rest of us just had to live with it.

Damascus' whole life he'd been trying to make up for the mother he believed he'd taken from Damascus, first with the seeds, and now with Ivy. He'd loved her enough to give her a mama, but I didn't know how Damascus would ever understand this. And I'd done nothing but complicate the problems in her family since the day I got here.

She was the one I loved, and I'd betrayed her. All that longing for her daddy, all that disappointment, it was made a thousand times worse in the moment she saw him holding me, only to learn he'd given her away.

When Will left to go figure out what to do about his fractured kinfolk, I did the only thing I knew to do. I hung the bone charm on the porch. I cut Delia's herbs and scattered them by the light of a new moon, wielded my broom, banishing all threats to the border of the conjure woman's yard, making my own protective ring.

I pushed the shattered pieces of glass from beneath the bottle tree. They shone at the yard's edge, a shimmering boundary, dangerously beautiful. With one swift flick of my broom, I did the one thing those vanished natives thousands of years ago had not done—I changed to survive. I left an opening big enough to slip through.

Chapter Nineteen

Roslyn

I was barely able to get around the next day. My knee was swollen and stiff, and my hip ached like fire. It was Saturday. Mama and Jackie would be cruising up the highway toward Atlanta. More than anything, I regretted not taking Mama up on her offer to caravan home. Half the night I'd imagined a hundred different things I could have done differently, and the other half I worried about Damascus and wondered where Urey had gone to lick his wounds. I couldn't imagine he would really just leave the island. If he did, I knew no one would ever see him again. Ivy was coming home today, and at least that made me hopeful for Damascus.

Most of my things were packed, and I was taping shut the box of Grandpa Byrne's poems, ready to be shipped to the self-publisher. It remained to be seen if I would actually be able to drop them off, but I believed it was the right thing to do. Just like leaving today. I'd struggled with the impulse to barge in at Nonnie's and strike whatever crazy deal I had to with the devil to make things right between me and Damascus. But really, I had no faith in Nonnie's magic. And precious little in myself.

For one last time, I climbed the trail up to the plateau of the shell ring to look down on the water and the small island that had somehow become the whole world in such a short time. I had the last sculpture from Mama, intending to leave her up on that high place where she could watch over this place I now loved.

I knew Urey wouldn't be there today. Wherever he'd gone, it was far from here. All I saw was the blue horizon, the wide oaks sheltering the house below, and a small brown rabbit that skittered out of sight so fast I almost missed him. One of the babies we'd seen that first day I'd come here? The snake didn't get him, and neither had Elder. He was a lucky bunny, and there was just no accounting for fate.

"I figured you'd be up here." I turned to see Ivy coming up the hill to stand next to me. "Thinking about jumping?"

"Rolling over, actually. Somebody told me once, islands do that. It's harder than I thought," I said. She smiled. "You're back."

"I am. And I guess I should have called to tell you what was happening."

"I wish you had," I said, unable to hide my hurt. "But it wouldn't have mattered," I admitted.

"I didn't know if Urey'd go for it, and I was waiting before I made any noise about it. If I'd known how this was going to go, I'd have done different. He told me he'd wait to talk to Damascus until I could be there."

"Have you seen her?"

"She's still with Nonnie. She's not ready to talk yet. It's going to take some time with everything going on at once."

"Urey's gone."

Ivy looked around us, out across the water. "I don't know. He was always disappearing one place or another, but if I was a betting woman, I'd say he's not as far as he'd have us think."

"What did you do to make him agree?"

She shrugged. "Told him he was just like Daddy. I'm not proud of it. But it was all I could think of, and I couldn't stand watching this go on with that child anymore. She's growing up, and it may be too late already to turn this thing around. I said I knew he'd always hated Daddy for abandoning us, but I'd always been glad. Urey was my daddy then, and he loved me and took care of me and Mama when he was way too little to be doing it. I just said he had to be that kind of daddy to Damascus now. She deserves better than somebody who's just working out a grudge. The road to hell, and all that.

"He knows he's still her daddy. He's welcome to see her any

time. He's doing the right thing, and she's going to know it one day. I hope sooner rather than later."

"I had no idea so much was going to change so fast. You're moving, so I guess the job worked out?"

"I got the training. I'm working at a Kroger pharmacy. It's going to take some getting used to, the kind of hours I'll be keeping and helping Damascus settle in someplace unfamiliar. But it's new to all of us, so that's got to level the playing field some. We won't go 'til the pumpkin is brought in, of course."

"JB's probably told you about what's gone on there. We've got about two hundred pounds of frozen pumpkin in the deep freeze. He's cooked up a big legend about how haunted this farm is and how it's magic that grows the pumpkins. The kids at the marina all want to meet Damascus. He's working miracles. I swear he needs a stand and a tip jar."

Ivy's mouth twisted in a begrudging smile. "Shyster," she said under her breath. "So, it wasn't all bad, then. JB told me about what you did with Otis."

"It wasn't a big deal. But I think I'm going back to school. Physical therapy makes sense."

Ivy laughed. "I'm glad something does."

I stood there another moment before I sighed. "I'm going now. You're back, and with everything that's happened it's just not a good idea for me to stick around."

"You're going to see Damascus?" Ivy said.

"I don't think so." I tried to avoid more explanation. "Could you take the kitties? Or see if they'll take them at Sunrise Hills?"

Ivy cocked her head and narrowed her eyes. She'd noticed the sculpture I was still holding.

"She wouldn't want to see me right now," I said. "I'll come back, I swear. I'll find some way to explain so she can understand nothing happened between Urey and me. What she thinks she saw."

Ivy raised her eyebrows.

"He kissed me, but it wasn't what you think."

"What was it?"

I shrugged. Placing the sculpture at the edge of the steep ledge that dropped to a wide beach below, I stepped back to take in her view of things. I supposed the origins of the shell ring would remain a mystery, but I felt a stirring each time I came there. What it had been no longer mattered.

"Well, you might not know this since you've been gone, but apparently, underneath this banged up, crazy-ass exterior, I'm a red-hot flaming goddess. Good for granting safe travel, bountiful harvests . . ."

"Grace?"

I shook my head tiredly. I shouldn't have been surprised to hear Ivy use that word. "I think you have to be able to forgive yourself before you get that goddess badge. I guess you could say your brother was due a blessing, and he came to the right house."

"He always was a lucky son of a bitch." She sighed over the lie. Ivy looked at the sculpture and back to me. She was the expert on blessings, after all. She knew exactly what they were worth. She took up the spot beside me so we both looked over the water, letting the wind blow over us, through us. I bit my lip hard and felt Ivy lace her fingers through mine.

"Now then," Ivy said. "Where from here? Atlanta? Your mama's?"

"I've not really decided, but neither, I think. Maybe I need to do a little wandering."

"Wandering, huh? That's what the goddesses are doing these days? In that case, can I return the favor? Somebody pointed me in the right direction once. She said I already knew where I was going." From her pocket, she pulled out the scrap of paper on which Trish had written the address and time for the singing at Bethany Baptist.

"Where'd you get that?"

"God." She grinned. "And He said tell you to take a cab because JB took your car for a tune-up."

"Mama," I said, a little breathless when she picked up.

"Roslyn? Is something wrong?"

"Nothing's wrong, but I need to tell you something. I just wanted you to know . . ." I had to lean my head hard against the cool metal of the refrigerator door. "I know why I did it, burying the baby like that. I've thought about it and thought about it, how it was just a crazy thing, and it didn't make any sense."

"Oh, Rosie."

"No, just listen. I need to tell you this. I was putting her away, like Granny put those poems of Grandpa Byrne's away, or you put the Kellers away. When she died, and we couldn't go back there, it felt like punishment because I'd failed at so many things. I didn't want anybody seeing that. Not even you, especially you. I'm telling you this because I need to say, I'm not ashamed of her. I'm not ashamed anymore, not about any of it. When this summer's over, things are going to be different. I'm different. I'm not coming back to Dalton, Mama. Not right away."

After a moment, Mama's voice sounded tinny and distant when she said, "Well, I guess you've got your money's worth down there. I'm sorry it took all this for you to come to the big conclusion that I've made you ashamed of yourself."

"That's not what I said." I sighed. I'd said it all wrong, but there it was. Truly, like it or not, Mama and I had things to be hashed out that went much farther back than the day my daughter died.

"You always harped about not sitting up in the house, letting somebody else do all the hard work while we just took all the benefits," I said, "but that's what we did. We left Glenmary, and we sat up in that house in Dalton, and we left Granny. We left the hard stuff back there. I sat up in Dalton when I was dancing because it was so easy, Mama, to just do what you wanted. I loved how you looked at me when I was up on a stage someplace. I thought I was making Granny proud, and that was better than being with her. It was the only time I was sure you really saw me, just me. I knew when you watched me dance, you were proud of me. You weren't thinking about the life you might have had if you hadn't gotten pregnant with me. You weren't remembering him, wishing I wasn't a constant reminder."

"Oh, Roslyn." Mama's voice was shocked. "I never said any of that. Why on earth would you think I ever didn't want you? I never even talked about that man."

"I know, and I'm sorry. I'm sorry you couldn't. I should have told you how I felt. I was a kid. I was afraid. And then it seemed like I had it all under control because that's what my whole life was about, controlling an image. But, Mama, we should have talked about him. You should have told me the truth, whatever it was. I wasn't happy, and I hid that, too. I blamed you and Granny, because I was too much a coward to walk away from dancing. Because I thought it was enough, making the two of you happy, I thought maybe one day if you were happy, if you didn't feel like you'd disappointed her, it would make things right between the two of you."

"Now, that was not your responsibility, Roslyn."

"No," I said quietly. "But it wasn't all about you. I was trying to make something inside me right, too." I took a breath. "We should have gone to Glenmary, Mama."

She made a shuddering, airy sound into the receiver. I could hear she'd been crying when she said, "Roslyn, that's water under the bridge. You can't get obsessed with all that right now. You can't change it. You need to come home and deal with what's real."

"Like you're dealing with Jackie and what's happening to him? I'm not running anymore. I've let other people handle my whole life for me. That's why I can't name her, Mama. I've never taken responsibility for myself, how could I be responsible for her?"

"You didn't want me to handle it?" Her voice sounded hoarse and high-pitched.

Panic rose in my chest. "No, of course I wanted you to. I let you handle it. I thank God you handled it! I was out of my mind, Mama. But that doesn't make it right, what I did. I never spoke to Stephan. I left there, and maybe I should have stayed and faced things, put that stone up and been honest about myself."

"I said call him," she said, obviously angry. "I told you, call

Stephan. Now, I don't know what good that would do anybody now, except stir things back up."

"I know. And he never wanted anything from me, Mama, but that's the thing. I owed it to him anyway. I don't know how I'll make it right, but I'm going to start with asking if he'd like to help name her. She was half his." Silence. "Mama?"

"We better just talk about this when you get home, Roslyn." She sounded stiff. I'd hurt her, but she had to know I was right. I wished she wouldn't take everything as an accusation.

"We will. I'll come see you." I pressed my fingertips hard over my lips, but there were things that needed to be said, that wouldn't wait anymore. "Mama, did you ever worry about the color of my eyes?"

"Well, what on God's earth kind of thing is that to worry about?" she yelped.

I smiled through my tears, knowing how wrong I'd been. I should have trusted her love more. The same way she should have trusted Granny Byrne. The way she would have to trust mine now.

"Everything's going to be all right, Mama. I'm going to be all right. And I love you." I heard her breathing and wished I could lay my head on her breast and listen to her heartbeat the way I had as a child, reassure myself of her constant presence. "I've found something I'm thinking of doing, and there's a training class in two weeks in Atlanta. We'll have time then. But listen, there's one more thing. I'm going to a singing today. And then I'm going to Glenmary."

She hung up.

I was remembering what Ivy said to me the first night in the conjure woman's house, how we're like window screens that life passes through. That's how I felt about Mama and what had passed between us. For the first time, I was beginning to believe I could let her need blow through me without fear, and that someday maybe she would be able to throw herself open to me, too.

But my heart was in my throat as the taxi pulled into a pine-shaded gravel parking lot only thirty minutes later. The church was much closer than I'd expected, only a small clapboard building with covered front steps and a simple steeple above. I didn't know if I could get out of the car.

"This is the place?" the Hispanic driver said, looking back over his shoulder at me, still sitting in his cab.

"I really don't know what I think I'm doing here."

The sound of the choir could be heard even with the windows up. It was a familiar drone that vibrated in my belly. I put my hand there instinctively, and it occurred to me that the hollow place had gone from me. What filled me now was a sense of anticipation, as though I were about to step off a very high place. But I knew what it would be to walk through those doors. I knew I would be carried into the rafters.

I dug money out of my wallet to pay the driver, and, for a second, I doubted myself. "You hear that, right?" I asked when I put the money in his hand.

He made a face. Of course, it was impossible not to hear this music. I smiled at him and got out of the car.

Checking my phone for the time, I saw it was still an hour before the singers would likely break for lunch. I'd either have to find a place to sit out here, or slide in the back and try to be as inconspicuous as possible. The song was loud and lively and I recognized it as Number 222, "Ocean."

No one turned when I walked in. The sound swept over me like a wave, and I automatically held my breath as though diving deep while I slipped into an open spot. Several folks standing along the back wall made room for me.

It was exactly as I remembered it. This church was much the same, sparse on furniture and filled with the same plain-folk singers, their faces full of concentration, unabashed joy. The tips of my fingers and toes warmed with the feeling that I'd found my way back to a lost land after a long journey. When the song came to a close, the older man beside me let out a breath and said, "That was a good one. Yep, a good one."

He was wearing soft blue jeans and a light cotton

button-down, but he smelled mildly of soap and hay. He smiled at me, but he was paying attention to the number of the next hymn being called from the center of the hollow square. The old man's fingers were large and arthritic, but he flipped with ease to the page in his dog-eared, scarred copy of *The Sacred Harp*. The maroon-colored, oblong books were held open in every lap with one hand, while the singer's other hand moved up and down to beat time.

I'd forgotten that, the bobbing along.

I'd only wanted to watch from a corner, sneak in and out like a thief. And I felt like a thief, like I didn't deserve to sit among these people. Certainly I couldn't open my mouth and join them. I was silent throughout the next song, Number 65, "Sweet Prospect."

When the throng of hungry singers headed downstairs to the fellowship hall, I managed to follow without anyone paying me any notice until I made my way to the drink table. I clutched my little loaf of pumpkin bread, unsure whether it was worth the offering.

The elderly went first to fill their plates. Everyone else formed a line. The voices of so many talking sounded like a hive of bees reaching a fevered pitch. I took my sweating plastic cup of sweet tea and tried to take it all in from under the radar, but the lady behind the table cocked her head and gave me a good look.

"There's not no chance you're Philadelphia Byrne's girl? From up Tennessee way? 'Cause if you're not, you got a double walking around. I ain't seen none of them in years, but you've got the look of a Byrne."

I could've lied. It occurred to me. But she was already out from behind the table calling for somebody named Buell. She looked over the crowd, raised up on her wide, flat feet. She was stocky and determined, and the crowd parted for us as she pulled me to the next table and a the man she was looking for.

"Buell," she said, "is she not the spitting image of Granny Byrne?"

A tall, thin man with mousy hair and a longish nose reached

to take my hand in both of his. Thus far, I was a complete stranger who had neither denied nor confirmed my identity, but based on the sheer fact that I looked like someone they'd once known, I was being embraced. Buell's soft hands covered mine in a gentle shake, and he gave my fingers a squeeze.

"Well, I'll be," he said. "You must be Rachel's girl. What a surprise it is to have you here."

"Is that right?" Buell's wife asked. "Buell, she's not even told me her name."

"Yes," I admitted. "I'm Roslyn Byrne."

They appeared pleased, but there was a quick glance from wife to husband that I didn't miss, although Buell looked a little confused.

"I haven't seen Rachel since we were just girls," the woman said. "Lord, that's been a thousand years. I'm Carol Beth Sevier. She won't know me that way, though. She'd know me as a Hyde. Hyde was my maiden name. I just hate we couldn't make it back up there when your Granny passed this spring. Honey, we're real sorry about that. People said that it was a beautiful service, and it ought to have been. That woman was beloved by many."

"She had her place in the square." Buell blinked at me kindly.

"Thank you," I said. "I appreciate you saying so."

How could I admit I hadn't seen that service either? Her own granddaughter?

"I know it's been hard for your mama," Carol Beth said.

I was still reeling from the shock of being recognized, but I realized quickly that Carol Beth obviously knew some about the history between Granny Byrne and her only daughter. "She hated how it happened," I said.

Carol Beth's expression was one of sincere sympathy rather than judgment, and I relaxed a little when she said, "Well, none of us can choose that. Now, we're just so glad to have you."

There was the question in her voice.

"I've been spending the summer down here, and someone told me about this singing. I always loved it. I hope it's okay if I just came to listen."

"Listen?" Buell chided. "Honey, if you can manage it, you'll be one of the few hard-hearted souls. You sit by me. It'll come back to you."

"Oh," I said, suddenly remembering the bread. "I brought this."

Carol Beth took it from me like it was gold. I smiled, remembering what Damascus had said. It made all the difference, having something to give. The thought of her made my heart ache.

After I'd stuffed myself to the point of being uncomfortable on the home-cooking of Brunswick ladies who encouraged me to pile my plate high with chicken casserole, fried okra, lima beans, baked rice and a rare treat, hominy, followed by a generous portion of rum cake, I did sit with Buell. If only because I couldn't walk fast enough to get away. He'd have nothing else.

His tenor was loud and clear. It wasn't long before I was humming. I learned about the Seviers between songs. They were mad at their daughter for moving down to Brunswick with their grandkids after a divorce. They'd finally decided if they were ever going to see them, they'd have to move themselves. Buell retired in the fall, and they'd been in Brunswick almost a year.

"It's been good," he said. "Carol Beth was about beside herself not being able to get hold of those grandbabies."

"I can see that," I said. There was the grief of the grave so near Mama's house, but it was bearable now. It was what it was.

"We've been real blessed," Buell continued. "This little church has been real good to us."

He flipped to the next hymn and helped me find it in the book I was borrowing.

Later he said, "I tell you, the hardest part was leaving the house. The market like it is, it's just sitting there. About breaks our hearts. Lived there thirty years. You know the place?"

"Oh, I don't know if I'd remember."

"It's out Bell Road. Just down from your Granny a couple miles. They's a creek runs along through there."

A little gasp escaped my lips, and Buell looked concerned.

"With all the daffodils?" I asked.

Buell's face lit up. "That's exactly right. My mama helped put out all those bulbs. They about took over that top field every spring. And you remember that?"

"I think about it every year when the flowers start coming up. Granny Byrne took me there one time, and I picked so many we could hardly carry them home. I told her I was going to live there when I grew up so we'd always be neighbors." It all rushed out of me, and he laughed. I was overwhelmed to find someone here who remembered Glenmary as I did, who knew who we were then. "And that's your house?"

"It surely was," he said.

We sang through the afternoon, and it wasn't until the light began to fade that I remembered I would have to catch the last ferry back to Manny's Island. Truth be told, I hadn't thought of anything all day, except what was going on right there in that hollow square. Now that I did, the rest of my life seemed a little removed from reality. The leader called up the next song, "Sweet Canaan."

The familiarity of the Sacred Harp family had displaced all the troubles of the Trezevants, and I had to admit that the intense weeks I'd spent on the island were such a brief time in the whole of my life. My time in the square had given me perspective and brought me back, as it always had, to earth.

I slipped outside to call the cab, and Carol Beth joined me as I was hanging up. She had a plate of desserts for me to take.

"I just can't tell you what a surprise and a joy it's been to see you. We get to missing Glenmary something awful," she confided, her chin quivering. She waved a hand to dismiss any undue concern. "Buell would get me for acting like this, but we do miss it. Of course, it's changed. It's not what it used to be. Folks is up and gone that we knew when we was there. But your Granny, there wasn't ever anybody so good to me and Buell. We loved her. Now, didn't her house go to one of the cousins?"

"I'm not sure," I admitted. "I think so."

"She was real proud of you and your mama. Every time she'd see us she'd tell us something you were up to down in

Atlanta, how smart you were getting. Buell said you remember
the daffodils out at our old place? Now what about that? This is
just like Old Home Day." Her eyes took on a look of gentle
concern, and she took me by the elbow. "You look good,
sweetie. We heard some about that accident. Buell and me, we
said you were made of stern enough stuff, you'd pull through. I
hope you're doing okay way down here by yourself. You know
you can come see us now we've all found each other."

It was hard to keep the tears from starting up. "That's real
sweet of you, but I'll be going up to Glenmary, in fact, for a few
weeks," I said this with no hesitation, knowing now that it was
where I'd been going all along. "My mama's not going to be
happy about it," I sighed.

"Maybe she'll surprise you. Mamas just want their daughters
to have it better than they did. I wouldn't have picked Brunswick
for my daughter over the seventh level of hell, but if
Linda—that's my girl—is happy there, then I'm just working on
sharpening my horns and pitchfork."

Carol Beth hugged my neck when we saw the cab coming
up the road. "You call us then," she said. "I put my number right
on the back of that paper plate for you. And say hello to your
mama for me.

"We'll have somebody open the house if you'd look in on it
for us. You're welcome to stay." She rushed to say, "Now, don't
feel any pressure, but most of our stuff's still in the house. You'd
be real comfortable. We always thought we'd just figure what
we'll do with it all when the time come. Except, it's *you* that
come." She giggled. "Oh honey, I'm just being a silly old
woman, but I love that place. Maybe it'll feel so good you just
won't want to leave."

I smiled back at her, encouraged by the warmth and
assurance of this day. "The truth is, Carol Beth, I never did."

Delia's grave was impossible to find, just as a conjure
woman's grave should be. I'd walked up the road near the ferry
dock about a quarter mile from Cain's. Since I'd left the church,

I'd been thinking about what to say to Damascus, and I still didn't know how I would make her understand. I was hoping Delia might have an idea.

But there was no sign of where she rested, and no advice to be had, only the wisdom of my own heart and the echo of the Sacred Harp. I watched a locust flit from one blade of grass to another. A breeze rustled the tall sea grass, but Delia was not there.

"She gone home."

It was Nonnie, standing a few feet from me as if she'd sprung up from the ground.

"What do you want, Nonnie? You want me to leave? I'm leaving. You don't have to threaten me with spells. I know you're not the one who scared Otis Greene. I know I've screwed everything up."

For the first time, Nonnie smiled. A big, wide, full smile that showed large square teeth. As she made her way to join me, she said, "The bone, it works."

I'd have died right then, rather than admit I had one of those bones in my pocket.

Her smile faded. "A man's coming to drag the alligator out. She's gone down to pitch a fit."

I felt terrible. Another loss for Damascus and it was because of me. I was the one that turned that animal into a pet.

Nonnie scowled and made urgent, jabbing motions with her hands. "I told you, all I done is try to help you, 'cause I seen all this. I know what you come here for. Don't you love that girl? Ain't you going to help her?"

The peace I'd felt at the singing evaporated. I saw then what I'd been missing, a thing I should have understood from the very beginning. Nonnie's devotion wasn't to the house or to some imagined inheritance, but to Damascus herself. She loved her. It was Damascus she was protecting.

"I don't know what to do. I can't change what Urey's doing. I'd do it, too. That alligator shouldn't have ever been there in the first place. And I know you think I brought it there. Well, whatever. I should have known better than to let her get attached to it. I shouldn't have let her get attached to me, either. Look where that's got her."

"The alligator's going to do what he do," Nonnie said. "He's an alligator. Who are you?"

My ears throbbed with the blood racing through my head. Since I'd left Mama's, I'd been asking myself that question. "I don't know."

I'd believed my identity was my dancing. Then it had been my grief. And finally, I'd looked back to Granny Byrne and the girl I'd been in Glenmary. But the answer wasn't that simple. I was all of those things. I was more, so much that was completely unknown. What kept me from being able to run to Damascus now was the same thing that had stopped me from finding out who I was all along. I was afraid I would not be enough.

"What is it you think is going to happen?" I needed to know.

"All I can say is what I seen. I cain't say what people are going to do about it. And what I seen was you cross the water. You was up on the alligator's back, and he carried you. I seen Damascus, and she lost to you. Her daddy's calling and calling her, 'til he ain't nothing but a voice, nothing but the river."

"That doesn't tell me anything. It doesn't even make sense." I was confused and overwhelmed by the same feelings I'd had that day in Mama's bathroom when all my choices seemed wrong.

"That's what I seen all these years, and now here the day's come."

"But I'm leaving. I'm packed. I know where I'm going. You told me the only reason I was here was to name my baby, and that's what I'm going to do. I just came back here to get my things and leave. It's better for everybody right now."

It was a lie. I'd made a promise to Ivy, one I'd really believed I could keep. But I was ready to run again. The difference was, this time I was running toward something stronger than my fear.

"I done told you," Nonnie said as she turned to walk away, "you ain't going to be able to help yourself. You was born to help her."

It was the first thing she'd said that I knew for truth. And I followed her.

Chapter Twenty

Damascus

Every day she'd watched for what Otis said, to see the pumpkin change, grow, turn into something new. And it did. Faithfully. And that was how she was sure she was doing it right. She'd done everything her mother asked of her.

You just watered, you just weeded, you just kept the bugs off and the worms out, and you just knew when they'd gotten to the point where they weren't going to grow any more. They were full. She had this awesome pumpkin to show for it.

But that was all. She felt as hollow and distant as a planet.

The man Daddy'd called came to capture Spook, and that's when Damascus took her opportunity to get away. She'd begged for the alligator to stay. She'd done her best, made deals with everything she had, but Daddy wouldn't change his mind. An alligator that'd eat up a poor old skin and bones mama cat, wouldn't think twice about taking a chunk out of a little girl, he said. And so she'd lost Spook the same as she was losing everything else she cared about.

Now she had to hurry. In her hot little hand, she clutched a knife she'd snuck out of the kitchen, a big one, the biggest she could find for the biggest job of her short life.

The pumpkin crouched in the shadows like an enormous toad. Sunlight beat down on the top of her head, heating her up so she could hardly think. Damascus lifted the knife and jammed it deep into the thick shell. It sank to the hilt, and she had to use both hands to work it free and repeat the action again and again. At last, she'd cut a complete circle around the top of the pumpkin. She dropped the knife in the sand and went to work twisting and pulling and working the makeshift lid off the top, using the vine still attached to the rest of the plant. She didn't cry. She'd cried over this all she was going to a long time ago.

Her arms and legs strained, the bones of her spine seemed to pull farther apart. Finally she felt the pumpkin's flesh begin to rip. Damascus cried out, as though it was an injury to her own skin, but she did not stop pulling until she was exhausted. She let go of the vine and sat down hard on the ground.

She could hear voices carry through the grove of oaks, now. She tried to not think about whether they'd caught Spook. Whether they'd drugged him up, whether he was sleeping, traveling miles and miles without knowing that when he opened his eyes again, he'd be far from his home, in a place he'd never been. To Damascus, it seemed like he had more right to the farm than any of the rest of them. He'd been born here. He'd kept to his hole. To Damascus, it seemed unfair. Nothing was turning out the way she'd thought it would.

With the knife, she went at the fibrous insides of the pumpkin, slashing at the wet, slippery innards, feeling the lid popping free a little at a time. Damascus was covered in sweat, and her small chest was heaving, but she had to get it done fast. She was careless in her thrashing, and the blade bit the tip of one finger. She stuck it in her mouth, tasting the sharp tang of blood mixed with the mellow juice.

Damascus scrambled to her knees. In a rush of panic, she plunged her arms as far down as they would reach into the slimy stuff and grasped with her fingers, but found nothing solid to hold onto, aside from the hard little seeds that slipped through her grip. Handful after handful, she emptied the shell until there was nothing but the smooth, glistening bottom staring up at her. The pile of sticky fibers was almost as big as she was, and there must have been five thousand seeds.

But as enormous, as truly goliath as the spectacle was, Damascus did not find any wisdom there. She did not know any more about life and death than she'd known before.

What she found was a vessel, large enough to hold a little girl.

She thought she heard Nonnie, and then she was sure it was her name being called. They'd finally missed her, but they were too late. She stood and hefted both legs over the rim of the pumpkin and slid herself inside the shell marked with her mother's name, settling down inside and feeling the juices soaking through her clothes, squishing between her bare toes. She wrapped her arms around her knees and tried to ignore the sound of Roslyn and Nonnie desperately calling. Her name, said over and over like that, began to lose its meaning. Pretty soon she could imagine their pleading had nothing at all to do with her.

And she began to rock. She rocked herself so that the round bottom of the pumpkin began to gently sway atop the sandy ground. She didn't know when she'd started crying, but it was hard to clear her face with the ruin of the fruit sticking to her skin, caught in her hair, threaded through her fingers. She was covered in it, as surely as she was covered in sorrow.

Damascus remembered staring down at the seeds in her mother's hands. She'd loved the way her mother smelled, the way her beautiful fingers curled up at the ends, protective around the seeds, how her lovely, solemn eyes looked down at Damascus and the seeds with so much hope. All the hope that was left.

Damascus had put away the truth of how her Mama died and thought only of that perfect memory when she planted the seeds, did everything right.

Her mother had taught her long ago how to say her prayers at night, a little sing-song habit that she had given up when Mama died. What good were prayers to God if you could be a perfect girl, beg and promise and still end up with nothing but pumpkins? Still, inside the shell Damascus found herself whispering, "If I should die before I wake, I pray the Lord my soul to take."

"Take me." she said. Then cried, "Take me where?" All she could do was rock harder in her strange cradle of life.

A sudden lurch made Damascus brace herself with her arms. Her intentions had started something, put something in motion she could not take back. And with a strange thwack, Damascus and the pumpkin came to a halt. Or not. The motion was still there, only it changed, no longer rocking. Now she swayed.

Damascus held her breath and didn't blink an eye. She knew where the pumpkin sat along the bank, and how the earth dropped off toward the river. She knew the motion of the pumpkin for what it was. Damascus was floating.

Carefully, she inched her legs underneath her until she could raise herself up and poke her head out. All around her was the river, and she was moving with the current, a girl in a shell, crossing the water.

Damascus' heart beat harder than it ever had. She couldn't catch her breath. All her life it seemed like she'd been sitting on the riverbank watching the water disappearing round the tip of Manny's Island, going places she couldn't even dream up while she stayed still, just the same. Now everything was happening to her at once, and it was more than she'd ever imagined.

She took several seeds and put them in her pocket, careful not to lose them for next season—wherever she might be by then—before she pulled one arm and then the other through the hole and held them high overhead. The water rushed past, shining in the sunlight. She rode along, stretching her arms out in elegant arches, swaying as Roslyn had taught her, drawing rainbows, watching the riverbank pass by as the tug of the currents pulled her farther away. She was leaving the shallows behind for the deeper waters, going where the sky above reflected so blue it was hard to tell where the earth ended and heaven began.

It was an effortless journey, and she might have gone on like this forever, Damascus thought, had she not heard the music. It was faint, coming from somewhere behind her, the sweet, high tone of a fiddle. The secret blessing of the Seminoles. And then, her name. This time Damascus' heart lurched in her chest.

It was her daddy's voice.

In that one word, she heard what she'd been listening for

her whole life.

Her breath came fast even as she turned slowly, careful of her precarious balance. How far she'd drifted in such a short time. The sound of his calling was ragged, desperate. She tried to call back to him, but the rush of the water carried her voice away. The farm was disappearing fast. And ahead, the river wound around the tip of Manny's Island where Damascus knew it would open up to the salty vastness of the Atlantic, a water so wide and strong that if she got that far, she might not get back. Suddenly, she knew the truth.

Water was only ever water, pulling in and out with the tide, flowing the same as it had for all time. It was never the river that was changing. It was the people watching it.

No secret language of forgiveness could bring back the daddy she had known. Life had rolled over, like the island. Just like she would have to do, because she was a girl, not a river. No magic, no woman, man, or even an alligator full up on broken hearts could turn back time or hold back the tide. Just like the moment she'd looked at her mama's letter and suddenly she could read, Damascus looked at the river and knew she had to choose.

Mama was not out there. That's what the pumpkins had been about. They'd taught her a thing has to fight to be alive. It's not some lazy game. She remembered JB's advice, the courage in his hand when he'd made that terrible cut to let one go so the other could live. But she wasn't ready to let go of her dream. And she didn't know if she could be the girl they were talking about at the marina, the girl who could grow a miracle.

Damascus reached to see if she could get an arm in the water, to try to guide her route, but when her weight shifted, she nearly pitched forward into the river. Starting to panic, she tried again. This time she eased the pumpkin far enough onto its side so that she could paddle with one hand. Damascus worked her arm hard against the water's pull. She couldn't tell if she'd made the least difference. The riverbank seemed as far away as before.

She hadn't thought of this, that she might not be ready to go. The pumpkin pitched and threatened to flip over with every desperate stroke, and her muscles burned like she'd been set on fire. The oak grove and the rest of her father's farm were slipping away, and she knew now that there was nothing else in the world she wanted, except to get home.

She hadn't thought how hard it would be to fight the tide, or how tired she would be or how weak against the nature of the river itself. "Mama!" she screamed, some habit of the heart that rose to the top. "I'm sorry! I can't go, Mama!"

But even as she called that sweetest of names, Damascus knew there would be no answer. She would have to do this for herself.

Chapter Twenty-One

Roslyn

The dirt yard was quieter than usual. I turned to look again at the
hole and began to feel uneasy. I could see nothing of the
alligator. Spook wasn't in his usual spot. I backed away from the
swampy spot and cast quick nervous glances all over the ground,
searching for the drag marks of his departure or any sign as to
which way he'd gone. I felt entirely too exposed, and in that
moment I realized just how right Urey had been about having
the animal removed, how in denial I'd been about the danger.
Finally, I found the faint trail Spook's heavy body had left
behind in the dirt.

Atop the rise sat Damascus' pumpkin. Or what was left of
it. I let out a terrible moan. The pumpkin itself was completely
gone. What was left on the riverbank was nothing but the
innards, scattered and glistening, horribly tender and alive in the
sunlight. Tossed to the side, a knife lay in the sand.

Damascus' name tore from my throat as I shrieked for her.
I ran the edge of the river and called over and over, but heard no
response. I looked out over the wide water, looking so hard,
seeing it rush past with the outgoing tide, but I saw no sign of
the little girl.

I made a circle, running around the house, limping when my
leg started to give out. She was nowhere. But Nonnie met me
before I could go any further. Somehow, she had Urey's gun in
her hand. She pulled me firmly by the arm. "She is there."

I turned to search wildly, following Nonnie's steady gaze
until I could see Damascus on the river she loved, the river she
was named for, her mother's one gift. The girl and her pumpkin

shell, like something from a fairytale, floating away on the tide, the morning light glowing around them like the inside of a shell. I could think of no way to stop it.

Nonnie nodded when I looked at her. "You go to her."

There was no time to argue that she was crazy, or to question her part in any of this. It was too late for that. There was only one way I knew to reach Damascus now, and it wasn't any alligator. I scrambled down the bank to where she and JB had left the canoe and shoved with all my might, crawling into the boat at the last minute, half-soaking myself. The current did most of the work for me, but I pulled with the water, working the paddle until my arms burned. I had no breath left to scream for her, but suddenly she looked up as though she'd heard something. I watched as she began to struggle and fight to get back to the bank, but the current was too strong this time of day.

Then I saw the shell tilt, and Damascus disappeared into the water.

All the reasons I was here rushed in on me, as though it were me drowning. My lungs ached, and my muscles burned as though my skeleton had turned to lava, and I thought this must be what it felt like to be one of Mama's sculptures. But I knew I would come out of this fire. I would not lose this one I loved. This time I could fight. I could pull her back.

Then, only a few feet from where she struggled to hold onto the sinking shell, I saw the wake. Something large and dark, just beneath the surface and so close to the girl it might devour her.

Nonnie must have seen it, too.

My scream was drowned out by the sharp crack of the rifle when Nonnie fired. I did not see if she'd hit her mark, and there was no time to take care for myself. I reached both my arms into the water up to my shoulders, grabbing hold of Damascus, pulling her over the side of the canoe. Exhausted, we collapsed in a heap, and I slammed my head against the side of the boat. But once I knew she was okay, nothing else mattered.

I fought the current. Even when it seemed I had no strength left, somehow I got the boat near enough to shore that I got out and dragged it the rest of the way. We lay there in the marsh grasses and sucking mud, unaware for some time before Nonnie found us.

"You got that child?" she kept said when she helped us stand. "You got hold of her?"

It was the first time I'd ever seen Nonnie scared. When I looked back toward the river, she said, "Ain't nothing back there. What it was is gone."

We climbed into the golf cart so she could drive us back.

She looked sideways at the house, but she would not come inside.

"Thank you," I said. "I'll put her to bed, call Ivy and tell her what happened. And Urey. I'll find him."

I didn't know what had happened, really. But we were all okay. It was over. I hesitated only because of something about the way Nonnie looked at me.

"Don't thank me none. I told you I seen you. All my life I seen you just like this right here. The way you ought to be."

But I shook my head. "But you were wrong. I didn't name my child."

It did not seem so important anymore, I thought, as she walked away, toward the shell ring, taking her secrets with her.

We didn't say much, Damascus and I, only got out of the wet clothes and lay down, exhausted. But I lay facing Damascus, looking at her face, pushing a strand of wet hair off her forehead when she opened her eyes to look at me just before falling asleep.

"I heard him," she said. "My daddy. He was calling me, my name."

"Your daddy?"

"He was in the water. He sent me home." She shivered. Her eyes were soft and clear, full of life, green as the river. "Mama give me that name," she said.

"I know," I whispered.

After a long time, when I'd almost drifted off, I heard her say, "But Daddy give me them seeds."

I lay awake the whole night long, listening to Elder's cry, eerie and lonesome. I'd called everywhere I knew, but no one had seen Urey. Instead, there was his dark little shadow, hovering over us. Finally, I'd gone outside to search the treetops. I'd wandered to the edge of the yard, looking up, when something bit into my foot with a sharp sting. I bent down and pulled a thin piece of glass from my heel, a broken sliver of the bottle tree.

The moon was full and bright and the ground glittered. The owl's strange call sounded almost overhead, and I jerked around at the rush of wings, but what I saw was the form of a man in the shadows. He stood on the riverbank, too far away for me to see his face. I knew him anyway, just as I'd known he was out here, close by all summer.

I felt strange, like I wasn't awake, but I knew I wasn't dreaming. When Urey didn't speak or move, I started to go to him, but in the soft breeze and the changing shadows he seemed to shift, undefined, and I realized he didn't stand on the riverbank, but beyond it somehow. He was the water, the shadow. I didn't want to believe what I felt must be true as he regained his shape, and the breeze died away. But I understood I could not go to him.

"She knows the truth," I called softly. "She knows you loved her."

Something drew my attention away, and immediately I saw the outline of the rifle carefully leaned against one of the oak trees. I gasped, faced with the realization of what he was asking. He'd always protected them, from themselves, from the world, with all his strength, with his life, with his soul. But Urey's mercy came at a high price, not just to him, but to those he'd lain himself down for since he was a boy. He'd carried a debt no one could know or even understand. Who would that debt fall to now? When I turned back, I was alone.

I took the gun to the spot next to the house where Delia's herbs grew. The ground was soft there. I'd done this before. I knew sometimes you buried a thing for the right reasons. This time, I knew I wasn't crazy or selfish. I thought of the child sleeping inside. I dug a hole deep enough to protect those she loved.

"Grace," I whispered. I never held much with mercy.

Sometimes our most beautiful gifts are our heaviest burdens. And I cried for us both, and prayed this old haunted riverbank that judged the hearts of those who dared walk its paths, would keep our sacred secrets.

An hour later, the security guard sent over from High Dunes looked miserable with the task of delivering the news. Urey's body had been found washed up near the shell ring by the woman who worked the register at the island grocery. The police speculated he'd drowned. They found no damage to the body, something remarkable to anyone who knew the Little Damascus. It was a sad comfort to Damascus, who mourned him quietly, and a miracle to me, the woman who'd buried the gun.

But I knew without a doubt, the news was no surprise at all to the conjure woman who stood watch since I came to the island, laying roots and blessings at my door and keeping watch along the shore of the shell ring all her life.

Chapter Twenty-two

Damascus

Damascus knelt to fish out the seeds she'd left scattered on the riverbank just below the conjure woman's house.

Roslyn was packed to leave, and JB was helping her load the cart. Aunt Ivy, who always came when Damascus called, who always listened like she'd never wanted to hear anybody's thoughts so bad in all her life, was waiting for her. Aunt Ivy had registered her for public school, like it or not. Things were changing.

She'd be living with Aunt Ivy and Uncle Will and JB now, leaving the island, but this time, not being left. Somehow, that seemed harder to believe than her daddy being gone.

"I was just thinking," Damascus said. She couldn't hug Aunt Ivy, but she leaned her head in so it her forehead rested against Aunt Ivy's shoulder. "You and me's got the same eyes. That's something, ain't it?"

Aunt Ivy didn't hold her. She knew better than that. "I know, baby," she said. And she told Damascus how their grandmothers were women of a lost tribe who'd never really been lost at all.

"Aunt Ivy," Damascus said. "I know you got to take me, 'cause Daddy had the law say so. But did you ever think, maybe you might want a girl?"

Aunt Ivy's arms came around Damascus now and this time she did not let go. "No, honey. I never did. I wanted you."

Roslyn wasn't so thin anymore. She didn't look like you could knock her down with a stiff wind. "Come on," she said. "Show me where you're going to plant next season."

They stood on the little rise where the pumpkin vine lay. Soon it would brown and crisp and before she knew it, Damascus would look and the vine would be gone. You wouldn't be able to tell the difference between it and the earth where it grew. She put her fingers in her pocket so she could touch the seeds she was saving. Next year, when the days grew long and the moon was right, she knew just what to do.

"Remember that favor I wanted to ask you?" Roslyn said. The breeze stirred her hair, and Damascus thought she was beautiful.

"I wonder if you'd take the kitties to Sunrise Hills? Do you think they'd like having them?"

Damascus shrugged, trying to act like she wasn't thinking about things like the end of summer, how fast everything was changing, how much it hurt to think about what her daddy had done.

"You can go visit easier from Brunswick," Roslyn said. "And you know what else? I'm going to come back here next year for a singing. I'm taking you with me."

Damascus groaned. "Not that hollering again. I thought you'd quit all that."

Roslyn laughed. "You're going to love it, Damascus. Wait 'til you hear. It sounds just like the river."

It was time to leave for both of them, but Damascus looked out at the river instead. This was the part she didn't know how to do, the weeks and months between now and next season.

She reached to take hold of Roslyn's hand. She grabbed it too hard, but the soft, warm touch reminded her of something Roslyn had told her once about having something to give.

Wait 'til you hear. It sounds just like the river.

She pulled Roslyn to her so she could whisper in her ear. A name.

Chapter Twenty-Three

Roslyn

Summer in Glenmary was nothing like the island. The air was crisp and warm, and the road curved back on itself as Damascus and I climbed into the thick green hills of southern Appalachia. I'd finally convinced her to come see the house in the valley.

I'd been in Glenmary for the better part of the year, with visits back to Mama and Jackie every few months. Jackie's kidneys had begun to fail him in the last months, and, while he was at the dialysis center flirting with the nurses, Mama had taken up visiting the baby's grave every Saturday. She told me she hoped it gave me comfort to know she kept the flowers fresh.

I took some of my own when the daffodils came in the spring, not as abundant as I remembered, but come fall I would set out new bulbs.

I loved the quiet at the hollow, just south of the Cumberland River. I loved the herb garden I'd put in at the back step and the odd pieces of furniture I'd picked up to fill the spacious rooms, a few antique pieces that once belonged to Granny Byrne. I wasn't sitting up in the house in these hills, but it wasn't like what Mama'd always said. I'd come home. I was living, working locally holding Benevolent Ballet sessions and going back to school for my degree in physical therapy.

I'd given Mama a CD that Will Cain burned of the song he'd written using Grandpa Byrne's lyrics.

"Now, what in hell made you think to do that?" she said, smiling.

"You took him off the shelf," I said.

Later, after the book had come in the mail, all of Grandpa's poems bound and printed beautifully, she called me once.

"I see what you mean," she said. "I never really read these old things before. But they sound just like him talking. You know, I've never said anything so this may shock you, but there's been times I've sworn I can just hear those two singing that crazy music."

"No. I'm not surprised at all."

I'd given her the rattler. I hoped she'd come to Glenmary someday and sing again. For me, the Sacred Harp was part of everything now. I'd remember my story, even as I watched to see how it would surprise me from day to day. I sang with the church in Glenmary, and sometimes traveled to singings nearby. But the bone charm dangled from my rear view mirror, a reminder of where I'd been. I never wanted to forget that story, either.

When I thought of my daughter or Urey, I didn't know why life was sometimes cut short. But I knew there was a place in the square for me. We would, all of us, meet again. We would sing together soon. And maybe even dance.

I'd finally called Stephan about a month after leaving the island. We met at a coffee shop near Atlanta, and it surprised him when I hugged his neck. He gave our daughter her middle name, his mother's. I gave him a little box full of soft, yellow crochet squares. He said I'd changed. He looked small to me, but I was comparing him to a man I'd once seen command a river.

Damascus had changed, too, grown tall, the bones of her face strong and beautiful like her father's and her aunt's. I could see the promise of the woman she would become, and Ivy's influence in the little things like the careful way she was pulling her hair back, grown long and shiny now. She was someone's daughter. The line of concern was between her eyes, but she was eager about what I'd brought her here for, even if she tried to hide it.

We pulled off the highway onto a narrow lane that led to the gravel lot where a tall black gum tree stood over the church. Even before I cut the engine, I could feel the sound in my bones;

I vibrated like a tuning fork.

Listen.

Damascus turned to look at me with wide, expectant eyes. I smiled. I knew just what she felt rising up inside her. In a sure and wise voice that had been there all along, she said, "Tell me you can hear that, too."

Acknowledgements

This book sprouted from a very small seed. A lot of people had to come along and take the time to care for it and for me in order that it should reach full fruit. Without their generosity and patience, it would have been impossible to make it to publication. I'd like to thank the readers of previous versions of this novel, Gail Fortune, Pam Mantovani, Brandi Stagg, Dorene Graham, Tanya Michaels, Nicki Salcedo, Ingrid Knowlton, Jenny Bent, Kimberly Whalen, and the indomitable Karen Johnston; esteemed authors Terry Kay, Joshilyn Jackson, Kieran Kramer, Sharyn McCrumb, Karen Spears Zacharias, Susan Gregg Gilmore, Jackie K. Cooper and Karen White for their support and encouragement; the unflagging faith and sage advice of Patti Callahan Henry; and the enduring friendship of Misty Barrere, who took me to the island and poured the sangria.

Inspiration also came to me through Sheila Lehner, whose fall prevention program for the elderly, Benevolent Ballet, changes lives daily. And from Sherry Austin, whose book, Mariah of the Spirits and other southern ghost stories, haunted me and first raised the question of ghosts as regrets.

Enormous thanks go to Deborah Smith and Deborah Dixon for their incredible enthusiasm for the novel and the opportunities they create every day for established and debut authors, alike.

Thanks are also due to Lynn Coddington, my editor, for seeing promise in this story. Her brilliant ability to mine the depths of character and theme transformed this disjointed work into the novel you hold in your hands today.

Thanks to my family for enduring life with a spacy kid, endless plays, rotten poetry and bad math grades.

And of course, all my love to my husband, Daniel, who patiently understands when my mind wanders midsentence, and to my beautiful children, Claire, Paul and Morgan, who will always be my greatest joy.

Lastly, to an old seed sower who taught me how to plant, and how to play checkers, and sometimes let me win. (Matthew 13:3-8)

About the Author

Kimberly Brock's writing has appeared in anthologies and magazines. After studying literature and theater, she earned a degree in education. She lives north of Atlanta where she is a wife and mother of three.

Visit her website at kimberlybrockbooks.com for more information and to find her blog, *Tales of a Storyteller.* You can also find her author page on Facebook at Kimberly Brock, or tweet her: @kimberlydbrock. She is currently at work on her next novel.

CPSIA information can be obtained at www.ICGtesting.com
Printed in the USA
LVOW12s1720170913

352858LV00005B/860/P